PROTON

By

Robert V Aldrich

To the denizens of artist alley

Cover designed by Robert V Aldrich, with help ^___^*

This book is a work of fiction. Names, characters, places, and incidents either are products of the author's imagination or are used fictitiously. Any resemblance to actual persons, living or dead, events, or locales is entirely coincidental.

References to characters appearing in comic books, video games, television & movies, and other forms of entertainment, are intended only as cultural references relating to the artform of cosplay. Their use is intended only as homage and are in no way a challenge to their respective copyrights.

Robert V Aldrich
Visit my website at www.TeachTheSky.com

Printed in the United States of America

First Printing: Aug 2017

ISBN-13 978-1981874194

TABLE OF CONTENTS

CHAPTER ONE

Front or back, Kate couldn't decide where she most needed her cape. Worn like normal and she could scarcely remain standing, her was shivering so bad. Draped across her chest instead and she bounced up and down to mitigate the blistering drafts across the back of her thighs. There was no escaping the cold.

Abandoning comfort, Kate Harbough through the cape back over her broad shoulders. Dressed in the costume of the DC Comics character Power Girl, she tugged the fabric against her thighs before tucking her hands into her armpits. Doing so rested her arms on the large hole in the chest of her and helped to cover the pronounced hole in the white long-sleeved one-piece. Kate was standing outside with a dozen other Power Girls on the palatial hotel steps. Situated on the waterfront, the massive hotel & convention center was playing host to Comic Party International, the largest comic book convention in the world that weekend.

"Geez, come on," Kate said at the photographer at the base of the steps. "I'm turning blue. I'm legit turning blue." She uncovered the hole in the front of her costume and said, "See? I swear, they're turning blue."

Denise Wallace laughed cynically. Dressed like Batgirl, she was enjoying the warmth that came from a full-body costume, unlike Kate's Power Girl that was devoid of pants or leggings. Denise was standing away from the Power Girls, part of the crowd of other DC Comic Book heroes waiting for their turn before the photographer's lens. "Yeah, but inside, you're okay, whereas I'm melting," Denise told her friend, no wholly immune to the cold. "And I've got swamp ass for the rest of the weekend."

"Yeah, I know," Kate agreed, giggling before Denise shoved her. Kate adjusted her carefully-styled blonde hair against the pulses of cold wind coming off the wintry water. She, like the others on the steps, waited for the photographer to get her camera working. An elaborate and expensive set-up on a tripod, she was frantically trying to get the high-end camera to focus properly with a wide lens.

"Okay!" the photographer shouted abruptly, sounding cheerful and looking panicked. "Got it working. Everybody, take a pose!" The dozen women in white bodysuits, blue boots, and red capes, all struck different superhero poses atop the epic stone steps. The camera flashed a dozen times in a few seconds. "Okay, now…" A long list of commands and suggestions followed, all directing the poses and orientations and emotions. Each suggestion was immediately accompanied by a dozen or so fluttershots. The caffeine-powered photographer then froze like a statue. She studied the last still, the only indication of life being the tufts of white breath from her mouth. New commands, new shots, rinse, repeat.

After almost ten frigid minutes, the other cosplayers were directed to join in. Over fifty cosplayers from the convention, fans dressed as their favorite comic book characters, took over the steps. DC Comic Book superheroes and villains from across almost eighty years of publishing history took pose after pose together before the photographer.

The final shot taken, the crowd converged on the photographer and her staff. Shivering, they relayed emails and social media contact practically en masse. Kate, her hands still in her armpits, slipped in through the crowd and handed over a business card. She didn't even bother to say anything to the photographer, she was so desperate to get inside. The shoot had garnered a small crowd of onlookers, all of whom were more dressed more warmly than Kate. On the outskirts of the crowd, Kate paused to look for Denise but couldn't spot her among the post-shoot chaos.

"Hey, can I get a shot?" asked one guy, cell phone in hand. Kate smiled instinctively and struck a pose as he snapped the picture and said, "Thanks." Surrendering to shivering, Kate pulled her cape around her as best she could and ducked into the gigantic hotel complex. In one of the lower hallways, she bent over in the warmth, trying to speed her dethawing.

As she regained the feeling in her fingertips, Kate overheard, "Giant lesbian make-out." She looked up through her natural blonde strands and saw some guys a few yards down from her. Lanyards and badges of the con dangling from their necks, they were looking out the windows at the cavalcade of cosplayers. "Man, twenty Power Girls is my idea of fuckin heaven," said one of the other boys. The window they stood in front of was fogging up. Kate winced and departed in disgust.

The convention had generated a huge turnout. The complex was choked with every variety of enthusiast: comic book fans, movie aficionados, gamer nerds, otaku, casual followers and ardent loyalists. They all walked about, creating a buzz of geekdom. Through this crowd, Kate passed expertly, heading for the heart of the convention: the giant dealer's room.

With a flash of her badge, she slipped in through the double-doors and entered a sprawling site of commerce and creativity. Booths and tables filled almost every square inch of the massive convention hall. Every possible art, craft, and type of merchandise was available and on sale. The din of foot traffic, general conversation, and ongoing retail, was a white noise and siren song at the same time.

In the dead center of the expansive market, Kate arrived at a table covered by a light red bedsheet. She pulled the sheet off with some flair, causing only a few prints to glide off. The tables on either side were indifferent to the accomplishment, but the feat made Kate feel like a wizard. She balled up the repurposed bedsheet and tossed it into one of the folding chairs behind the small table. Kate began to straighten up the display and freshen up the table's presentation. Shared with two other cosplayers who formed their informal stable, postcards, pages, and even a few posters covered the table; all prints of the three women in costumes from comics, anime, and video games. A whiteboard on a standup display listed the times of the weekend when they'd be wearing what costume. Right now, afternoon of Saturday, Kate was cosplaying as Power Girl from DC Comics.

Looking over her mercantile accomplishment, Kate turned to look out at the aisle of her table. More than a few customers were walking by but none seemed interested in buying, or even considering. Kate swished her lips from side to side, trying to hide disappointment. She slipped behind the table and sat down. She began to dig through her backpack when Rachael arrived. The team's resident costumer, the Rubenesque women kept pushing dyed blue hair back under a baseball camp. "How'd the shoot go?" she asked Kate as she came around the table, bumping it and knocking over prints Kate had righted only a moment ago.

Kate didn't bother to protest. "It was fine," she said as she pulled out a sketch pad and a few grocery store-brand colored pencils.

"Did you--" Rachael started to ask when she looked Kate up and down and asked, "Are your boobs blue?"

"It's February. It's, like, thirty outside," Kate dismissed. "Denise was still out there. Where's Emily?"

"Shopping for her dad's birthday," Rachael said as she sat back in the other chair. She pulled out her phone and resumed her video game. Kate looked around at the not-quite-bustling dealers room. She sneered a little as she bounced her crossed legs to try and warm up. "Idealism gone already?" asked Rachael without looking up from her screen.

Kate shook her head, not in denial but in the truth of Rachael's question. "I swear, every con is the same. You come in, walk through the doors, and it's like 'this is gonna be the one'."

"The one what?" asked Rachael, only now glancing up.

Kate sighed. "Just...the one." Rachael looked up from her phone more seriously know. "The one where IT happens. We sell out big time. The one where we get noticed or something. I don't know. It. It happens. This will be the one where it happens."

Rachael nodded, gradually getting with Kate's thinking. "You want to get laid," she said as she returned to her game.

Kate rolled her eyes and resumed trying to get warm. She was about ready to chastise her friend when a small gaggle of young girls showed up. "Hey," she said with a friendly smile and tone to the girls as she sat up.

"Hey, can we get a photo?" asked one of the girls, clearly a group of sisters.

"Sure," Kate said, standing up. She puffed out her chest and stood tall, her hands on her hips. She flashed a big smile and turned her head subtly. The girls all snapped pictures with their cell phones and then let out a wave of 'thank you' before they jostled off. Kate watched them go and said futilely, "Prints are $5, $8, and $15." She grumbled and sat back down. She looked at the merchandise on the table to the tune of distant sales being made. "Think we need something under $5?" she pondered towards Rachael as she continued to try to get the feeling back into her extremities.

"The $5 price point is optimal," Rachael maintained in the well-tread discussion. "Any less and we cut into profits and the customers don't take the purchase seriously. Any more and it ceases to be an impulse buy." Her eyes never left her video game.

"Yeah, but nobody's impulsing," Kate griped.

"Everybody's got a cell phone," said Rachael without worry. Sensing Kate's growing discomfort, she put the game momentarily away. "Come on, you know how this works. Nobody buys on Saturday afternoon. The eager people buy ASAP on Friday; everybody else waits until Sunday. And Sunday is usually the big stuff. That's when the guys come buy and get one of everything so they can hang a picture of you over their bed."

Kate stuck out her tongue. "Ew."

"And the girls who are into cosplay realize how good ours are and they buy our pics for inspiration," Rachael maintained.

"The one to beat or a masturbation aid, joy," Kate grumbled as she looked around. "Welcome to cosplay."

"Welcome to cosplay," Rachael agreed cynically.

A loud gurgle came from Kate's stomach and she covered it with her hands. Rachael, incredulous, gawked at her. "Sweet lawd hammery, woman!" she exaggerated, Kate laughing with her. "What you got in there, a pitbull?"

"I'm hungry!" Kate defended with a laugh. "When are we getting dinner?"

Rachael went back to her game. "Soon as I go and buy it."

"We didn't get access to the green room this time, did we?" Kate guessed, hopeful she was wrong.

Rachael shook her head. "I might be able to sweet-talk Jeffrey into getting us something out of the con suite, but not until tonight." Kate shook her head and settled in. Her stomach gurgled again. Rachael sighed and put away her game. "I'll go get us some wraps from Chipotle." She opened the money box and began to count the precious cash.

"Do we have enough?" asked Kate.

Rachael looked less than encouraged. "Yeah, but we need some sales to do breakfast. That or risk not having gas money to get home." Kate scoffed, knowing which she'd prefer between returning to home or eating breakfast. Rachael stuffed some money into her pocket and said, "I've got to swing by the room first. Need me to get anything from up there? I doubt I'll be back before the panel."

"No, but send Denise or Emily by if you see one of them," Kate said with a shivered.

"Do you need to pee before I go?" offered Rachael.

Kate shook her head, then realized what she'd been asked. She glared at her friend. "I'm thirty years old. You don't have to ask me like I'm an infant."

Rachael cocked an eyebrow up. "Do you?"

Kate averted her gaze. "I didn't until you asked," she grumbled before getting up.

Kate exited the bathroom, having to bite her left dark blue glove to slip it on. Biting the near side and tugging on the far side was the only way she was able to pull on the second glove for some reason. The right never gave her such problems. As she headed towards the door to the dealer's room, a woman with a huge photography rig asked, "Can I get a picture?"

Kate nodded and backed up to the wall so traffic could continue to flow by. She struck a powerful pose, flexing her right arm. Her bicep stood up even beneath the costume's sleeves and Kate relished in the look of genuine surprise before the photographer snapped the shot. "Do you workout?" the photographer gawked as she snapped a few more pictures.

"Kettlebells," Kate said as she performed her best overconfident smile for the photos.

As Kate was about to disengage, several more people stopped and began to snap pictures without a word. Kate scrambled to get back into a pose, but this one was more awkward than the professional posture she'd just struck.

In the span of a few dozen feet between the bathroom and the dealer's room entrance, Kate was stopped twice more, and then a third time inside the dealer's room itself. Practically floating on enthusiasm, she returned to the table and sat down next to Rachael with a huge smile. The non-costumed member of the team noticed and asked, "Good publicity?"

"I should go to the bathroom more often," Kate said, trying to sound confident. Realizing how that sounded, the two women looked at each other and tried and failed to stifle the silly laughs that followed. "Go get dinner," she urged her friend. Her stomach vocally agreed.

Rachael nodded and disappeared into the crowd. Kate sat behind the table in thoughtful stillness for a moment. She turned her sketchpad over and looked for a drawing to work on, but found nothing captivating. She dug out her phone from her backpack and scrolled through social media but found nothing worth discussing, nor anything engaging enough to distract her. She put it away and again faced the crowd that moseyed on by. The dealer's room was bustling but not as crowded as it had been. Mid-afternoon was setting in and much of the crowd at the convention had begun to break off, engaging in panels or preparing for the main events that would come with the evening.

As Kate watched people come and go, she saw a little child wander up to her. The toddler, no more than four, looked up at her with a big smile and his eyes shone. Dressed in a white onesie with a red cape, the little baby giggled and waved shyly again at Kate. She waved back, smiling huge at the tiny cosplayer.

The baby's mother came up behind him. "He loves your costume," she said, picking up her son under the arms. "He loves Power Girl. Don't know why; maybe it's the boob window," the mom joked. The little boy reached for Kate and she shook his hand with a giant grin, thoroughly entranced by his unguarded smile. "Can we get a picture?" the mom asked.

"Of course!" Kate smiled. She accepted the baby and held him on her hip. The little boy, fingers hanging out of his mouth, laughed as she held him. As the mother set up with her cell phone to snap a picture, Kate stood tall and flexed her arm. The baby laughed and did the same, the two paired off in their giant smiles.

"Oh my god, that's so cute," the mom squealed as she accepted her baby back. "Thank you," she told Kate. "Do you have a photo for sale?" she asked, as if the experience wasn't perfect enough for Kate.

Transaction complete and the team one sale richer, Kate settled in her seat again, but only for a second. Emily Donovan came rushing to the table. The third cosplayer in their stable, she was dressed as Fran from Final Fantasy XII. A wig of white hair stood out against her dark brown skin and black armor that accentuated her body more than concealed it. "Where's the glue?!" she panicked.

"Glue?" Kate repeated, jarred by the transition from one experience to another.

"The costume's coming apart!" Emily freaked. She leaned over the table to reach into the cosplay repair kit behind it. Doing so left little to the imagination, an advantage more than a few passersby took by snapping beyond-candidate photos.

Kate grabbed up the fishing tackle box and opened it to access the multitude of improvised solutions. "Where?" Kate asked, getting out the rubber cement. Emily turned and pointed at the small of her back. Kate leaned close and saw the break in the Wonderflex armor. "What happened?"

"I sneezed," Emily admitted as Kate did the quick repair. "How bad is it?"

"We'll need to make a new one," Kate determined as she glued it.

"Dammit!" Emily cursed. She started to move but Kate held her in place so the glue could dry.

"Wow!" exclaimed someone. Kate and Emily's heads both snapped up as several fans slowed, already getting out their cameras. Without a word, they began to snap pictures of the two cosplayers dressed as characters from radically different communities. Emily and Kate quickly scrambled to salvage the situation and strike some semblance of a pose but the people were off. More were there to take their place, though, as a blockade formed before their table. Both cosplayers abandoned the repair for a moment in an attempt to generate good photos.

Well over a dozen photos taken and not a single sale.

As the crowd dispersed, Kate dove back down to re-glue the interrupted repair job. "Will it hold?" asked Emily.

"If you stay still long enough," Kate assured her, holding the pieces together. "Stop breathing!" she joked, making Emily laugh. After a moment, Kate removed her hands and then rose up. "I think that'll hold."

Emily tried to move a little, more reminding herself of her mobility limitations than testing the repair job. "Sheesh," she finally griped. She turned around in the impossibly high heels only a video game vixen would wear and checked her rabbit-like ears in the table mirror. "I'm sticking to Anthy next year."

"I still think you should do the Batgirl cosplay," Kate insisted.

"I'm not dealing with another 'Batgirl's white' flame war again," Emily tossed off. "Maybe for Supergirl but not Batgirl." She laughed. "Barbara Gordon ain't worth that." She shuffled awkwardly on the platforms to come behind the table. "Where's Rachael?"

"Getting dinner," said Kate.

"Subway?"

"Chipotle," Kate answered, Emily nodding. "Want me to text her your order?" Kate offered.

Emily shook her head. "Nah, I'll hold off until the parties. Besides, I brought a bunch of--"

Super Sayan Goku from Dragon Ball Z strutted up to the table. With thick, almost comically oversized white gloves like they were clearly repurposed from a Disney cosplay, the familiar face picked through the photos on the table, looking at them with a subtly condescending approval. "Hey ladies," he said.

"Hey Eliot," the pair said, neither of them terribly enthused to see him.

"You girls like it?" he asked, turning around. The blue leotard with hard plastic armor looked right out of the anime series. The cosplayer, a little less so. Eliot had pale pink skin and while his arms looked the part with impressive size and definition aided with not-so-subtle makeup to bring out the individual muscles, his shoulders were a little less impressive. As was the rest of him, especially the slight gut held back by a girdle comically shaped like a six-pack. After he'd done a quick turn, he held his arms in an unnecessarily dramatic pose and flexed, then flashed a cocky smile that Kate hoped was sarcastic. The flexing caused his foam hair to shift, revealing a few dark locks beneath.

"Nice," said Kate, trying to be diplomatic with the convention staple. She leaned across the table and looked close at the leotard that formed the basis of the blue combat armor. "What is that? It's not nylon or spandex, is it?"

"No, it's a metallic lycra hybrid we're working on at my work," Eliot told her with a haughty tone. He turned around again, almost pushing his butt into her hand. "It feels like denim but it stretches fine and it can support a lot of weight." Kate withdrew her hand and regretted asking. Eliot took off the glove and handed it at her. "Here, give it a try." She smiled politely and shook her head. "It feels really natural but it's super-sturdy too." He put the glove back on and affected a sudden modesty. "We're working on a bunch of stuff. Government gets it first, of course, but we're gonna revolutionize cosplay in a few years, but I can't talk about it."

"Right," said Emily with a slow, diplomatic smile. "Your place should do a fabric demo at a con sometime."

Eliot laughed a little too loudly. "Hey, that's a good idea. I'll tell my bosses. I'll bet they'll love it." He grinned with an enthusiasm that Kate couldn't place as sarcastic or just overly sociable. "Yeah, we've got all sorts of stuff," he went on, as though discussing his work was his natural state. "The military application stuff is really, really cool, too. But I can't talk about it."

"Yeah, we know," Emily nodded tiredly, smiling tight-lipped.

Eliot looked down at the pictures again and made a show of considering a few different prints then said, "I'm going to swing back by after I've gotten a good look at what's here."

"No problem," Kate told him as she rocked in her chair. Eliot headed off and she translated, "I'm going to use the excuse that there might be something better to buy so I don't have to admit I don't want to buy any of your stuff."

"Pree-tay much," Emily agreed. She readjusted some of the prints that Eliot had shifted, then settled back to watch the crowds come and go. After a long silence between the pair, Emily asked, "How are we on change?"

Kate dug out the money box from under the table, stashed under the four women's backpacks and other supplies. She counted the few bills inside and declared, "A one, a five, and two tens and some twenties."

"Where'd the ones go?!" Emily panicked.

Kate shrugged. "Rachael took them to get dinner?"

"We need ones! And fives!" Emily further panicked.

"Calm down," Kate assured her, taking out a stash of twenties. "I'll go get some change."

"Where are you going to—" Emily started to ask but Kate slipped away too quickly, eager to escape the claustrophobia of the table. Clutching the money like a child rushing to the store, Kate tried to not get distracted by the arts and crafts on display in the dealers' room. Everything from original art to blankets to home-made video games were available, crossing and mixing all fandoms and interests. The full spectrum of quality was to be found, from masterpieces to works that could only be described as optimistic, from the over-priced to the worth-every-dime to the tragically unvalued. With the convention dealer's room, for better or worse, everything could be found.

Kate's red Power Girl cape trailing behind her, she made her way to the front of the dealer's room towards one of the giant professional booths. While the majority of the dealers' room was taken up with a single folding table for each vendor, capping the ends of the aisles were multi-table professional booths for the headliners of the convention. Most were for major distribution companies - selling DVDs and similar professional merchandise - but at least one was a professional cosplayer.

At the giant and crowded booth, a small team of salespeople were moving costumes, prints, and various implements of cosplay. At the very center of the convention stand the size of a small store sat Yaya Han. Dressed in genuine metal and leather, she was costumed as Simon Belmont out of the original Castlevania game. Made by her own hand, the costume of the classic gaming character was adjusted to accentuate her own comic book proportions.

Kate approached the table, growing nervous. She tried to avoid getting the attention of any of the salespeople so that she could appear within the field of vision of her idol. The instant Yaya Han glanced in her direction,

Kate smiled huge and waved. The biggest name in cosplay waved back with a big, friendly smile, then resumed signing a print for auction. Kate felt her stomach drop a little.

"Can I help you?" asked an older boy. Kate looked to the teen and couldn't tell at first if he was a fan or one of the people working the table. "Did you want to get a print?" he asked, gesturing to the vast array of prints of Yaya Han in every imaginable costume and looking perfect in each.

Kate glanced from him to Yaya and back. "No, I...actually..." She hesitated nervously. She was furious that she was so star-struck. "I...wanted to say hi to Y—Mrs. Han. She and I did two shows together this past summer." The salesman looked a little confused. "I mean, we were at the same shows. She and I gave panels on the cosplay track at Anime Time-Con," Kate explained. She glanced back at Yaya Han and hoped to catch her eye again. "I, uh, I just wanted to say hi. We've got a panel during the Masquerade, so we wouldn't be there."

The salesman nodded and said, "I'll be happy to tell her you came by."

Kate felt genuinely embarrassed. "Yeah...thanks," she acknowledged before turning away. Feeling like a rank amateur and a stupid fangirl, Kate turned away and cursed herself for being such a novice.

Furious with herself, Kate returned to the table. Emily spotted her approaching and could tell something was wrong. Kate sat unceremoniously and stared at the table. Her friend gave her a moment to glare before asking, "What happened?"

"I'm just being stupid," Kate dismissed. She laughed angrily at herself. "I think Yaya Han's my age. How can she be my role model?"

"Yaya Han?" Emily asked. She immediately looked in that direction of the dealer's room. "Is she at her table?"

"Yeah," Kate grumbled. She handed Emily the money and said, "Go see if you can get change." Rather than argue, Emily took the money and jumped up. Stomping away on half-foot platforms, she left Kate to settle in for a long afternoon.

As moments dribbled away, Kate watched the way the convention attendees flipped through the book of prints. Most of the girls oohed and ahhed over the costumes at the front, where Kate had put the photos of her more technically-demanding outfits. They gushed at the custom-made shoes, the hand-carved props, the elaborate visuals created by carefully-selected fabrics. The intricate designs used to create the visual affect garnered momentary awe before the next page was turned. And then the girls always walked on, marveling at the graphic artists Kate and her friends were sandwiched between.

The guys always flipped to the back. There, Kate had stashed the more revealing, more risqué outfits. There was Mai from Fatal Fury, Cammy from Street Fighter, and all the others whose costumes worked less as an outfit and more a framing device. Most of the guys gawked and then looked at her, in the same way patrons at fast food restaurants compare the food on their tray to the food in the picture. Some even had the audacity to say, "This doesn't look like you."

Few bought.

Kate's stomach gurgled as she sat on the folding chair, her butt aching from the cold metal. Everyone stopped by the table and looked at the documentation of Kate's hard work, appreciating the beauty and near-mastery of her craftsmanship in creating not just the costumes but the pose and the presence of the character. The hard work that went into capturing the character in their essence was always noted…and then bypassed for the work of someone else.

She watched enviously as money changed hands near-constantly with the print factory at the table to her left. The crew of three people had set up PVC pipes to hang a wall of 8x11 pictures. Beautiful prints of photoshopped masterpieces, Kate didn't question the graphic skills needed to produce those works. She watched though as they sold dozens of pictures every hour, doing business nonstop, twenties and tens being handed over with little change in return. All the while, Kate's lockbox stayed shut.

To her right, a more modest business was at play. The girl behind the table was doodling on a computer tablet, drawing right on the screen with the help of a stylus. Her table had wire frame shelves nowhere near as elaborate as the PVC rig on Kate's other side. The girl young enough to make Kate feel insecure and unaccomplished had framed pictures showing off her incarnation of popular characters, drawing people in to flip through her display book. She did far less work and made far fewer sales, but by taking commissions, bigger payments came through her table. All the while, Kate's lockbox stayed shut.

Two girls appeared in front of Kate's table. They began to flip through her book, gasping at one costume after another. Kate smiled happily, watching them look. The older-looking girl, a tall brunette with high school gawkishness and wearing a Power Rangers t-shirt, smiled at Kate. "These are so amazing." Kate beamed. "Do you have any nude ones?"

Kate's pride shattered like a pane of glass. "Wh-what?" she stammered, completely taken off-guard.

"Yeah, do you have any showing your boobs?" asked the younger girl, whom looked for all the world like she was in middle school.

Kate's jaw hung open, completely stunned. In the absence of a quick answer, the girls wandered off, heading to the table to Kate's right, asking if the artist did hentai commissions. The girl responded with a bright "Of course!" and took an order. Kate couldn't stop herself from staring.

A couple approached the table, the guy sipping from a smoothie and his obvious girlfriend clinging to his arm like a sloth. Kate watched them, a little surprised that the guy could even walk with such an attachment. The guy flipped through the book for a bit and stopped on a costume Kate had made two years ago. "Who's this?" he asked.

"Original character," she told him with some pride. "She's based off the armor you see in fantasy games like Warcraft, but taking influences from the mecha designs of Moriki Yasuhiro." She pointed to the spaldings of the armor, about to go into the specific details of the construction when she noticed the guy had developed a disapproving look. He muttered a 'thanks' and wandered off, his barnacle girlfriend still leached onto his sleeve.

Kate could only sigh. She looked down at the picture and said, "The armor took me over a month to construct and cost almost four hundred dollars." She turned the page to show another picture of herself in the armor. "It was fully moveable and was featured on eleven different cosplay websites. I won best up-and-comer on Cosplay.com." She looked into the crowd where the guy had disappeared with his lamprey of a girlfriend. "But I also have Cammy from Street Fighter if you'd rather see my ass." She sat down with a pronounced glare.

Kate was having a hard time focusing as she sat behind the table at the panel.

Her team of cosplayers had lucked out into being in one of the largest rooms in the convention center, but audience space was made up of more empty chairs than attendees. The ratio spoke volumes as to how much the four women had over-anticipated their attendance. The echo off the convention center carpeting made the microphones unnecessary and the dearth of questions didn't help either. So Kate sat with her sketchbook open and doodled. She'd filled the front of the book and was now working on the back of the pages. She wasn't actively designing anything, only sketching aimlessly to keep her hands busy.

Denise stood at the podium next to the table and talked about the chemicals needed to make molding putty harden. She'd gotten lost in a tangent about how certain paints could undo the reaction and make the putty loosen and even liquefy and she showed examples from her and Kate's own not-so-early efforts. "Isn't that right?" she asked Kate, turning to her suddenly. She laughed a little when she did. She seemed to be the only one laughing. The audience members were either taking notes or texting.

"Yeah, the best part was when we tried it on," Kate laughed, trying to go along with the joke, trying to pretend to be awake. "It tinted the skin on our…" She fell playfully silent, feigning modesty. She mimed her hands over her neck, collar, and then a bit lower. "Well, you know." There was some laughs and giggles. "A good boob joke always gets a reaction," she whispered out of the corner of her mouth to Rachael, who nodded.

Kate returned to her drawing, trying to get lost. She found herself imagining a long dress with slits up the side and along the back. Deciding she was drawing some variant of Jessica Rabbit from Who Framed Roger Rabbit, Kate took the design into a diesel-punk direction by adding some flourishes of bygone technology. Anything to forget the mundanity of the panel, the convention showing, all of it.

The panel over, Kate and the others piled out, checking the status of the world by way of their phones. "According to Twitter, Cassie Adams got Best in Show," she alerted the others. She grumbled and put away her phone. "I guess Yaya Han liked her Chun Li."

"Yeah, because she spent five hundred dollars on the fabric alone," Denise griped as she carried a wand, a bow, and two swords she'd used as props in their presentation. "We should—"

"Can we get a photo?" asked somebody none of them spotted. Conditioned to instinct, the trio instantly put their conversation on hold and set aside their belongings with stunning efficiency. Fran, Power Girl, and Batgirl all struck a pose together. Mostly they were just smiling for the shot but they did so in a manner appropriate to their respective character. The illusion of the persona was all.

One photo turned into several, which turned into a cadre of fans and amateur photographers all readying their cameras and phones as someone else was taking the picture. The crowd of photographers swelled like a malignancy, blocking off the flow of traffic along the normally-spacious hall of the convention center. People were fully blocked by the photographers stopping to get a picture of the three cosplayers.

Finally, it seemed the people had their fill and began to filter off. The instant the photos stopped and Rachael – the only one of the four women not in cosplay – ushered the three quickly around the corner and down an alcove. Down the hall where convention center staff could disappear into the back halls and isolated from the thoroughfare of the con, Denise resumed, telling Kate, "Your Chun Li costume cost a quarter of that and looked better."

"Visual texture versus looking good in a photo," Kate griped. She looked into the crowd that passed by and her shoulders slumped. "Guys, I don't know if I can go back to the table. Between the dudes who just want a photo of my ass and nobody buying..."

"Yeah, but the masquerade just got out," said Rachael, keeping track of a million different things on a cell phone so oversized, it bordered on a mini-tablet. "Everybody will be flooding the dealers' room, thinking about cosplay."

"Yeah, I know," Kate groaned. She looked down and tried to think of a counter. "But they'll go buy from Yaya Han and Jessica Nigri and that's it."

"We need to sell prints," Denise insisted, Emily agreeing with an eager nod. She half-laughed, half-joking when she said, "I want breakfast tomorrow!" The four girls all laughed, less out of humor and more desperation at the situation.

"Yeah, how have sales been overall today?" Emily asked Rachael. Kate grew self-conscious, as if by proxy. Somehow, she felt that the unimpressive answer was directly her doing. Or lack of doing.

"We've sold eleven prints," Rachael reported.

"Like, eleven of the 8x11s?" Denise asked, hopeful.

"No, eleven total," said Rachael. "We've sold three 8x11s."

An unsettled hush fell over the friends. "We've got to get to the table and move some units," Denise insisted. "We've got to try and recoup some of the costs we've already—"

"I know," Kate told her, unable to look anyone in the eye.

"Kate, we've got to make some sales!" Denise told her forcefully. Emily slipped behind Rachael, afraid of the tone being batted around.

"I know," Kate acknowledged. She closed her eyes, struggling to face the crowds. She covered her face like she was brushing her blonde hair from her eyes. "I just…" She realized she was going to start crying if she had to stare out at another faceless mass of people. "I just…" She tried to keep calm but the thought of the football field-sized dealer's room quickly unnerved her.

Kate's position not lost on her, Rachael saved the day by checking the convention guidebook on her phone. "Actually, the dealer's room closes in half an hour," she said, cross-referencing the time. She threw up her hands. "I like them having a closing time for the dealer's room, so we don't try to keep somebody there all hours of the night, but closing at 8pm at an anime con seems crazy."

"So does having a Cosplay Crafting panel opposite the Cosplay Masquerade!" Kate grumbled. "I still think we should have entered Emily's Fran cosplay. We busted our asses on that." Emily looked at her faded black armor and felt self-conscious and she wasn't sure why.

"Panels like this build the resume," Denise told Kate. "We've all hosted a Cosplay crafting panel. We can use this to leverage the next con to—"

"Yeah, at the next con so that we can use that to leverage at the next con, to leverage at the next con," Kate interrupted, emphasizing the cyclic nature of it all. The pair began to argue, Denise snapping at Kate for her negativity, Kate exclaiming that she was shouldering the workload, and Emily trying to and failing to referee.

It fell to Rachael to silence them and silence them she did. "Hey!" she barked at her friends, glaring at them until they fell silent. Twice as heavy as any of them, she was also half again as short and was the only one wearing pants or a shirt. "Reopening the table might net us a few sales, but we've got a bunch of parties we need to be at." She looked squarely at and to each woman. "Let's go back to the room, unwind a little." She looked specifically at Kate. "De-stress a little, and go have a good time, huh? Network a little?" The three cosplayers looked among one another and sheepishly began to apologize, peaceably at first and then sincerely. "I think we all could use a drink after today," Rachael insisted before leading them towards the elevators.

CHAPTER TWO

Kate had to jump a little to get the mini-skirt over her hips. She jostled, shimmied, and wormed her way into the tight skirt until it finally passed over her hips and slid up to her waist. A little out of breath from the effort, she took a second to re-adjust her breasts in her bra, and then righted the skirt that had shifted a little laterally in the process. Looking from afar in the hotel room mirror, Kate turned and checked over her shoulder at her butt and glowered. Doing her makeup in the corner of the mirror, Denise saw her expression and asked, "What's wrong?"

Kate grumbled, "My butt's getting too big."

"No such thing," Denise dismissed, going back to her eyeliner.

"Yeah," Emily concurred as she walked by in a towel, her hair still wet from the shower. "Besides, your ass is muscle, not fat."

Kate continued to study the contour of her skirt. "Yeah, but there's, like, a point of diminishing returns when it comes to asses. If it's too big, it becomes booty and booty doesn't pair well with cosplay."

"It does if your Cammy," said Racheal. The only one of the women not getting tarted up, she was sitting on the hotel bed, doing the books and checking the schedule at the same time. "If you think your butt's getting too big, maybe we should shift some of the cosplays you're doing. Something butt-centric."

"Something ass-pecific?" Denise punned. Emily threw a sock at her.

Kate gave up and went into the now-available bathroom. She wiped the steam off the mirror and opened her makeup bag. Leaning into the mirror, she studied the lines on her unadorned face. Seemingly bland eyes and pale lips sat unremarkable on a face that looked far older than she felt like it should. Unable to tolerate herself without makeup, Kate quickly began to apply foundation.

As the makeup went on, Racheal called, "So we've got six invites tonight. Do we go as a group, or do we split up?"

"Group," all the girls answered in unison.

"'Kay," Racheal accepted immediately and a little surprised. "Do you want to try and hit all six parties, or do we only go for one, or what?"

Kate leaned out of the bathroom. "Go to the most promising, and leave if we start getting bored, and go to the next-most promising."

"Yeah, that," Denise agreed, the others echoing her support.

"Okay, fine," Racheal said, not getting answers she could work with. "How do you want to decide which party is the most promising?"

"The one with the most professionals there," said Denise.

"The one with Elliot Thompson," said Emily. Kate leaned out of the bathroom again and stared incredulously at her. "What?" Emily defended. "He's got that really good fabric stuff. Being friends with him has benefits."

"You can be his friend-with-benefits," Denise disregarded.

"Not that kind of friend-with-benefits!" Emily yelled across the room at her.

"That's the kind he wants, I promise you," Denise called as Kate returned to the bathroom. "That guy's a creepy perv."

"All guys are creepy pervs," Kate assured her. Denise snorted and nodded.

"So, the party with Eliot and the party with all the professionals," Rachael weighed, checking the invites. "Hey, Kate you…" She got up instead and crossed to the bathroom. She stood in the doorway as Kate worked on her eyebrows. "You think you can play nice with the American Cosplay Reviewers people this year?"

"I'll try," Kate told her as she made weird faces necessary to the application of makeup. "Tell that asshole not to tell me he'll give me a cover story if I blow him." She turned and said, "I still think we should have filed sex harassment charges."

"Yes, but it would have been he-said-she-said and there was no evidence he said it, but there was evidence that you punched him," Racheal reminded her. The reminder made Kate smile.

Silence filled the halls of the convention center.

There was no lack of noise but a din kept at bay by thick carpeting and sound-absorbing construction. Rooms in four-pack vestibules marched down the hallway in dizzying consistency, solitary lights standing guard over the gaps between openings. Each vestibule was identical except for the trash and room service trays that marked the floor outside the doors. The hallways were endless, extending into the distance in either direction. Steps seemed to cover less distance than they felt like they should, thanks to the overwhelming and dizzying uniformity.

The four women passed by one of the elevator stops that faced the inside of the massive convention center. They spotted two cosplayers and half a dozen ravers already getting their late-night party started with glow sticks and impromptu dancing as they waited on the elevators. Eliot was among them, talking to a raver girl who was sucking on a pacifier and twirling her sticks and her hips. Whether she was listening to him was anyone's guess but the four dashed by to avoid getting dragged into his conversation.

The hallways beyond were every bit as surreal for the four. After the glut of people of a convention, with the noise and the constant attention upon the cosplayers and their costumes, the relative silence of the hallways was unnerving. Even more was the stillness. So used to a hundred eyes on them at all times, the awareness and sensation of being watched didn't disappear the instant they were alone. Awareness warped into a deranged paranoia, compounded by the echoless hallway.

Contrasting with the silence and stillness, coming from more than one room was throbbing techno and electronic dance music. The pulsing tracks that were more rhythm than melody created a thick white noise, negating what little sound there was in the nighttime halls. This left the golden-brown hallways with throbbing air but an absolute absence of sound, even between the women as they walked together.

Kate and Denise ahead of Rachael and Emily, they reached the crosspath that connected the two different sides of the convention center. In the very center of the hallway was a line of people, standing at the door into a single hotel room. As the women passed, the door opened and inside was a room filled with blue light, dubstep, and absolutely crammed full of people. The departure of one person prompted the bouncer to let in two more, as if the two-bed hotel room was some kind of exclusive club. Based off the line that stretched almost the end of the hall, he wasn't the only one to think so.

They crossed to the opposite hall and headed on towards the suites at the front of the hotel, overlooking the waterfront. They gathered around a door and Kate took a breath, readying herself. Emily, seeing this, remarked, "It's just a party."

"No, it's a job interview," Denise told the youngest girl as Racheal knocked.

The door opened and a tall, bearded man was there. He took one look at the women and exclaimed, "Rachael!" He bent down and gave her a huge bear hug.

"Hey, Dougie," she said, hugging the man almost twice her height like he was her little brother. Once they'd released, they feigned royalty kisses to both cheeks. "I believe you know my ladies," Rachael said dismissively to the three cosplayers-turned-club-goers.

"Your harem, yes," Dougie acknowledged with a harmless grin. "Come in, come in!" he told them, stepping out of the way so they could enter the room.

Hardly the saturated club they'd passed on the way over, the suite was still a serious party. About two dozen people were milling about, helping themselves to the buffet of cheap junk food, talking in pairs and small groups, or watching the two dancers moving around an improvised but functional dancing pole.

"Who are they?" Denise asked Dougie, pointing at the dancers and speaking up to be heard over the music.

"A couple of cosplayers from Costumed Babes," he told her, shimmying a little to the dance music. "Want to dance?" he asked like a dork.

"After I eat," Denise promised him. The three cosplayers, like a pack of wolves, descended on the snack buffet. Conscious of what they grabbed and how much, there was no mistaking the hunger with which they went over the table.

Kate went for a large handful of peanuts and forced herself to stop there. She tried to eat slowly, to enjoy the meal as it were, but she was too quick to scarf down the salted peanuts until her palm was empty of everything but the memory and blissful scent.

Rather than risk further temptation, she entered the crowd, hoping to see someone she knew but finding only strangers. She tried to bop a little to the music but couldn't find the rhythm so she went outside. Through a pair of glass double-doors, Kate exited onto the narrow balcony that looked out over the street beyond the hotel convention center. Down into the freezing night, she saw some cosplayers walking with brisk, quick steps towards the nearby pharmacy. A similar party of convention attendees exited the all-night supply center, each carrying bags of candy. Kate resisted the urge to hop the balcony railing and fight them for the Peanut M&Ms she saw several in the party carrying.

She turned around and leaned against the railing and tried to enjoy the moment. The dense, sweltering heat from the packed hotel room mixed with the frigid, fresh air of the early spring nighttime. The point of mixture was invigorating and right where Kate found herself. At least until a quick draft of cold air found its way up her miniskirt. She let out a quick shriek and exited back into the party.

For Kate, parties went one of two ways: every guy hit on her (sometimes right in front of their girlfriend/wife) or everybody ignored her. There was no middle ground. She wasn't sure if it was a bad case of resting bitch face or what, but something about parties never fit with Kate and she never fit with them.

She wandered around the room, gravitating towards people, trying to pick up enough of their conversation to dive in. Usually, though, she found them discussing some personal matter that she had no real way of understanding. By the time she'd circled the room twice, she'd concluded that everybody in the party was sharing their own private experiences with their close friends and had little use for a straggler.

Even her own friends were finding conversations to join, but whatever skill they had to strike up conversations, it was one Kate lacked. So instead, she got a bottle of water from the ice-filled sink and went to the dancers in the middle of the room. She sat on an ottoman and watched as the two women shimmied and shook, swaying to the music as if they were born from it.

It didn't take long for Kate to begin feeling self-conscious. The two girls were half her size in almost every respect. Slender, soft waists made Kate self-conscious about the six-pack she sported between her halter-top and her miniskirt. Narrow shoulders and thin hips made the two girls look like nymphs from some fairytale. Kate felt like a lumbering ogre by comparison.

By the time the second song had ended, Kate felt ready to cry. She rose from her seat and went to find Racheal, but couldn't spot her anywhere. She looked around the room, growing tense and a little desperate. She realized she was in a sea of people she didn't know, the room expanding into an ocean of strangers while at the same time closing in on her like it would choke her.

Kate began to panic and she rushed to the kitchenette of the hotel suite. She grabbed up a handful of the ice water and splashed it into her face, scrubbing vigorously to shock herself into calm. The sting of the water helped but she couldn't escape the sense of chaotic uncertainty. She leaned over the sink, trying to fight back the fear and control the anxiety. She breathed deliberately, trying to will her heartbeat to slow down.

"Hey, you okay?"

Kate jumped when addressed. Thinking herself alone in the alcove kitchenette, she was stunned by the dark-haired guy in a suit, sans the tie. He held up his hands in surrender. "Hey, whoa, sorry," he said quickly and genuinely. Kate felt even more self-conscious, now that she'd startled a stranger. "Didn't mean to sneak up on you," he told her as he gave her space.

"No, it's fine," she waved off. She dabbed at her face, relieved her makeup wasn't running.

"You okay?" asked the gentleman, testing the possibility of getting closer, like he was trying to check her eyes. "You look a little freaked."

"I am," Kate admitted. The alcove kitchenette afforded them some modicum of privacy as well as a slight buffer to the music. "I was--" She fell silent when he leaned close and shone a tiny penlight straight into her left pupil. "What are you doing?!"

He smiled self-consciously but he didn't relent. "Making sure you're not on drugs," he admitted. "I'm Devon," he introduced as he checked both eyes. "Your pupils aren't dilated. I saw you freaking out." He lowered his penlight and, standing a bit taller than her, he looked relieved. "I was afraid maybe you were having an adverse reaction to some meth or X."

"No, sorry," she told him, both of them pressing against the far wall as another partygoer slipped past them to get a beer from the fridge. "Are you a cop?" she asked loudly over the music.

He shook his head and corrected, "Doctor."

"Well, doc, I'm Kate," she said with some sarcasm.

He laughed, blushing some. "Sorry," he said, like this wasn't his first violation of social norms, or blown first impression. "Aaaand let me just go ahead and apologize now. I'm not an MD." Kate nodded, as if expecting the retraction. "I am a doctor, though," he maintained. "Just not a medical doctor. I couldn't do the sleepless nights. Pharmacology."

"Still," she allowed with a shrug. Deciding he seemed harmless, she offered as the closest anecdote she had, "I was studying to be a personal trainer. Once."

He smiled warmly, which made her smile in return. He had a slightly darker complexion than her, with black hair and strangely endearing asymmetrical expression. "You do these parties?" he asked, the sound of his voice seeming to wake Kate up from what she realized was her staring. Her response was a confused glance. "The cons, and the, the con-parties," he clarified, having to speak up now that there was a new song playing louder, like they were being punished for trying to converse.

"Yeah, they're kind of a job requirement," she yelled, leaning towards him to be heard, him leaning an ear towards her to hear. "I'm a cospla-a professional cosplayer." In the back of her mind, she felt uncomfortable with the exaggeration. Semi-professional was a stretch.

"Wow," he said with a grin before taking a sip of his drink.

She nodded and then said, "You have no idea what that is, do you?"

"Oh no, I know cosplay," said Devon, laughing at the suggestion otherwise. "I do have other interests aside from chemical interactions."

"Oh?" she posed.

"I'm also an illustrator," he said, like it was trivia. "Put myself through school doing commissions."

Kate laughed, both astonished and not sure she believed it. "Really?"

"Oh yeah," he nodded, not entirely sure he believed it either. He emptied his cup and went for a beer bottle from the sink-turned-cooler. He got two and offered her one, which she accepted. "Of course, with the crap I ended up drawing most of the time, I'm pretty sure I'm on some FBI watchdog list."

Kate laughed in total sympathy. "Yeah, I know how it is, believe me."

"I'm glad to hear it, and I'm sorry," he said, blushing a little. His nervousness made her blush a bit as well. "Look," he ventured nervously. "I'm sorry to be forward, but…but this place is kind of loud." He nodded at the air that was throbbing with music. "You want to find somewhere a little quieter?"

Kate's heart skipped a beat, and she wasn't sure if it was fear or something else. "Sure," she smiled.

The stairwell was warm, with alternating tufts of chilled air and hot breezes going up and down like ghosts walking passed. Kate sat on the top step of the fifteenth floor, facing Devon who was one step below her, his back against the metal railing. Her legs were crossed along the step, matching his as they both sat casually. She was swishing her longneck bottle in her hands as she listened to his tale.

"I'm not sure comics are for me," Devon admitted with a bit of a sigh. "I mean, I always wanted to be an illustrator. I've always been drawing. Since I was a kid, I drew." He snickered. "I remember the first time I saw a computer with an illustration program. A friend of mine in school, his dad had one. I was entranced. Mesmerized. I remember telling Santa Claus that instead of toys, I wanted a computer with Photoshop." Kate laughed.

Devon grew bittersweet. He shook his head and sipped his own beer. "I don't know," he lamented. "I've just…I've been trying to get into the industry for forever. Trying to get my break and I've just never quite gotten there, you know?" It was too hard for Kate to answer. She looked instead into her beer.

"I've gotten close, and you know what I've seen?" he asked rhetorically. The heavy bottom of his bottle clinked loudly when he set it aside. "It's not worth it." Devon shook his head and looked into the distance at his disillusionment. "I know guys that work for Marvel, for DC, and they live hand-to-mouth like somebody working at Walmart. Okay, maybe not that bad, but it's still carefully balancing their pay until the next paycheck, one that they hope will come on time. Big name guys that are still selling prints at artists' alley. Still taking commissions."

"Yeah, I know," Kate agreed solemnly.

"Nobody becomes an artist to get rich, but…" Devon lamented. "But, I mean, I thought there was a point when there was no longer a monetary concern, you know? A point where you got to forget about worrying about going hungry. A point where you were like 'well, at least I don't have to worry about paying the electric bill next month'.

"Or rent," Kate concurred bitterly.

Devon looked at her with the realization that he was dealing with a truer kindred spirit than he knew. He toasted her beer with his own. They sipped in melancholy silence. Well after their echoes had faded down the stairwell, Devon asked, "So how'd you get into cosplay?"

Kate just shrugged. "Geek, born and bred." Devon smiled wide. "Mom was into Star Trek and D&D and Speed Racer. I loved comics and cartoons and video games and…" She shrugged and had more beer. "When I discovered conventions and was like 'wait, you mean there's a place people go and just be geeky? Well, hell, sign me up!'" They both laughed. "First one I was at, I saw this woman in a 'Borg cosplay from Star Trek the Next Generation and I was just Ahhh," she sang like a heavenly choir. "So, I did a bunch of those. Star Trek originally. Then I discovered comic book cosplay, and then my boobs hit."

Devon nearly spit out beer, he laughed so hard. "Your boobs hit?!" he repeated incredulously. "You make them sound like muggers or something."

"Yeah, well!" she laughed at the absurdity but not inaccuracy. "I developed late. Or actually, I developed early and they developed late." She looked down at her breasts like they were separate entities. "When I was, like, sixteen, I was visited by the titty fairy." Devon looked about to drown, he was laughing so hard. "It was over a summer, too. Everybody at my school thought I'd gotten breast implants."

"Oh god, that's awful," Devon sympathized, even as he chuckled.

"For the most part, yeah," she agreed with a laugh. "I mean, I'm not going to lie, having big boobs definitely has its benefits at time. But my back hurts constantly and I have to pretty much give up on ever finding bras that actually fit."

"How big are they?" Devon asked with a smirk. Kate leveled a comically disappointed look at him. "No, really, I'm curious," he defended. "I'm a guy. I don't know anything about Ds and double-Ds and, and cup size to…to whatever."

"I'm double-E," she told him.

He stared for a second in amazed disbelief. "Geez," he finally accepted. "What does that…is that…like, what's a 32-EE or…"

"The number is the size of your torso, sans the boobs," she explained with some expertise. "You take a tape measure and go under your breasts, like you'd measure your waist or something." Devon nodded, following. "The letters are the cup size, the size of your actual breasts. So you can have a person that's 32-A and they've got the same torso size as a person that's 32-D. The person that's 32-D just has bigger boobs. That's it."

"Huh," Devon nodded. "Wow."

"You didn't know this, doctor?" she teased. He shrugged, not sure how to defend his ignorance. "How do you become a doctor AND an illustrator?"

"By hating free time?" he asked with a laugh. "No, I've just got more than one passion. And it's hardly unheard of. Osamu Tezuka? The guy who basically made anime?" Devon searched Kate's expression to see if she'd ever heard of him.

Kate was a little offended and her temper got the better of her. "My mom raised me on Kimba the White Lion and Princess Knight." Devon seemed genuinely impressed. "Yeah," she told him, not unhappy to see contrition in his eyes.

Devon's efforts to resume the discussion started with some blubbering but he recovered. "Um…yeah, Tezuka…I mean, he was a medical doctor." He had the decency to phrase the statement as rhetorical, not informative. "His series Blackjack was all about a medical doctor and Tezuka drew extensively on his experience in medicine."

Again, Kate nodded, feeling slightly guilty for her abrasive tone a moment ago. She looked at the metal door out of the stairwell, able to hear the conflicting music from the different room parties nearby. It was all a din of unintelligible sound, but it crept under the door like smoke from a fire. "I still can't get over the bra thing," Devon said, with a snicker. "Guys have…we've got nothing like that. Even athletic cups come in one size fits all." Kate snickered at Devon's naivety. "And your back hurts?"

Her answer was, "Hang a kettlebell from your neck and walk around like that all day, and see how your back feels."

Again, Devon shook his head in awe. "Have you considered having reduction surgery?"

Quipped Kate without hesitation, "Every time the Advil runs out." A little more seriously, she looked at her reflection in the dark glass of the longneck bottle. "But it costs money. Like, a lot. And cosplay doesn't come with a health plan. Plus…" She grew reticent. "Plus, I think half my popularity is linked to my cleavage." She'd meant it as a joke, but it stung to hear herself admit it aloud. Beer was needed. Now that she'd said it, though, there was no stopping it. "Sometimes I worry that it's not my cosplay that's popular, it's my boobs that are, you know?"

"A little bit," Devon said. A strange anger welled up in Kate as she tried to imagine what a man could know that was comparable. He expounded, "Like I said, I've done – I do – a lot of commissions and comic book art and stuff. I draw women dressed in clothes and nobody notices. I draw them dressed in what amounts to bondage regalia and suddenly I'm brilliant." He snickered cynically. "I can draw Batman vs Captain America better than Alex Ross and I'll get a dozen likes on Facebook. I draw Spider-Gwen pressed up against Mary-Jane in t-shirts in a cold room and I'm called 'the next big thing'." He shrugged. "Sex sells, I guess." Kate fell silent in grudging agreement.

As though desperate to pick things up, Devon smiled at her. "And hey, some people have to recognize the quality of your stuff? The details you put into the costumes, how accurate they are, stuff like that, right?"

"I hope so," she concurred.

"And plus, maybe you just need to get regular backrubs," he added.

Kate's left eyebrow went up. "If that was a pickup line, it was pretty obvious."

"It's supposed to be," Devon told her with a smile that was equal parts harmless and charming. "It does no good if the woman doesn't know she's been hit on. The goal is to be charming about it. Charming and clever. It's supposed to flatter her a little and entertain her." He told her this like he was instructing a pupil.

"Ah," she nodded. Sip of beer. "Well, it was smooth, I'll give you that."

"Thank you," he accepted with just a bit of blushing. Awkward silence ensued.

"I'm not having sex with you," Kate sort of blurted out. She was instantly worried about his response but he just nodded, as if he expected it. That surprised her. "You seem…"

"What?" he asked.

"Sorry, I didn't mean to be rude," Kate said almost as an apology. "But you seem…okay. Not surprised."

Devon shrugged. "You came in here, with me," he said, nodding to the stairwell, "knowing I was going to hit on you. So it's not like it was a surprise. Just the same, I knew you might say no. You were probably likely to say no. Heck, you may have decided before I even tried my clever-yet-adorable pick-up line."

Kate laughed a little, relieved. "Most guys think if they've gotten this far with me, they're going to close the deal," she admitted.

Devon dismissed that. "If guys have gotten this far with you, and are disappointed that they don't get farther, then they don't understand what they're missing." She looked at him curiously. "You saying no isn't some failure on my part," he told her. "And it definitely isn't some kind of...of, shall we say, unsociableness on your side either." Kate gave him an appreciative nod. "You're cool. You're interesting. You're...you're the kind of person I come to cons to meet. Sure, I want to hit that," Devon said vulgarly, looking her up and down, making her laugh, "but I want this," he said, gesturing at the space between them, "a whole lot more. I want...conversation?" He looked unsure, like the word wasn't adequate.

"So you don't mind being friendzoned," she teased.

"If anybody comes to consider me a friend, I'd feel very fortunate," he told her. Kate looked away, taking a sip of her beer. She was blushing. She found herself thinking him too far away from her and that worried her a bit. She also noticed she was chewing on her lip, which worried her even more.

"Although, I do think you should let me give you a backrub," he told her. She looked hesitant. "Pharmacology means I know anatomy very well," he advocated. "And I dabbled in physical therapy, Ms. Trained-to-be-a-personal-trainer." That got a laugh from her. "We can go back to your room if you want. You can call some of your friends to meet us there. But I'm not giving them back rubs too," he warned in advance.

Kate inhaled deeply, trying to keep her rational mind in control. "I don't know," she hemmed.

Devon leaned forward and took her beer bottle by the lip, guiding it from her hand. Her smile faded and her desire swelled. He set the beer aside on a lower step and took her arm. He placed his fingers on her shoulder and her upper arm and began to rub. Almost immediately, she felt tension slide from her hand and fingers. "Wow," she whispered, in awe of his quick work.

He dug fingers and thumbs into points across her shoulder and upper arm, the effects immediate below her elbow. Devon only rubbed for a moment, then he released her arm and retrieved her beer. He set back down on the step beside her and said, "And that was just your hand." He gave her a comically suggestive wink. She laughed further and covered her own smile with her hand. She turned away, she was blushing so hard. "What do you say?" he asked disarmingly.

Kate took a sip of the beer, to crunch up her courage to accept his offer. She smiled and said nothing as her world suddenly went black and she passed out.

Kate awoke sharply, without any grogginess.

For a second, she thought maybe she'd just blinked, until she realized she was staring up at a cement ceiling and not looking across a hotel stairwell. She tried to get up but she couldn't move her limbs. Feel, but not move. Her hands were draped above her head on a hotel bed. Her feet were likewise motionless and pulled tight. She wasn't just restrained but rendering completely unable to move. Like her limbs, her waist and hips were beyond her control, as motionless as her neck. She had no ability to move or wiggle in the slightest way.

She had no sense of her orientation. She wasn't entirely sure if she was laying down, or held back, or even hanging from above. There was noise all around her, like a waterfall, but coming from all sides. Light splashed across the ceiling over her and she heard someone enter the room. "Who's there?" she shrieked in a panic. She bucked against her restraints but to no avail. Amidst the sound of metal and wood shaking, Devon appeared over her. "What did you do?" she asked, more angry than scared. She tried to tighten her fists but only her face responded to her will.

"It's what I'm going to do," he told her, his words insulated from the noise of falling water. He seemed contrite and apologetic. He began to speak, stopped, and then started again, like he was deciding between conflicting truths. "I've given you a paralytic. Its effects will wear off. You can still feel; you just can't move." He looked almost afraid when he explained, "Feeling is going to be important...I'm afraid."

"Why?" Kate demanded, determined to move and still unable to do more than speak and scowl.

"I've found something," he told Kate like it was a confession, heavy conflict clear in his expression. "I've found something in you." He held up a hammer and a plastic box full of tiny construction nails. "I'm going to let it out."

Kate's heart stopped.

"I don't know where it came from," he explained as he moved into a better position over her. "I personally think it's a toxin that's been building up inside of us, all of us, for ages. But whatever its origins, it's there." He looked down at Kate and seemed fully aware of how insane he was acting. Aware and genuinely sorry for it. "But some of us, some of us, can release it. Or, it can be released from us."

"No, stop!" Kate pled as Devon put the tiny metal nail against her face, just off her nose and beneath her eye.

"Don't move," he warned her as he lifted the hammer into view over the nail.

Kate awoke with a start.

She was in her hotel room, in her hotel bed, naked. Denise, Rachael, and Emily were nowhere to be seen. The room was dark and totally quiet. The endless wash of the waterfall noise had become so constant, not hearing it made everything terrifyingly still. Kate touched her face and she felt wetness.

She scrambled out of her bed, hysterically kicking off the covers as she rushed. She fell over the entangling comforter and the litter of cosplay parts and makeup and dealers' room goods all over the floor. Her panic overrode any sense of care as she scrambled through the bathroom door and hit the lights.

She looked fine. Exhausted, but fine. There were no nails sticking out of her face, her body, anywhere. There was no sign of the violent, mutilating assault by Devon. She was okay. She started to leave the bathroom, her whole body aching, when she felt oily wetness on her face again. She turned back to the big mirror in the bathroom and noticed a tiny little dot next to her nose.

Not even the size of a droplet of sweat, it seemed to appear from out of nowhere. Kate leaned close to her reflection and touched the blue spot. She looked at her finger and studied the strange liquid. Barely the size of the head of a pin, it had a thick consistency, less like water and more like blood. It was thick and oily and sharp, royal blue.

Kate looked again at her reflection and saw the tiny dot had reappeared on her face, precisely where she had just removed it. She watched it bubble larger, the size of a tear now. Movement drew her eye to the other side of her nose and she saw a second dot of blue bubble up.

Rapidly, more spots appeared. Her skin began to give way as more dots of blue appeared from within her own face. She looked down at her hands, her arms, her chest and her stomach. All over her body, blue appeared, dribbling forth from within her. From every place Devon had driven a nail, blue was beginning to issue forth.

A sickness overtook Kate. A violent sense of betrayal and violation collided with a very real vertigo and she fell to her knees. She gagged on violent revolution within her body that threatened to spew up through her. Frantic, she crawled onto the toilet just in time to throw up. The violent gastric release was mottled by the blue oil. It was less like throwing up and more like regurgitating digested foam. It was thick and abrasive and unyielding, like vomiting out a pillow.

Kate could feel the blue running down her face and down her body, the puncture points bleeding freely and endlessly. Soupy red and harsh blue clashed, gushing down her skin as she felt like she was deflating. Kate couldn't even sob between violent vomiting. She tried to control her expulsions long enough to pull herself into the shower. She hit the water handle and the shower began to spray all over her.

Kate continued to vomit in the tub, bleeding out from the puncture marks. The water coursed down on her and she realized she was absolutely burning up because the hot water felt chilly. She curled into a ball and continued to expel violently under the flow of water. Sickness and violent exhaustion stole her away from consciousness.

The elevator doors parted with Denise and Emily both scowling inside. "Good grief," grumbled Denise as she got out. "What was his problem?"

"I don't know," Emily agreed. "Who says that? I mean really."

"I know!" Denise agreed as they walked down the hallway. "I don't even know if a reverse oreo is racist, but it sure as shit sounds racist."

"It was a reference to a sex act, so I'm guessing it wasn't racist; just awful," Emily said as she slipped her keycard into the lock. "Rachael better not get into trouble."

"Trouble? She talked us out of breaking his head; she better get a medal when she's done smoothing stuff out..." Her voice trailed off as the door opened. They were greeted with a foul stench and the sound of running water. Emily peaked in through the open bathroom door and saw Kate half-submerged in the standing water of the tub. "Oh god!" she shrieked as she ran inside. She hit the shower controls to silence the lukewarm water and she pulled Kate out of the tub. A wave of murky water went splashing over the sides and washing across the floor of the bathroom. Her shoes gave out beneath her and she fell back, Kate collapsing atop her on the soggy floor.

"Kate, KATE!" Denise yelled. She shook Kate in Emily's arms and tried to get a reaction. "Kate, please god, tell me you're okay."

Kate loosely awoke. Her eyes resisted opening but they relented to her efforts. "Wh-what..." Her head rolled from one side to the other, lacking the strength to even lift up. Wet hair was matted in knots to her neck and back.

Emily looked into the tub, seeing the murky, draining water was tinged with red blood. "Oh my god, I think she tried to commit suicide."

The word meaning death got Kate's attention and she looked around blearily. "Sui...who did?" She looked at the tub and saw the water draining out. "Oh god," she whimpered, "is that me?"

"Come on," Denise said as she pulled the barely-conscious Kate out onto the floor of the hotel room. She grabbed a towel and began to dry her off. "God, she's cold as a..." She couldn't finish.

Emily turned Kate's hands. She inspected her whole body, finally noting, "There are no slash marks." She looked back towards the tub, then at Denise. "What happened?"

CHAPTER THREE

Kate's hand was shaking. It made the contents of the bottle of complimentary water slosh inside the cheap plastic, a few drops splattering onto her fingers. She put the bottle to her lips, but felt a shiver go through her. She practically spasmed and pulled in tight, tugging the heavy wool blanket around her. She shivered and nearly cried out in pain.

The other women watched her, none of them able to process what to say, much less how to say it. So a circle of silence ensued as Kate tried to regain control of her body. When the shivering finally passed, Kate stared at nothing, not even the air before her. "I think…" she whispered. "I think I was raped."

A pallor fell over the other girls. Rachael grew angry, the others not far behind. "Who did it?" Rachael demanded. "I'll cut his fucking nuts off."

"I don't know," Kate said, utterly dazed.

"What did he look like?" asked Emily.

"I don't know if I was raped," Kate said. Under the blanket, she reached between her legs. "I feel…" She shook her head and shivered some more.

"What happened?" Rachael asked.

Kate was numb, in a daze as physical as mental. "There was a guy…" she recalled distantly, her words unsteady and just slightly slurred by the struggle to recall. "We were talking…we were talking…and he, and he stabbed me." She closed her eyes and tried unsuccessfully to focus. "No, we…we went to the stairs. Why did we go to the stairs?" she tried to reason. She fought to have a single thought she could focus on, but they all slipped through her consciousness, like trying to grab water. "A guy, stairs, then…" Terror filled her gaze. "Oh god, he stabbed me." She felt at her face. She grabbed her cheeks and forehead, jaw and scalp, horrified beyond all reason but touching only smooth skin.

"Where did he stab you?" asked Denise. She knelt before Kate and brushed blonde strands from her face.

"All over," Kate said as she touched her face and neck, like she was trying to find the wounds that didn't exist. "He…he used…there were these tiny nails. They were almost like needles. He, he used a hammer." She dropped the bottle unthinkingly and bolted up from the blanket. Naked, she ran into the bathroom and checked her reflection, but there was no sign of a single puncture wound anywhere on her body. She turned this way and that, checked under her breasts and behind her ears, studied every inch of her skin but found only unblemished skin. "Where are they?" she asked her own reflection.

Kate looked to the others who had crowded the bathroom door. They were all as worried as she was confused. She looked at the tub, only vague hints of blue left within. "What was in the water?" she asked weakly.

The others were hesitant to even speak. "We don't know," Rachael braved. "Emily and Denise found you in the water. There was blood and--"

"Blue," whispered Sam, unsure what was recollection and what was imagination. "It came out of me." She looked to her reflection, like it might know, or at least know how she knew. She reached to her face and slowly, painfully, recalled. "It…it bubbled up…up out of me. It sort of popped, like a zit that's too, too big." She halfway gestured the bursting motion all over, as she continued to try to piece together the mystery with just a bit more clarity than before. "All over," she recalled. She looked into her reflection. "Little blue…they just kind of, came out. All over." She began to check her body again, then looked at the tub. "What is it?"

"Okay, honey," Rachael said, crossing the threshold into the bathroom. She took Kate's hands and led her back into the bedroom and down onto the bed. She sat Kate down and Denise returned the wool blanket over her shoulders. Emily stayed a step back, chewing on her thumbnail. "Kate, honey," said Rachael, "I think somebody roofied you or something, Okay? I need you to think."

Kate could hear Rachael, see her in front of her, but couldn't quite process the words that she was saying. She squinted at her friend and tried to understand. "But I..." She reached between her legs again. "I...I don't think I was raped."

"They may not have been able to do it," Rachael rationalized. "I don't know. I don't know what happened, but we need to call the cops."

Kate stared for a second and then nodded. "Yeah, okay," she agreed absently.

Rachael jumped into action, already dialing with her cell phone. As she excused herself from the team, Denise took Rachael's place kneeling before Kate. "Do you remember what the guy looked like?" she asked in a consoling tone.

Kate blinked, staring. "Guy?" She tried to think. "He, uh...he was a guy. He had..." She closed her eyes and then began to shiver again. She tugged the blanket close and shook as she tried to keep away the cold. "Oh god!" she cried out as her whole body quaked.

When the shiver passed, Kate opened her eyes with a strange sense of clarity. "No," she realized, speaking firmly. "I don't..." She licked her lips as she thought. "No, I don't...he..."

"Did he have light hair? Dark hair?" Emily pressed.

Kate strained to answer but could only shake her head. "I really can't remember," she confessed with shame.

The male police officer standing over Kate mostly wrote in his palm-sized notebook. "And you don't have any recollection of your alleged assailant?" He didn't look up from the small, lined pages when he spoke at her. He only kept scribbling with a golf pencil.

"No," Kate repeated, a word she was becoming too comfortable saying. Dressed now in jeans and a tanktop, she still had the wool blanket pulled over her. The shivering had stopped, and though she still felt cold, it wasn't nearly as bad as it had been. It wasn't a surface cold, but one that had seeped into her bones, or deeper yet. Her fingers still burned from the chill, as did her ears and her chapped lips.

"And you say you had been drinking?" asked the officer. At the door, the other officer glanced inside. An older man, he checked on his partner, with only interest in Kate to make sure she wasn't becoming a threat. Two con goers stopped at the door and looked inside, looking right at Kate, but the officer at the door very lazily waved them on. They took their time passing. "Did you do anything to illicit a response from this man?" asked the interviewer.

Kate's eyes narrowed slowly, confusion tinged with just a hint of madness. "Did I...do...what?"

"Did you do anything to lead him on?" explained the officer as his eyes traced the scribble of his pencil. "Did you do something that gave him the impression you were interested?"

Rage.

"Did I do something that said 'yeah, I want you to drive fucking nails into my face?!'" she screamed at the officer.

"Ma'am, no need to get hysterical," the uniformed officer told her, looking at her for the first time. Kate just seethed. He flipped the notebook closed and informed her, "I will file a report, but without a physical description and no sign of the injuries you claim to have incurred..." He gestured over her body as evidence and nothing more. "I don't think there's much we can do."

"She was attacked!" Rachael exclaimed from the bathroom doorway.

"Some guy—" Denise argued.

"Did what?" asked the officer coldly. He looked down on Kate. "Your friend looks fine. There's not a mark on her."

"Take her to the hospital," Rachael insisted. "Get a rape kit done. Inspect her for sexual trauma."

The officer responded with confusion, as if the proposal was farcical. "She says she doesn't remember being raped and that she doesn't feel—"

"She's projecting!" Rachael exclaimed, storming from the door to get into the face of the officer a foot taller than her. "You think she got nailed in the face? Maybe not, but she got fucking nailed!"

"Ma'am, I'm going to need you to calm down," the officer told her in a patronizing tone.

"You're going to just—"

"I'm going to start arresting people if you don't calm down," the officer told Rachael directly. Rachael backed down but fumed visibly. The officer turned back to Kate. "We have your contact information. If we decide we need anything else, we'll be in touch." He left without another word. He patted his partner on the arm and the pair departed, not even bothering to shut the door behind them. The cold indifference of the hall and world beyond was left plain as the door slowly drifted shut on its own. Kate watched the door shut and felt numb but not from the cold.

Denise secured the deadbolt and stood facing the door, practically vibrating with rage. "I can't believe that son of a bitch," she cursed, her balled-up fist shaking.

"Fucking cops," Rachael growled. From the corner of the room, Emily watched the whole exchange like she'd witnessed her parents fighting. It was a corner she wasn't leaving anytime soon. Rachael came over to Kate and knelt before her. "Honey, I'm so sorry."

Kate just nodded. She asked, "Can we just go to bed? I'm really, really tired."

"Sure, honey," Rachael assured her. "Just lay down."

"Okay," Kate agreed, giving the faintest smile for the first time. She slid back on the bed and crawled under the covers. She shivered still as she pulled the pillow close and closed her eyes. She was aware of the other girls talking about her, discussing the event, but she tuned them out. She felt sore all over, and cold. Yet she felt the conflicting sensations of wounds all across her body – a million tiny puncture marks left by hammer and nail – and also the total lack of any damage, any puncture marks, any violation, anything at all.

She fantasized that she imagined the whole thing and found the slightest solace in that thought.

Well before dawn, there was a knock at the door. Kate's eyes opened unwillingly and she looked at the clock on the bedside table between the two queen beds. Showing 5:37am, Kate closed her eyes, only to hear knocking again. She rose and looked at her peers, all of whom were fighting the good fight to stay asleep and all slowly losing.

Kate rose and shuffled towards the door. "Who is it?" Rachael growled from beneath her pillow.

At the door, Kate peeked through the peep hole and saw a woman in a blazer over a t-shirt about to knock again. She had a walkie-talkie in her hand. Kate was worried but opened the door. "Yeah?" she asked, blearily.

"Hey, I'm Elisa Henry, the con-chair," said the professional-looking woman with clipped hair and a haggard expression. Kate looked confused for a second, so Elisa clarified. "Co-con chair, with Jeff Ackerman." Kate thought for only a second, then removed the chain and opened the door.

Allowed a more complete audience, Elisa went on in a hushed tone. "I just got word that you called the police about a sexual assault?" Kate rubbed her face and nodded, leaning against the doorframe. The con chair began to say more, then asked, "I know it's early, but can I come in and talk?" Kate sighed but couldn't think of a reason to say no, so she turned from the door and returned to the room. She grabbed up her pillow and hugged it, waiting for whatever else was going to happen.

Elisa shut the door as Rachael turned on the bedside lamp. "First of all, I am so sorry," said the convention representative, her voice shaking with genuine shock. "I don't know how something like this could happen at our convention, but when Jeffrey relayed what happened..."

"Jeff's taken good care of us, so far," said Denise, yawning from her and Emily's bed.

Elisa got down to business immediately. "Okay, did you file an official police report?"

Rachael got out of bed and took charge. "We called the police. Two officers came and one of them took a statement, barely."

Elisa followed, "Have you gone to the hospital?"

Kate looked down at her pillow and whispered, "No."

"I really think you should—"

"I don't have health insurance and I can't pay for the rape kit," Kate told her without looking up from the pillow she was holding. Elisa was taken back. "I'm not even a hundred percent sure I was ra...I don't think I, I..." She only shook her head.

"Why didn't you report this to—" the con chair began to ask.

"I'm really tired, okay?" Kate told her rather bluntly. "I've got to be back at the table in, like, three hours, so...can we please talk about this then? Or never?"

Elisa swallowed fearfully but nodded. She took a card from her back pocket and laid it on the drawers, next to the TV. "I know you guys are friends with Jeff, but email or call me if you need anything. The hotel wants to send a representative." Kate clamped her eyes shut, already dreading it. "I'll try to head them off for you if you want."

"Have them talk to me," Rachael said, Elisa nodding.

"Thank you," Kate told her.

Elisa nodded and said with genuine sympathy, "I'm sorry. I am so, so sorry." Kate only nodded and held the pillow tighter. The con chair saw herself out and the four women slowly returned to their beds and their sleep. Except Kate.

In the predawn darkness, the sky outside the window drawing to a brighter darkness before the first beams of sun would pierce the sky, she stared vacantly into the empty air of the hotel room. A distant sadness crept through her as she thought, "I want to go home."

***

It felt weird for Kate, getting dressed in her Cammy costume from the Street Fighter Alpha video game. She checked the paint on her thighs and turned to see the way the costume rode up high on her hips. Everything looked in place but it didn't feel right. Kate looked at her reflection and felt weak. Cammy was strong. Wearing the beret, the oversized hard plastic armored gauntlets, and the matching teal-blue costume, Kate didn't feel like she was cosplaying or even playing pretend. She felt like she was faking.

A tear dribbled down her cheek and Kate reached for the costume. It felt like a lie painted on her. She grabbed at it, but she stopped herself before she ripped the fabric. Her hands shook as she lowered them slowly and deliberately. She put them down on the sink basin and leaned on the counter. "I want to go home," she whispered to herself as she tried not to ruin her makeup with more tears.

She stood up, shuddering as she rose. She looked at herself in the mirror, stared into the woman's eyes, and slapped herself. A big, red imprint on her cheek made her chin quiver at the pain. "Stop it," Kate told herself. She slapped herself again. "Stop it," she rasped angrily at herself, furious that she was crying and furious that she was beating herself into submission, and furious that she was having to beat herself into submission. Kate let out one more sob of "I want to go home" and then took a deep breath. She buried all the fear and all the tears down deep and her face was a mask. She wasn't Cammy but she was someone else. She was someone pretending to be Cammy. The important thing was now she could smile, which she did. Now she could go outside, which she needed to.

Sunday panels at conventions were always poorly attended. Taking place at hours too early for most fans, and with the added handicap of taking place right after the usual debauchery of Saturday night, they were often highly-niche panels or ones unlikely to be all that popular. That there was anyone at all in the tiny room where Kate and her team were speaking was nothing short of miraculous.

Kate watched the sparse cluster of people as Denise talked about the benefits of different fabrics for presenting on camera versus in person. This led to her transitioning to talking about fitness routines and why dance classes were better than martial arts, especially for posing like characters from action games. Kate glanced down the table at Emily. Dressed as Rey from Star Wars: The Force Awakens, she was again on her phone. The slight chuckle she gave suggested it wasn't social media she was scanning.

"So how do you get a nicer butt?" asked one girl in the audience, rather tactlessly.

The question jerked Kate back into awareness thanks to its forwardness. Denise, dressed as one of the blonde bombshell dancers from Captain America: The First Avenger, turned and looked at the others at the table, eager for someone else to talk for a change. "You're our resident exercise person," she teased at Kate. "What do you recommend?"

"Deadlifts and swings," Kate sort of cursed without any preface. Denise and Emily looked down at her, a little surprised she'd spoken, much less so curtly. "Get a good kettlebell and swing a lot," she told the girl. "Comfortably difficult. You want it to be challenging, but not hard. Swing a lot. Hundred swings a day, lot. Or deadlift. Work up to a bodyweight deadlift and your butt will take care of itself." With nothing else to add, Kate turned back to her sketchpad.

"Uh...yeah," Denise slowly agreed. With a self-conscious chuckle and a smirk, she faced the crowd and tried to expound on Kate's brief explanation.

At the merchandise table, Kate couldn't get comfortable. Every time she closed her eyes, she could see a nail. She could see the positioning of it against her skin, the slight sting of its cold puncture paling to the dread of the impending agony when the hammer would fall and drive it through her skin. No blood; just pain.

Kate would open her eyes, frantic to drive away the thought. She would bang absently on her knee, like the physical movement would and could distract her. It sort of worked, but it left her in the waking world with a giant dealers' room full of people who paid no attention to her. They walked by the table of posters and prints, barely sparing her a glance. On the off chance that they did look to her, there was a haunting knowledge in their eyes. It was like every single person who walked past her, every single person who even glanced in her direction, knew. They knew she'd been attacked. They knew what had happened to her. And their looks were little more than confirmation that here was a woman who had been ruined.

Emily arrived, her full costume complete with sleeves and pants making Kate jealous. "Hey, how's it going?" asked the younger cosplayer. Kate didn't bother to answer verbally. Instead, she held up the noon-afternoon page of the ledger, showing only two very casual sales. "I'm sorry, but Denise needs you up at the front desk," Emily told her. Kate's heart began to pound. "There's an issue with the checkout."

Kate leapt up and practically sprinted out of the dealer's room. She ran through the hotel, shooting past everyone like they were standing still. She skidded on the smooth floor of the lobby, but her cosplay boots gave out and she fell, sliding into the wall. Too panicked to worry about embarrassment, she scrambled up and walked briskly to the front desk.

Rachael and Denise were both there and glanced back at Kate as she arrived. They looked worried and genuinely apologetic that she was needed. "What's going on?" Kate asked quickly.

"Ms. Harbough?" asked the woman younger than Kate who stood behind the counter. "I'm afraid there's been an issue with the checkout. Because of damages done to the room—"

"What damages?" Kate interrupted immediately. She glanced back at Denise and Rachael, both of whom were wary.

"The bathtub was heavily stained, according to housekeeping," the young woman behind the reception counter explained with a polite smile. She had to speak up a bit due to the crowd of people checking out in the convention center lobby. "Due to the excessive cleaning that will need to be done in order to clean and sterilize it, we have had to charge your card with an extra fee."

"How much?" Kate asked.

"They want five hundred bucks," Denise told Kate.

"Five...what?!" Kate exclaimed, her shriek stopping the entire lobby.

"Ma'am, please keep your voice down," the girl tried to reason.

"Five hundred dollars for a bathtub where I was FUCKING RAPED?!" Kate shrieked again. She jammed her hand over the girl's shoulder. "Manager. Now."

"Ms. Harbough, I am the—" the girl tried to explain.

"Then get the district fucking manager. Now." Kate glared.

The girl glanced back at the office, then looked down at her computer. She thought quickly, looking around the lobby full of people trying to checkout, most of whom were now staring. She practically whispered, "I can do a $50 charge for the cleaning supplies alone," she offered.

Kate wanted to scream further but an exhaustion passed over her and she shook her head. She wobbled a bit, Rachael and Denise both noticing and readying to catch her if she fell. "That's fine," Kate relented, desperate to get it over with. "Charge my card." She turned to Rachael and asked, "Can I borrow twenty out of the group fund? I don't have fifty in my account and I don't want it to get overdrawn."

"Yeah, sure thing," Rachael quickly agreed. Kate nodded and just walked away. Her head was throbbing and she felt like she was going to throw up. She ducked into the bathroom just off the lobby and practically dove into a stall. There, in a moment of isolation, Kate closed in on herself. She grabbed her arms and shivered tightly. Her teeth chattered and she practically spasmed. Back and forth she rocked as she tried to ride out something neither physical nor emotional. After a moment, the chill passed and Kate was left positively exhausted. It took some will to not collapse onto the floor of the stall and sink into unconsciousness right there.

Kate rose on unsteady feet and exited the stall. The white bathroom echoing with the chatter of people in the convention hall beyond, Kate took off her gloves and quietly washed her hands. She meant it just to help her wake up, but as she ran her hands through the water, she saw droplets of blue bubble up. She began to shiver out of fear, but drove the terror down deep, pushing the hallucination away. She inhaled deeply and exhaled slowly, determined to stay in control. "I want to go home," she told herself like a meditative mantra.

"Mommy, look!"

Kate glanced back in the mirror and saw a mother and her young daughter entering the bathroom. The little girl pointed right at Kate and squealed in delight, "Cammy!"

Kate fought with every ounce of strength to smile brightly at the girl. "'ello," she said to the girl in her best British accent, winking at her. The girl's face lit up and her smile widened. Positively beaming, she watched Kate put on her gloves again. "See you out there," she told the girl with confident smile. She strolled out, sparing the mother a glance, who gave her a thankful smile in return. Kate slipped out of the bathroom in full character.

The instant she was through the door, though, she gasped and nearly fell over. She clutched her fist to her chest, trying desperately to keep in control. With another shudder, she forced her eyes open and powered herself to walk, adamant not to let the weekend win.

Kate looked over her shoulder with an intense glare, clenching her fist tight. The amateur photographer snapped her camera while four passersby clicked with their cell phones. "Cool, great, thanks," said the professional, paying more attention to the screen on his camera than to Kate or the crowds walking passed. Kate tried to speak but all that came out was a nod as she slipped back behind the table. She didn't quite sit down, instead smiling happily while obfuscated by the table, she pulled the bottom of her one-piece out of her butt.

The photographer grinned with pride at the results and turned the camera awkwardly for Kate to see. She glanced at the screen and smiled, not interested in scrutinizing the image. "Very nice," she said as genuinely as she could manage.

"I'll post this on the site tonight," said the woman. She handed Kate a card and said, "Check it out when you get the chance."

Kate accepted the card and said, "Will do."

She settled back into the folding steel seat and watched the photographer head off. She looked down the aisle and saw people milling about the large event room that was emptying quickly. The neighbors on the right were already beginning to pack up. "You guys leaving this soon?" Kate asked them. "It's not even three."

"Got to get ahead of traffic," said the girl of the duo as she took a scarf down off the rack. "Plus, I have to be in the office tomorrow and I hate getting less than eight hours of sleep." She wound the scarf carefully and put it into a plastic bag. The man, her husband Kate assumed, was dismantling the shelves that had displayed their goods while simultaneously helping to block Kate's table.

"Well, be safe," Kate told her with a big, sunny grin.

The woman nodded and promised she would, but Kate barely heard her. Instead, she fixated on the small pins the woman was pulling out of a corkboard. Tiny slivers of sharp metal, they were just a breath thinner than the nails Kate remembered clearly but could find no context. She remembered screaming, pain, and passing out in a tub. It made less sense each time she remembered it and each time, it made her clinch her eyes and look away from the world.

"What's wrong?"

Kate looked up and saw Eliot. Dressed in regular clothes, she almost didn't recognize him. It was the ill-fitting shirt that gave it away. Tight on the arms, as well as the round stomach, it was only flattering to his biceps. He had a large cardboard box full of figures, most of which were from classic anime and all of which were scantily-clad. "You okay?" he asked. "Eat something that gave you gas?" he teased.

Kate smirked, relieved to have such a mundane irritation to deal with, to remind her of normalcy. "No, just..." She looked away and wanted to scream, cry, or just go home. "Just a bad dream," she lied as best she could.

"You should have told me you were gonna dress as Cammy," said Eliot, putting his box down on the table, covering most of the prints. Kate didn't have the energy to protest, only glare. "I thought about wearing my Guile costume last night. I brought it." He took out his cell phone and showed a picture to Kate of him modeling the decent costume in his bathroom. She looked at the screen and saw the costume she'd seen at half a dozen conventions just in the last year. She nodded and smiled, tight-lipped. "I always liked Guile and Cammy. They're my OTP." He laughed. "One True Ship, get it?"

Again, Kate nodded tightly. "Yep. I, I know what it means." She began to count to herself in an effort to keep from asking him to leave.

"I mean, they're both military. They both speak English," Eliot went on. Kate didn't answer or respond, only nodded.

Eliot smiled in the awkward silence for a moment, a silence that persisted well past the point of being uncomfortable to simply unpleasant. "Okay, well, I'm heading home," he told her, picking up his box, indifferent to or unaware of how it disrupted their prints. "I'll see you around, okay?"

"Will do," Kate told him, running out of steam for the day already.

"Bye," he told her, heading off.

Kate looked at the table he left behind, at the mess of the prints, and just sighed. She found herself without the strength to adjust them, to correct the chaotic arrangement. Something about the disrupted mess on the table felt appropriate to her.

But she couldn't leave it.

She leaned forward and began to straighten the pictures, organizing them as they had been. She fixed Denise and Emily's sets first, then her sets, then the group sets at the top of the collection. She leaned back in her table and sighed, wanting the day to be over.

It was late.

The convention was over and the four women were in the hotel bathroom, just off the main lobby. Kate and Emily were both at the sinks, dressed in casual clothes and scrubbing their faces. Rachael was standing with their stuff while Denise continued to change in one of the stalls.

Kate was scrubbing her face, trying to purge all the makeup from her skin. But with every stroke of her fingers that removed thick foundation, eyeliner, mascara, and blush, she felt like thick, viscous blue was coming too. She glanced into the mirror and spotted her face covered by streaming lines of blue, coming from a dozen tiny puncture marks all along her face and head. She shivered but kept scrubbing. "How'd we do?" she asked, needing to either change the subject or start crying.

"I've got a lot to tally but I think pretty good," Rachael said in that vague, noncommittal way that meant she was lying. Kate couldn't take any more disappointment this weekend, so she didn't push it.

Denise exited the stall, in jeans and a Henley shirt. Her hair was frizzing up, warning of rain. She looked painfully sleep-deprived and pale. "I feel like I've been run over," she said, the statement turning into a yawn.

"For real," Emily agreed, brushing her teeth.

"Let's get on the road and go home," Kate said, looking at her reflection in the mirror. Without any makeup at all, her skin was blemished around her chin and behind her ears. Freckles and darker spots dotted her face, the flaws of a normal human, blemishes in no way afforded a cosplayer.

Kate wondered if anyone outside of her three friends had ever even seen those spots.

Gathering up their bags and trunks of materials, the four girls began to make the long trek to the adjacent parking deck. Across the hauntingly empty hotel, the four women walked through spacious halls devoid of sound or presence. With the afternoon light fading fast, long shadows filled the halls.

With the clack of their feet and the rumble of the wheels on some of their luggage, the four women exited out into the blistering pre-twilight cold. The wind was blowing harshly, the wet air off the river behind the convention center biting at their fingers and ears. The girls shivered as one, too cold to even say anything as they crossed the empty valet parking section towards the parking tower across the street. The sky was already darkening. The white clouds were starting to take on an orange hue against the blue of the sky which was deepening towards purple.

"At least it's a pretty day," said Emily, trying to be the eternal optimist as she turned to look at the sunset.

"Yeah, to get stuck in rush hour," Kate grumbled as she and the others soldiered on.

"It's Sunday," said Emily. "They don't have rush hour on Sunday."

"Oh ye of little faith," Denise countered cynically.

They made for the elevators, only to find 'Out of Order' signs hanging on both doors. "Are you for real?!" Denise exclaimed. She kicked the door with high-laced punk boots, the thick platforms putting her just shy of Kate's height.

"Come on," Kate said, not even bothering with the energy for outrage. She bypassed the elevators with barely a break in stride.

They exited into the lowest level of the parking deck and began to draw their luggage behind them as they wound through the positively arctic darkness of the poorly lit deck. They walked up the traffic ramp, following the flow of traffic as if they were cars themselves. They remained quiet, simply too cold and too tired to even complain about being cold and tired.

Finally, they wound around the last turn and arrived in sight of Kate's car. A twenty-year-old four-door mini-sedan, the car sported several serious dings to the sides and the rear break light cover was cracked (though the bulb still worked). The rear bumper was dotted with stains where bumper stickers had once announced fandom proudly. Now, the bumper was an array of different stages of fading, while the paintjob itself was now chipping. The driver's side runner along the doors had fallen off, abandoned ages ago to the side of some distant road.

Kate hit the remote to unlock the car, but it didn't go. She pressed hard on the button, but still no release of the locks. "Oh come ON!" she groaned. She simply dropped her stuff, letting it clatter to the pavement of the empty parking deck. Doing so caused a wheel on her suitcase to pop off. "What the hell?!" Kate exclaimed as the wheel went sailing through the air, hit the rear wall of the parking deck, and ricocheted back to Emily. It hit her in the cheek, stinging, and disappeared under the car of somebody who clearly had the money to stay the extra night.

In the only reasonable tone such an event could necessitate, and saying the only appropriate thing at that moment, Kate yelled, "FUCK!" She kicked her suitcase in frustration, causing the dual pain of watching the latch give and making her foot hurt. Her clothes burst forth like a fountain, covering the oil-stained pavement of the parking deck.

Kate fumed for a second then abandoned her clothes. She left the pile behind and unlocked the nearer passenger side door manually, then the rear door. She unlocked the trunk, but had to shake the key to get the latch to release. She returned to her clothes and quickly gathered them up. With hastily repacked suitcases under her arm, Kate waddled towards the car where the others were waiting. She threw her luggage into the trunk, only for the broken case to open in air, spraying more of her clothes all over the ground as well as bouncing off the frame of the car and falling upside down onto the pavement. The others stayed fearfully quiet as Kate visibly counted to ten. She repacked her case yet again and shoved it into the trunk. Leaving the others to load their stuff, she went around to the driver's door and unlocked it.

The final door, the driver-side rear door, wouldn't unlock. As the girls loaded their stuff into the little car, Kate fought with the keys to get the tiny door lock button to raise most of the way. Normally a satisfying pop, the underwhelming elevation seemed to mock Kate further. She pulled on the handle, but it wouldn't open. "Oh, come on, for fuck's sake," she groaned, jiggling the handle and pulling on it. She began to genuinely cry in frustration as she pulled futilely on the handle.

"Kate, it's fine," Rachael told her, Denise and Emily watched petrified as she fought with the door.

"Fucking open!" Kate yelled at her car. She gave it a slap with her hand, then knocked it with her shoulder, causing the sedan to rock on its wheels. She pulled harder on the handle, not quite grasping what the problem was. She glanced at the other doors and saw them unlocked, then at this door and finding it unlocked and yet still not opening, she lost it. "OPEN!" she screamed through tears. She fell against the car, sobbing. "What the fuck?" she whimpered at the world. Her three friends were perfectly still, unsure how to respond except to default to sympathetic witness.

Erupting, Kate screamed, "WHAT THE FUCK?!" She yanked on the handle of the door, the manifestation of all that was wrong in her world. With a high-pitched squeal of metal surrendering before breaking, Kate's hold on the car door gave. She stumbled and fell back from her car, sobbing still. She landed on the pavement, the handle of the car door still in her hand. She sobbed quietly, unable to handle anything anymore. She curled into a ball, still holding the door handle as she cried. The harsh cold air stung her tears and ended her self-pity, uncaring for her condition. Her face stinging in the cold, she looked in utter despair at her friends.

They were all staring, nervous silence replaced with terrified shock.

"What?" she asked through the tears. She looked at the car, mortified to realize the door was gone. The frame warped outward, Kate realized that the car had been broken, the driver's side rear door clearly absent from the vehicle. She glanced around, trying to figure out what had happened to it, until she realized she hadn't pulled the handle off the door.

The door was still attached to the handle in her hand.

Kate looked at the car door she held, the metal warped and twisted. Fragments littered the pavement at her feet like shards of glass. Kate looked at the side of her car, the frame as warped as the door, then at her shocked friends. Her chin quaked and she simply whispered behind clamped eyes, "I want to go home."

CHAPTER FOUR

The most annoying alarm ever invented in the history of the world went off at 5:45am.

Kate slapped at her bedstand, her head still buried under her pillow. She finally caught her phone and pulled it under the pillow with her. "Ow," she groaned at the sound as she turned off the alarm. She set the phone aside and settled back under her pillow and comforter for a second. "No! No no no," she demanded, forcing herself to get up. She sat up and stared bleary-eyed at her room.

Clutter had accumulated into large piles in the corners and along the edge of the walls. The carpet in the middle of the room was mostly clear, though it had obviously not been vacuumed within recent memory. Or ever. The walls of her room, the same generic white of all apartments, were covered almost entirely by superhero posters. More than a few of the pictures were original works or commissions from conventions, some of which were yellowing from age. At the foot of her bed was a matrix of long cardboard boxes jammed almost to the bursting point full of comic books. New issues, such as ones collected from the convention, were stacked neatly-ish on top of the boxes. Dotting the room was an assortment of three-shelf stands of different styles that had been collected from charity shops and the apartment complex dumpster. They all held action figures, momentos, and other assorted brickabrack arranged somewhat neatly.

Kate swung her legs out from under her comforter, giving a light shiver in the exposed air. She managed to stand and felt around rather than look for the pajama pants she always kicked off during the night. She pulled on some Avengers flannel pants and shuffled out of the room. In the living room, the television was on. In one of the three recliners, all of which were frayed heavily at the edges, Deloris Harbough was watching the news as she sipped coffee. "Good morning, Nana," Kate said as she leaned down and kissed her grandmother on the cheek.

"Morning, baby," cooed the silver-haired octogenarian, tapping Kate's leg with a wrinkled, arthritic hand. "You got in awful late last night. Did you have fun?"

"I did," Kate said happily with a yawn as she shuffled towards the communal bathroom. She fished her toothbrush out from the medicine cabinet dominated with her grandmother's medicine bottles. Kate wet the brush, applied the toothpaste, wet that, and then scrubbed vigorously. Standing before the mirror, she almost fell asleep mid-scrub. She rinsed her mouth and brush, then leaned into her reflection.

Her jade eyes were still bloodshot, but that was nothing new. She had terrible bags under her eyes and a breakout along her neck thanks to the makeup she wore for Cammy. The limited exposure, though, kept the little red bumps to a minimum. Most importantly, there were no signs of puncture marks or other wounds. Whatever she'd dreamt at the convention had stayed there.

Kate got a hair band from the container full of them and put her frizzy, blonde hair back in a ponytail as she departed the bathroom. "Baby, where's your car?" her grandmother asked, craning her neck around the back of the recliner.

Kate froze mid-step and suffered a minor panic attack. She swallowed fearfully and pivoted on her heel towards her grandmother. "I left it at the auto shop," she said. "I need to call them." She felt the need to make up a lie on the spot for her grandmother. "We hit a pothole on the way back from the convention and the car's driving funny now."

"How much will it cost?" her grandmother asked, already wringing her hands.

"I don't know," said Kate. "I got to call them at lunch today."

"Will they be able to get to it today?" Deloris asked.

"I don't know, Nana. I expect so." A step towards her room and Kate backpedaled to the same spot and asked, "Why?" She suddenly worried about some forgotten chore or errand she needed to get to today.

"I just don't like us not having a car in case we need it," said the homebody. She wrung her hands for a bit more, even as she settled back to the first round of the local news.

Kate felt bad for worrying her grandmother, but she also began to get lost worrying about the car. She didn't even want to comprehend the cost of fixing the door. She began to play in her mind ways she might be able to play the loss of the door off as an accident or something, and get her insurance to cover it. Those thoughts turned into fears of what her insurance actually covered and her ignorance therein ran through her mind. Then she juggled the terms 'comprehensive' and 'collision' and she couldn't remember which was which and which one she had.

With a full-body shudder, Kate tried to put it all away and she went back into her bedroom. She shut the door and leaned against it. In the darkness, she almost fell asleep leaning against the door. With another shake, she pushed it all away and clicked on the overhead light, revealing with greater clarity the magnitude of her geeky collection. Toys and statues, cosplay props and pieces, and every assortment of fandom imaginable filled the room that was less personal space and more shrine to all things geek.

Kate went to the closet and slid aside the mirror door to pull out a 44lb kettlebell. Kate popped her back, then hoisted the kettlebell up and did a host of quick lifts at an easy pace with it, warming up until she began loosen up. Once she felt less cold and more awake, she returned the lighter bell and pulled out a 62lb kettlebell.

In the middle of the room, Kate began to snap quick swings with the bell, over and over. Hoisting the bell between her legs, she thrust her hips forward, practically throwing the kettlebell away only to keep it in grip as her body snapped tight for a split second before she hiked the ball back through her legs. Resting periodically, she did a hundred and then did a dozen slow get-ups, starting on the floor and then standing methodically and with hypnotic control until she stood tall with the heavy bell head aloft. She then reversed the movements in precise order until she was laying on the floor again.

Panting a little and with a sheen to her skin, not even sweating, Kate headed back into the living room and kitchenette that was the majority of the three-bedroom apartment. Bypassing her grandmother without a word, Kate fished out some eggs from the refrigerator and quickly began to scramble some while she hardboiled others. As the eggs cooked, she pulled out her phone and began to post all across the internet.

"Great time!"

"Thanks to everyone who came to the table!"

As she posted some of the earliest pictures from the convention and gushed gratefully about selling out of different prints, the master bedroom door opened and Lauren Harbough came shuffling out, just as bleary as Kate had been twenty minutes ago. "Hey," she said with a yawn.

"Morning, mom," Kate said as she typed in a cheerful, energetic tone totally antithetical to her actual mood.

Lauren went for the cabinet and fished out a Star Trek mug. She shuffled into the opposite direction with a snort and filled her blue mug with coffee, the heat causing Commander Riker to appear on the color-sensitive surface. "You got in last late night," her mom remarked as she added cream.

Kate nodded, still typing on her phone. "We got away late is all."

"Good con?" asked Lauren as Kate scraped eggs onto a plate. "Did your panels go well?"

Kate decided pre-dawn was not the time for a nuanced answer. "Pretty well," she told her mom with a smile. Lauren rewarded her hard work with a kiss on the forehead, then returned to her gloomy disposition as she took her coffee back into her room.

Kate took her plate into the living room and sat with her grandmother, watching the news. A science correspondent was being interviewed about some astral event, but Kate paid very little attention. She was too busy cross-posting on every social media platform that existed. She linked to her friends' pages and shouted out at everyone imaginable. She responded to every comment, even with just a Like, and made the convention sound like a success, both professional and personal.

"Did you hear about this, baby?" her grandmother asked.

Kate glanced up, but the news cut away to a cute dress maker that was selling fashion based off African tribal designs. "What was it?"

"There's going to be an asteroid coming by," explained Deloris. "The man on the news said that we'll be able to see it with a telescope."

"Cool," Kate said with a smile, even as she went back to her phone. "Does anyone actually own a telescope?" she muttered to herself.

The instant she'd chewed the last bite of her eggs, Kate was back in her room. One glance through her closet doors and she confirmed the ugly truth of how little of her wardrobe was hanging from the hangers. Or even clean. She turned back to her room, sighed, and went digging through piles of clothes. She pulled out every bra she could find, sniffing the cups until she found a tan bra that didn't offend her nose. Off came her tanktop and she affixed the bra behind her back.

Next, she dug out some khakis and a white undershirt, followed by one of her blue work shirts. She fished around the knickknack bin on the bedside table and found her nametag and affixed it over her left chest. She checked her reflection but because of her breasts' size, the nametag was practically facing straight up. She had to reposition it to make it even a little readable, but that resulted in it riding on the front of her breast like the least flattering pasty ever. Grumbling, Kate went into the bathroom and used that mirror to find a position that was functional but not comical. It took some work.

Just as she found the perfect spot for her nametag, something poked her in the ribs. She winced at the pain, then placed the familiar discomfort. "No!" Kate groaned as she began to feel under her breasts. She quickly found the break in her bra and the underwire that was poking out. Kate undid her shirt and tilted her torso up so she could lift up her right breast and see the wire poking out a bit. She stood up straight and moved a little, finding the spots that would result in her being stabbed with underwire. Deciding the risk was acceptable, she rebuttoned her shirt.

Kate ducked back into her room and grabbed a small black purse. She filled it with what little cash she had, her wallet, an extendable baton, her keys, and her cell phone, and ducked out. She leaned over her grandmother's chair again and kissed her saying, "Bye, Nana."

"Bye baby," Deloris answered, trying to pat her leg again but Kate had already stepped away.

"Bye, mom!" she called across the apartment.

"Bye!" her mother yelled through the bedroom door.

Kate rushed out of the apartment and locked the door behind her. The morning was positively frigid, but in a manner that promised the temperature to double before the day was out. Ignoring her visible breath, Kate dashed up the half-flight of steps from her apartment up to the sidewalk, and then down towards the main road. Cars were zooming by, illuminating her in flashes as she walked briskly towards the bus stop one complex up the street.

As she walked, the clack of her work flats keeping time with her breath, Kate fished out her cell phone. She quickly dialed after checking the time. "Anderson's Tire and Body," answered the man on the other end.

"Hey, this is Kate Harbough," she said as she walked, turning away from the loud traffic. "I dropped my car off last night. It's the one with all the duct tape."

"Oh!" laughed the guy. "That's your car afterall, huh? We were wondering who left a car with a door duct-taped on to it."

"Yeah, the door just...just popped off," she told them. She made a displeased face that she didn't have a better story for the damage.

"You didn't drive with it like that, did you?" he asked.

"The backseat looks like a spiders' web with a bunch of bungie cords," Kate warned him. "Just, you know, FYI. My friend Denise also kind of held it in place as we drove back so, there's...yeah." She looked nervously about before she asked, "Can you guys look at it and see if it can be put back on?"

She heard him clacking on a keyboard. "Um...yeah. We can get to it today, I think. Just a heads up, we're kind of swamped. I doubt we'll be able to affix it today, especially if there's any damage to the frame."

"Yeah, no, I get that," she said. A gust of cold air shot by her as her bus passed ahead of her, reaching the stop before she was there. "I'm headed to work, I'll call you later, okay?" She hung up without waiting for an answer and sprinted for the bus stop before the bus left her behind.

Kate stood in a circle with all the other opening employees. Given that it was Monday morning, the gigantic store was grossly understaffed. With more people working in the backroom than in the front to help the customers, most departments were staffed with a single person until the evening shift. At the morning 'pep rally', the employees stood in a circle as the store assistant manager did his best to explain how integrating the corporate sales goals into the floor team's daily work would make things more fun. Kate yawned, and wasn't sure if it was the early hour or the insipid talk.

Once the assistant manager was done wasting everyone's time, he had them all gather together and put their hands in like they were a basketball team. Kate hated sticking her hand into the pile of everyone else's hands but being singled out was never good at work. She endured it with a grimace she tried to make look like a smile. "Go team!" the assistant manager said with the enthusiasm found only in the extremely well-paid or extremely desperate.

The morning 'pep rally' over, Kate was able to head to her department: women's intimates. She paced among the aisles of bras and underwear, with everything from the high-end stuff that almost seemed worth the money to the ugly and barely functional but economical. Once she'd completed a quick walkthrough to confirm there were no major problems, she slipped to the edge of her section and glanced across the walkway that carved up the store. Adjacent to her section were the toy aisles. She peeked around and confirmed nobody – customer or management – was nearby and she crossed.

Kate headed right for the action figure aisle and went for the superhero toys. She quickly picked through the collection with expert speed, trying to spot any that she simply couldn't live without. Sadly, she found too many. As she always did. Kate selected two action figures for consideration: a film Supergirl, from the 1984 Helen Slater movie, versus the CBS television Supergirl with Melissa Benoist. Both did a poor job capturing their respective actress' likeness but at least the TV series Supergirl had something resembling an expression. The film Supergirl figure had only a vapid glare facing straight forward.

"Given the rarity of the event, it's believed these phenomena may be connected."

Kate looked up from the toys into the electronics section beyond. The wall of TVs against the far edge of the store were all tuned to the news, all showing the same reporter interviewing the same expert. Kate glanced back to confirm the intimates section was still a barren ghost town, then set aside the action figures and slipped over.

Rich and Derek were at the electronics counter, watching the TVs. They barely noticed when Kate arrived. "'Sup," was all Derek said. Rich was too engrossed to speak.

"What's going on?" asked Kate.

"That asteroid that's supposed to fly by in three weeks or something is going to cause all sorts of weird effects," Derek explained, the taller of the pair with wavy brown hair past his shoulders. "Like, electromagnetic stuff."

"We're supposed to be able to see the Aurora Borealis," Rich said as he watched. Equal in height to Derek's armpit, he had a similar complexion and disposition.

"Really?" Kate nodded with indifferent approval. "Cool."

"Yeah, they're saying some of the effects are already being felt," said Derek. "Satellite reception is tanking. There are places that are getting no reception."

An epiphany hit Kate. "I wonder if it can cause dreams." Rich and Derek both broke from the TVs to look at her oddly-specific hypothesis. "Like, nightmares?" she asked them like they were experts. She swirled her fingers around her head to demonstrate. "Like, what if somebody's brain got fuzzled by the asteroid and they had, like, a stupid-terrible nightmare?"

Rich nodded very slowly, very sarcastically. "Sure," Derek agreed, just as slowly.

"Maybe it—" Kate continued to speculate with relief.

"Guys," called Walter, the store's newest assistant-assistant manager. In a blue vest over a white turtle-neck, he practically rushed over. "Why are the TVs on the news?" He completely ignored Kate, for which she was grateful.

Rich looked at the TVs, then at Walter. "Because I put them on it."

Walter grew visibly angry at the insubordination. "They're not supposed to be on channels; they're supposed to be on the in-store demo." He looked at the TVs quickly and realized, "Wait, that's cable?" He glared at Rich. "How are they on cable? How are they even getting anything? We don't have reception back here!"

"You think they put me in charge of electronics for my people skills?" Rich asked him with an indifference to authority born from irreplaceability.

Walter glared, his chubby jaw twisting. "Kids from the school like to come in here during lunch."

"Right, 'Lunch'," Derek sarcastically agreed, adding the air quotes with his finger. "That's when they come."

"You think it's appropriate for them to see the news?" Walter aimed solely at Rich.

Rich looked at Derek then said, "Uh, yeah." Derek nodded his head in unanimous agreement.

Walter's patience was visibly wearing thin. "Switch it back to the demo right now." Rich set about doing so, though with positively no urgency. Walter then pointed back at Kate as she tried to sneak away. "And you."

"Dammit," she cursed, almost to the toy aisles, her route of escape.

"This isn't women's underwear," Walter asked. "Why are you out of your section?"

Kate shrugged. "I saw the TVs on and I wanted to know what was going on?" she asked, like she was hoping it was an acceptable answer.

"You need to stay in your area," Walter told her like it was his motto. He gestured for her to skitter off like a good girl, an act that made her want to punch him. Rather than do so, however, she did as she was told and went to waste the day among bras and thongs.

"What do you mean it's not covered?!" Kate exclaimed into her phone as she paced in the breakroom. Mid-morning on her break, she covered her ear as she attempted to speak in hushed tones in the small kitchenette.

"I'm sorry, Ms. Harbough, but your insurance is liability-only," said the insurance rep on the other side. "Incidental damage, especially of this magnitude, is not covered under your policy."

Kate slumped forward against the unpainted cement wall and took a few deep breaths. The rep on the other end of the line was continuing to speak, but Kate wasn't really listening. "Okay, thank you," she told the woman without a clue of what she was telling her. Kate didn't even listen to know if she'd interrupted the poor woman. She just hung up the phone.

Kate slumped down with her back to the wall, in the farthest of four dinette sets of the small, ugly room. She managed to sit down right in front of the vending machine. Stationed prominently in the very center of the vending machine, perfectly in Kate's line of sight, was a pack of butter crackers and peanut-butter. The thought of the taste she hadn't known in ages made her lick her lips. But the movement of her reflection in the front of the vending machine caught her attention.

Kate was staring at herself. In the store uniform of blue and khaki, the thirty-year-old could see the bags under her eyes, only half-hidden by makeup. She could see the frizz in her blonde hair and the clothes that had never been ironed. She saw every flaw, especially the wrinkles. Kate closed her eyes and whispered, "I want to go home." Alone in the kitchenette, she stayed behind her closed eyes.

Kate was putting bras on hangers.

With a box from the dressing room on one side of her and a box of hangers on the other, she rotely suspended the garments by their shoulder straps and set them on the handle of a shopping cart she'd pulled over. She moved on auto-pilot, a million miles away, thinking about costumes and comics, cosplay and conventions.

An ugly stench caught her attention and Kate crinkled her nose suddenly. She searched around for the source, only to realize it was the bra in her hand. The right cup had a pronounced stain on it and Kate blanched in disgust. She tossed the bra into the basket, just as Walter was approaching. "How's it going?" he asked, curious about the discarded bra.

Kate gestured at her empty section, which matched the rest of the empty store. "Fine?" It was a guess.

"We've got to cut some hours this month and next," Walter explained casually, like loss of income was no big deal. "Candice wants to keep from laying people off, so it's hours that get cut instead." Kate couldn't tell if he agreed with the plan or not. "We're giving people the option to take a leave, or to get cut back to part-time."

"I work thirty-four a week; I am part-time," Kate said as she tried to ignore the sensation of a brick in her stomach.

"We'd schedule you for probably one eight-hour and two six-hours then." He glanced around sourly and took a quick sniff. "Anyway, maybe three or four six-hours?" He was just guessing. "It depends on how the weekly schedule shakes out. Since most departments are mostly breaking even..." He said that and looked around, like he was trying to drive home the point that her department wasn't among them. "Do you have a preference?"

Kate swallowed and felt pathetic. "I really can't do a leave. I'll take part-time."

Walter nodded and crinkled his nose again at the rancid smell. "It'll just be temporary, until the summer push starts."

Kate muttered under her breath, "Yeah, right."

Walter started to leave, but stopped when he sniffed the air again. He pulled the bra out from the cart and grimaced at it as well. "We need to get this thing bleached."

"Oh god, you're not going to sell it?!" Kate exclaimed.

Walter didn't make a decision either way. "I'll..." He just turned and walked away, leaving Kate disgusted with everything about the exchange.

Just after noon, Kate was turned away from the handful of others in the store breakroom. On her phone, she asked "Isn't there anything you can do?"

"'Fraid not, Ms. Harbough," said the mechanic on the other end of the line. "The door is completely broken. Looks like the joints too. We're going to have to do some serious body work on the car's frame just to be able to reattach a new door, and it's going to have to be a new door. The strain placed on the old door warped the metal. I mean, yeah, technically, we could repair the door y'all duct-taped on there, but you'd be talking three or four times the cost of just buying a replacement door from a junk yard."

Kate sighed and covered her face. She was NOT going to cry at work. Not again.

"What happened?" he asked curiously. "The door was clearly pulled off. Somebody prank you with a Zamboni or a truck or something?"

"Something like that," Kate tossed away without a thought. "Look…I don't know if I can afford to get the work done. Can you…can you, like, weld the door on or something? Just get it to hold in there for a little while longer?"

"A little while longer?" he asked, surprised.

"Yeah, until I can…" Kate's entire world shattered when she realized she had no idea what she was trying to buy time towards. All she could think of was raising money by moving a whole bunch of prints at the next convention. It was a goal as common to her as breathing, and as rare as a good night's sleep. "Until I can…get paid?" she practically whimpered, knowing full well how little that would make a difference.

There was silence on the other end of the phone. Kate was afraid she'd been hung up on, but the mechanic finally offered, "Look, there's still some more stuff we need to check out on it to make sure it's street legal. Let me…let me make some calls and see what I can do." He didn't sound confident. "Maybe I can make something happen, okay? But no promises."

"Oh my god, thank you!" Kate exclaimed.

"Alright, I'll call you back Ms. Harbough," he said.

"Thanks, bye," she said before hanging up. She slumped forward, her head practically at her knees. "Goddammit," she muttered angrily. Her head hung low, she worked hard to keep from whispering 'I want to go home'. She was tired of how much she'd said it. Being tired of it, however, made it no less true.

It had been dark when Kate had left for work and it was dark when she arrived home. Hardboiled eggs at lunch had barely sustained her and Kate's stomach announced her arrival home before she could even call to her mother and grandmother herself. She covered her stomach in embarrassment as she shut the door behind her.

"Welcome home, baby," her grandmother said as she shuffled in from the kitchen. She immediately asked, "How was work?"

Kate lied with a happy smile, like she did every day. "It was fine." She unbuttoned her shirt as she expounded, "It was slowly, most. Some of the guys in electronics were watching the news about the asteroid."

"Oh yeah?" her grandmother said with a big smile. "I've been watching the news too. I keep waiting for them to say when we can see it, but they just talk about a fifty-percent chance of this and a thirty-percent chance of that. Make up your minds and decide!" Deloris tantrummed playfully, getting a smile from Kate. "Your mother just got home a few moments ago herself."

"That's never good," Kate said only semi-sarcastically as she headed towards the master bedroom at the back of the partial-submerged apartment. She knocked lightly on the bedroom door that was half-ajar and peeked inside. "Mom?"

A woman who could have easily passed for Kate's much-older sister was sitting at the desk at the foot of her bed. A jury-rigged desk/vanity made from concrete blocks and planks of wood, it supported a small collection of geeky-jewelry, most of which had lost some luster. Still dressed in the pant suit from work, Lauren Harbough was taking off her shoes and looked at Kate with an exhausted expression. "Hey, honey. How was your day?"

"About like yours, I bet," Kate said.

"I hope you didn't have to research briefs for your boss," her mom said as she turned to a makeup mirror and began to take out her earrings.

"I work in underwear, mom. Don't say 'briefs' please," Kate laughed.

Lauren chuckled as well. "Was the store rough?" The way she asked that made Kate feel marginalized, so she didn't answer. Lauren leaned against the doorframe as she yawned deeply. "I'm not sure what to do about dinner," she ventured in the wake of the posture-compromising yawn.

"I can cook something," Kate offered, quietly hoping her mother would take charge.

"We don't have anything, I don't think," Lauren thought, turning towards the kitchen. Her expression was a mix of certainty and lethargy.

All Kate could say was "Uh…" She looked vaguely in the direction of the kitchen as well.

Her mother surrendered to exhaustion and just exhaled. "I don't feel like going back out. Why don't we order pizza?"

Kate waged an immediate war inside her mind. Laziness and a love of comfort food fought against the love of a flat, defined stomach. She did a calculation with expert precision of every calorie and macronutrient in every possible pizza ingredient and pondered just what would be the best order to trick her body into thinking it was healthy. The grumble in her stomach demanded that she forgo health and opt for full. The battle was vicious.

When there was no response after a moment, Lauren looked curiously at her daughter. "Kate?"

She looked surprised. "Uh, yeah?" she asked, startled from her dietary mathematics and ethical quandaries.

"Do you want to just order pizza?" Lauren asked again with a drained, world-weary tone.

"Yeah, sure," Kate said, trying to sound enthusiastic and not like an overly picky eater.

"Okay," said Lauren as she stood up. She rolled her trick shoulder and grimaced. "I think I'm going to get a shower."

Kate died a little as she hedged. "Um, sure." She now did a very different breed of math as she tried to remember the precise dollar amount in her bank account. She turned to leave, then slowed, hoping her mother would offer her debt card. Instead, Lauren headed passed her into the bathroom.

Kate had a mild panic attack of sheer shame. She crossed the apartment into her square of a bedroom, trying to think of ways she could make a few dozen dollars in ten minutes. She slipped out of her overshirt and looked at herself in the mirror of her bedroom doors. Her mind flashed of every person at the convention that had stopped by her table and not gotten a print. She thought of every sale that she felt was just within her grasp but she'd said something poorly or not been engaging enough, so they'd left with their money rather than left her their money. She then began to feel guilty about being so obsessed with sales.

Everything spiraled in her mind until she just backpedaled onto her bed in a numb, paralyzing stupor of shame. She sat on the edge and just spaced out in embarrassment and self-resentment.

A soft knock on the door awoke Kate from her self-flagellating stupor. "Yeah?" she asked, quickly wiping her cheeks. She was afraid she'd started crying.

Deloris Harbough slipped into the room and shut the door behind her. Skinny and frail, she tended to hold her hands together in front, almost like she was some old world maid. "Baby, I wanted to know how the convention went." Even standing still, her voice tended to shake just a tiny bit.

"It went fine, Nana," Kate lied. She felt like crying.

"Did you sell a lot of pictures?" her grandmother asked, still by the door.

"Yeah," Kate continued to lie. She opted to not even bother with explaining the differences in pictures and prints. "My panels went really great, too. I was worried about it but we had..." She recalled the mostly empty rooms. "They went really well."

"Did people ask questions?" asked Deloris.

"Yeah, they really seemed to like us," Kate told her like she was talking to a child.

"Good," Deloris told her. She then struck on the age-old talk. "Did you meet any boys?"

Kate couldn't help but laugh. "Nana, I'm thirty. If meet any boys, I'd get the police called on me."

"Oh, you know what I mean," her grandmother chastised playfully.

Kate smiled as she got up and fished around for some different pajama bottoms from the stacks of clothes in her room. "No, no boys. " A pang of panic hit as she remembered Saturday night, but the ghosts of hazy memories were easily shooed away for once. "Not a lot of people looking for dates at conventions," she said. "Since people come from all over, it's kind of hard to make a real, lasting connection." As she sifted through the clothes, she muttered under her breath, "One night stands, on the other hand..."

"Well baby, I'm awful proud of you," said the octogenarian as she shuffled across the room. "I know things have been real hard, so..." She tried to surreptitiously slide a twenty-dollar bill into Kate's pants pocket. "You need more than eggs for lunch, baby."

Kate's body rebelled when she tried to block the cash. She was perfectly still, practically catatonic from her want, her need to deny it. "Nana, I—" She went silent immediately.

"I love you, baby," Deloris told her, leaning awkwardly forward to kiss Kate on the forehead. "I'm awful proud of you." She turned and shuffled out, closing the door as she went.

Kate pulled out the double-folded twenty and unwrapped it. For a long time, all she could do was stare at the money. She could see lunch for the week. She also could see one of the Supergirl action figures, an indulgence Kate hadn't enjoyed in a long time. She could at least imagine seeing part of the car door at the repair shop. She could see the pizza her mom wanted her to order.

She could see so many things, but mostly she saw more money than she had to her name.

Kate's vision blurred with tears. Her lip shook, then her chin curled in. She tugged her arms in tight and she stumbled backwards onto her bed. She became an emotional ball, quaking under the weight of her failure. She fell onto her side and grabbed the pillow, covering her face just in time as she began screaming painful, ugly tears.

She rolled her back to the door and cried. She practically spasmed, crying so hard from the shame. She hid it from the world under her pillow, clinging to it as the one thing she could trust. And as before, it slipped out through her sobs. "I want to go home," she whimpered between vomits of emotion. "I want to go home!" she cried to no one.

Abruptly, she sat up. Red-stained cheeks were slick with tears and her nose was stopped up. She sat on the edge of the bed, forcing herself to uncomfortable stillness. Her eyes were huge, mad, as she stared forward, seeing passed her reflection in the mirror. "No, no, no," she said again and again. "No, stop it." She dug her nails into the mattress and pushed down everything.

When her breathing subsided, she deliberately closed her eyes. "It's okay," she insisted. "It's okay, get a grip." She opened her eyes.

Superman was across from her.

Across the wall of her bedroom, at the apex of all the superhero and video game and anime posters on her wall, Superman stood most prominent. The iconic hero of DC Comics was standing tall with the American flag and looking proudly right at Kate. She stared jealously back at him.

"Bet you never cried like a little baby," she practically accused. Her eyes glanced down, in mounting shame, and she saw the twenty-dollar bill on the floor. "Bet you never had to spend birthday money on bills or use some extra crash on groceries. Or wear a nametag. Or realize you'll be homeless when your grandmother dies." She clamped her eyes shut. "Or realize how awful you are for even thinking about that." She began to cry again, collapsing in on herself.

She grabbed the pillow again and finally surrendered. She gave up on fighting her tears and sobbed, screamed, and howled into the pillow, no longer bothering to try and control her unmitigated shame. She rolled away from the door again and let her shame and embarrassment have their way.

***

A police flashlight shone down on the broken chunk of sidewalk.

Just off the main street that wound through the far shadow of downtown, the sidewalk curved down into a cul de sac in the housing projects. Tall, ugly buildings from a bygone era were covered with graffiti and disrepair, one step away from being condemned. Laundry lines were improvised outside of second and third-story windows and much of the parking lot was made up of cars that either didn't work or looked like they shouldn't.

Two uniformed police in the middle of the night were standing over the broken sidewalk, trying to understand what they were looking at. "Somebody take a piledriver to this thing?" asked the officer holding the flashlight.

The cement square had been broken dead center and driven down almost half a foot into the ground. Water from a line was seeping out, along with sparks and flashes from wires in adjoining routes. "You don't think that could cause electrocution or something do you?" asked the other, younger officer.

"Better get the power company out here quick," said the veteran officer as he bent forward to shine the light with more focus. He glanced back as ambient lights began to flicker. An entire building's lights died and a cacophony of displeasure came from the now-darkened windows. "Dammit."

"I thought the power company wouldn't come to these neighborhoods during the day," said the rookie.

"If we don't get them here, they'll start rioting," the veteran said derisively. The front door of one of the project buildings opened and out came two locals, both looking angry. "Damn," the veteran repeated, his hand inching towards the gun at his waist.

"Maybe they're just coming to see what happened," urged the rookie cop.

"Not these animals," said the veteran, starting to ready for trouble.

"Animals?" the rookie repeated, surprised. He looked at the two coming out the door, heading towards them. "Their power went out."

"Back inside," yelled the veteran cop, his hand readying his weapon. "Back inside, now!" he yelled.

Unbeknownst to the two officers, they were being watched by more than denizens of the neighborhood.

Nearby, hidden behind a dumpster in the shadows of one of the adjacent buildings of the housing project, two figures watched curiously. The male of the two, in a dark blue bodysuit and alabaster-colored skin, looked on, completely amazed. "Are they cowards?" he asked quietly. "Or are they violent? Do they seek turmoil, or do they expect it so certainly that they would prefer start it so that they may exert control over it?"

Behind him, a female twin watched, equally entranced by the two police and their exchanges with the two argumentative youths. She speculated, "Perhaps the locals are dangerous."

"Dangerous?" snickered the man. "Y'marda, these are the civilization's local warriors." He gestured at the police. "How can they fear non-combatants?"

The woman watched the exchange as the veteran cop stood off against the two young men, the rookie officer trying to act as intermediary. "Given the median age of the dominant species, the skill differential between professionals and amateurs is likely negligible," she suggested. She looked down at her own hands, opening and closing the fingers that lacked any prints or distinctive markings. "The uniformity of their bodies, likewise, seems like it could be an issue." The male of the pair looked back at Y'marda, surprised and curious. "We've both four limbs: two arms and two legs. We've both the same number of bones and organs. Eyes," she gestured.

"Our bodies are not identical, Y'marda," he told her, nodding at her breasts.

"Not identical, no, but uniform," she agreed. She stepped behind the building itself and shifted her body about, testing the joints and limbs. "My weight distribution is different than yours, Y'dosh. My body composition, too." She stopped moving and stood at a powerful height. "But these are negligible differences," she all but declared. "This race is practically uniform compared to all other middle-tier life." She looked at her hands. "It's a wonder they can even tell one another apart."

Y'dosh turned towards the two police officers, both of whom were retreating tactically towards their squad car at the front of the cul de sac, exchanging words with now a small crowd of young men from the housing project. Their hands were on their sidearms. "What bizarre creatures."

"The use of vehicles is hardly abnormal," Y'marda observed as the two police got into their car. She shifted her body, turning it this way and that. "It's a fairly unstable thing," she said, feeling her spine and hips. "I'll never understand bipedal forms." She touched her face, feeling along the oversized bridge of her nose and the shallow cheeks and brow. She touched her arms, almost as wide as her legs.

Y'dosh absently asserted, "They have their advantages." He watched the squad car disappear into the distance. He checked the doorways of the local buildings, spotting more residents. "Locals are beginning to rouse." He turned back from the corner, to Y'marda. "What are your orders?"

Y'marda surveyed the cul de sac and thought. In doing so, she sighed, an action that surprised them both. Slightly unsettled by the breathing anomaly, she checked her right wrist, consulting a small digital display on her bodysuit. "We've quite some time yet." She surveyed their immediate area; an overgrown half-yard between the housing project and a line of leafless trees separating it from the neighboring projects. "Our exposure will complicate our operation. Complicate and perhaps compromise."

"Then we hide?" asked Y'dosh.

Y'marda nodded, deciding, "Probably for the best." She turned away from the housing project and headed into the shadows, disappearing into the trees and the night beyond.

CHAPTER FIVE

"We can either hire a photographer or I can try and rent the camera," explained Rachael, her voice cutting out a bit over the phone.

Kate walked through the intimates' section of the store, pretending not to be wearing a blu-tooth earpiece on her ear and engaged in a non-work conversation over her personal phone. The underwear section was sparsely populated but she kept an eye on the handful of women eyeing reasonably-priced economy-quality unmentionables. "I'm still running the numbers and waiting for the final charges to clear," Rachael urged the others on the call, "but we really need to be looking ahead."

"We just got done with a con," said Emily like a tired child. "I don't want to deal with making products and sales minimums. I want to make some new costumes." Kate said nothing but nodded in total agreement.

"I think we need to splurge for a full photography suite," said Denise, also on the conference call. She was just a little louder than the other two, making Kate winced whenever she spoke. "We NEED some new stuff and we NEED some new prints. All we've got are reissues of older cosplays. We need to do a full group set, with some Photoshop effects or something. We need a BIG project." Kate could practically envision the hand gestures going along with the emphatic words.

"Yeah, but that's expensive as hell," said Kate as she turned towards a rack of bras and pretended to organize them. She was surprised to realize that she was, in fact, organizing them. She was also surprised that a nearby customer had overheard her and was looking at her in confusion. Kate held up a bra and feigned shock at the price. The woman quickly steered herself away. Kate let her get a few steps out of the section and continued, "We'd be looking at, like, a hundred dollars an hour or something. A hundred easy."

"That's twenty-five per person," Denise suggested.

"That's not too bad," Emily added with the optimism of someone with a college meal plan.

Kate scoffed quietly, shaking her head in irritation. "Twenty-five a person isn't...on top of new costumes?" She waited for a response and knew she wasn't getting one. "And what did you have in mind? Another Street Fighter group shot?"

"Maybe," Denise came back, a little confrontationally. "We could do Justice League if you want."

"Guys," Rachael jumped in. "Look, we're meeting tomorrow. We don't need to decide right now what we'll be shooting. But we do need to have something completed well before the summer conventions. And those will get here sooner than you think."

"I know," Kate said, as if Rachael had been speaking right at her. She then just blurted out, "But I simply don't have that kind of money right now. I don't know how much the car is going to cost to get fixed and, I'm sorry, that's kind of a priority."

"It's just the door!" Denise exclaimed. "How much does it cost to reattach it?"

"The door wasn't just busted; they think the body might have gotten damaged too," Kate argued with her, indifferent to the looks of the customers near her. "They have to check the hinges and the frame and..." She waved off the rest of any explanation.

"Jesus, She-Hulk, what'd you do?!" Rachael exclaimed.

Kate blubbered, really not feeling up to this. She was ready to argue but the walkie-talkie at her waist blared, "All associates, all associates, time for the mid-morning pep rally."

Kate sighed. "Guys, I've got to go. Meeting number two of six. I'll call you when I get off work." She didn't wait for people to say bye. She hung up and slipped her earpiece into her pocket with her phone as she dashed off.

Walter was droning on about something as Kate slipped into the circle of employees in the back of the store, just inside the doors of the undecorated work area. The backroom workers were sequestered away, under orders not to disrupt the meeting despite it taking place in front of the central door into and out of the store proper.

"And it's important," Walter explained as he walked like how he envisioned a general walking among his troops, "that we always make ourselves available for the customers." Kate really wanted to point out how that conflicted with the near-hourly team meetings but she kept her mouth shut. She instead looked around at the circle of a dozen floor workers, each as spaced out as she, each taking the meeting as seriously as she.

She spotted Derek a quarter of the circle away and slid over to him. "Wishing you were Rich?" she whispered while Walter was turned to the opposite side of the circle.

"Man, I'd quit this job so hard," Derek snickered to the fellow geek.

Kate laughed a little too loudly. "No, I meant Rich. Richard. He doesn't have to come to these."

It took Derek a second. "Oh!" he nodded suddenly. "Yeah, sorry, I'm kinda inhibited."

Kate glared comically at him. "You came to work stoned?"

"I can't think of a day I don't," he giggled, causing her to snicker as well. One of the women from the grocery section shhhed them both as their church giggles endured.

A different sound caught Kate's attention and she glanced to the door back into the front of the store. A customer was waving to Kate, calling her over. Kate broke away from the circle and started for the door. She made it just to the door when Walter asked condescendingly, "Miss Harbough, you have somewhere to be?"

The first-grade-school-teacher tone didn't sit well with Kate. In her mind, a fantasy of putting Walter in his place and quitting on the spot played vividly. Instead of acting rashly, Kate told him, "Yeah, a customer needs me." She didn't wait for his permission or even acknowledgement, though she relished the irritation on his face as she pushed through the door. "Thank you," Kate told the woman waiting for her.

The mother of two was confused but smiled all the same. "Um, okay. I had a question about towels?" the woman seemed to propose, gesturing towards the far side of the store. Kate, keenly aware of her ignorance on the subject matter but desperate for any way to avoid returning to that meeting, simply smiled and let herself be led away.

After five minutes of poorly managing the help request, Kate took as long as she possibly could returning to the back of the store. Seeing with relief that the meeting had concluded, she started back towards the intimates, again taking the longest route possible. The department store was full of the usual afternoon shoppers: people who got off early from work or didn't have work to begin with, kids from the private school a few blocks behind the store, stay-at-home parents finishing their chores. The daily almost-bustle.

Kate passed through the hair care aisle, considering different breeds of red. She pondered different uses for each, considering Black Widow from Marvel Comics. The thought of turning an old Power Rangers cosplay into a Black Widow outfit sounded like fun. She didn't really look like Scarlett Johansson or her movie version of the character, but that didn't mean Kate couldn't pull it off. Besides, she thought cynically to herself, all she had to do is flash some cleavage and it would get attention.

As Kate window-shopped, she heard a mother and her son. The mom picked up a dark brunette and considered it while her son said, "I want to color my hair."

"Baby, boys don't do that," she told the little boy.

"Why not?" he asked her.

"Because only girls color their hair," she told him. She took his hand and began to tug him off as he looked longingly back at the wall of hair color and the possibilities it presented. Kate watched him go and felt her heart sink.

With a sudden and inexplicable burst of anger, she started towards the mother and her son. She was ready to snap at her, but stopped just before she was within speaking range. The thought of the woman complaining to Walter struck Kate like a bolt of lightning. Walter wouldn't hesitate to fire Kate right in front of the woman, if only to appease her ego. Or is own.

A strange paranoia came over Kate and she looked up to the ceiling. Little black half-spheres dotted the ceiling, security cameras hidden within. Kate looked all around and acquainted herself with the sheer magnitude of cameras overhead. Kate was absolutely certain one of them was watching her right now.

Kate turned like she'd seen a ghost and returned with some speed to the women's underwear section. Her hands were practically shaking. Walter could probably see her right now, was certainly watching her disapprovingly. He knew how little time she actually spent doing anything useful, knew how much time she spent wondering over to the toys or electronics, or just window-shopping in other departments.

He could fire her.

He WOULD fire her.

It slowly hit Kate that, were she honest with herself, he should fire her. She glanced over to the other departments and saw other khaki-and-blue-clad workers helping customers. Everybody else was engaged, doing their job in some fashion. She seemed to be the only one doing nothing but standing still, confronted with her own employment mortality.

She quickly looked around the underwear section, desperate to find someone to help. She spotted a mother and her daughter and thought to approach. She was halfway to the two when she realized how much people didn't like being approached when looking at underwear. Kate stopped herself, but tripped and tumbled forward half-a-step. She caught herself on a bra-and-panties kiosk which clattered as it skidded off the carpet and onto the tiled floor of the aisles. Kate, blushing frightfully, avoided anyone's gaze as she righted the kiosk and then went to find a corner to curl up in and die.

In the breakroom halfway through her shift, Kate was once again sitting alone in the corner. Her phone out, she was typing in numbers on a notepad, doing math. "Rent, power, cable and internet, cell phone, insurance," she read off, double-checking the numbers next to them. "Groceries," she said, typing far too small of a number. "Gas," she realized. "Hosting provider," she added. Her shoulders sank. Her hand went to her lips and she stared at the numbers.

A glaring, red number sat at the bottom of it all.

Kate set the phone aside and focused on nothing for a moment. She set her chin on her fingertips and thought. The TV in the breakroom played an episode of Friends that two other employees were barely watching, providing her a modicum of white noise to think against.

"I get paid next Friday," Kate thought aloud. "That should be..." She tried to figure in the hours and the rate, estimating both generous and strict taxes. She got her phone again, practically sobbing at the mere thought. She checked the red number at the bottom of her calculations. Her jaw shook as she stared at it, then put her phone away. Her eyes glazed over as she thought.

She remembered having $20 a day ago, and again thinking how much money that was to her.

"Maybe Nana..." Kate ventured, but closed her watery eyes against the thought. She inhaled a ragged breath to control her emotions. She glanced nervously at the two others in the breakroom with her, but they weren't paying attention to her, thankfully.

She got up and headed across the breakroom for the sign-up sheet to trade shifts. Over two weeks old, it was mostly her name written on the left-hand column, looking for shifts. A few times, others had offered her their time but it had been a while. Putting on her best determined face, Kate wrote her name down once again.

She returned to her phone and checked the time. The glare from the overhead lights blocked the screen so she tilted it up to see. As the clock appeared, her reflection on the screen caught her eye and, with the way she was holding the camera, she could see down her shirt at the very top of her cleavage.

Sudden resolution took hold and Kate texted her mother and her grandmother. "Gotta meeting with the group tonight," she told them. "Be home late."

Kate's leg shook nervously the whole way along the unfamiliar bus route. Rather than take the bus back home, she'd headed across town instead. She'd left work towards twilight, but the bus ride had taken so long, it was firmly night by the time she arrived at the stop near the airport.

Across the street was another bus stop, this one for the inter-terminal shuttle for the airport. Kate ignored it and started her trek down the side of the street. She walked in the long grass along the side of the wide, two-lane road. There were no street lights at all, only the soft glow of the distant airport behind her and the shopping center up ahead.

In the late winter cold, right at the cusp of spring, Kate shivered as she walked. Her breath came out as a thick cloud, hanging in front of her before she walked through it. The area was clear on either side of the road into the horizon. The city was to her right, in the far distance. To her left were fields that stretched towards the airport's territory. She could just barely make out the chain link fences at the edge of the property.

A solitary car came by, but that was Kate's only companion. The cold got inside her work pants and even wormed its way into her jacket and she began to shiver. She contemplated running but didn't want to get sweaty or exhausted before she arrived.

At the edge of the shopping center, slightly removed from the rest of the buildings and secluded towards the back, was a large warehouse-looking building with few signs and fewer indicators that it was even a business. The parking lot was semi-full with an array of cars. Music could be heard through the walls. Kate headed for it, her heart beginning to race while her shivering grew to be less about the cold and more about her nerves.

Through a pair of double doors was a long, dark hallway lit with purple and pink lights, lined on either side by semi-nude posters of recent performers. Kate approached the first poster on her right, looking up at a semi-famous porn star. In the buff, her nudity was covered to the legal minimum with announcements of dates and performance times. She looked down at Kate with a sultry glower. Kate ignored the star-shaped schedule advertisements and instead considered the picture. She wondered about the lens used by the photographer and what makeup was employed, and how much of the photo was Photoshop. She considered the pose the woman was in and decided that the photographer was certainly crouching to take it. Kate imagined the photo shoot and her expression soured at how uncomfortable it must have been.

No stranger to the physical awkwardness of photo shoots, Kate felt a kinship to the headliner in the poster. That familiarity encouraged her. She turned and walked down the hallway, feeling slightly more in place and in control. The clack of her work flats echoed off the muffled dance music and the hallway walls spray-painted black. She headed down to the slight curve and found a desk waiting where a woman in all black was checking a clipboard. She glanced up when Kate approached and said, "Welcome to the Diamond Club."

"Hey," Kate smiled. "I'm, uh, I'm here to audition."

The woman nodded indifferently and gestured down the hall, towards another pair of double doors. "Go on in. Ask for Thom – that's 'Th-om', with an H – and he'll take you to the back."

Kate looked suddenly eager. "Just like that?" she smiled, hopeful. The red number she'd been staring at all through work and fixated on afterwards didn't seem so daunting now.

"For the interview, yeah," the woman nodded.

"Oh," Kate realized. She smiled and nodded, then turned and headed for the doors. Through them, she was hit with a wall of throbbing sound. The main floor was focused on a large octagonal raised platform at the back of a large room full of tables and chairs. A bar sat opposite the stage. On the stage, a woman in only a G-string was walking exotically around the pole in the very middle. The crowd of men weren't flocked to the stage like Kate had expected but were at the tables, mostly tending to their drinks. In fact, only a few seemed to be paying attention to the woman performing.

A little disheartened, Kate went to the bar where a goatee with a pair of shoulders was putting beers into a cooler. "Hey, is Thom available?"

The muscled man in a tight black t-shirt didn't break rhythm on his movement. "Thom!" he yelled over the music.

From down the bar, a smaller guy with a friendly smile approached and introduced himself. "What can I do for you?" he asked Kate.

"I was hoping to audition," she said, having to lean over a little to be heard.

He stepped back from Kate, nodding as he looked her up and down. It didn't feel invasive, like so often it did at conventions, but like a genuine appraisal. She wasn't sure if that was better or not. "Okay, come with me," he told her, gesturing for her to follow.

Thom led Kate around the large room full of black leather seats and inattentive men through a swinging black door. Back through there, the 90s Club Rock played by the DJ was rendered into a general throbbing white noise. Drinks were stacked to be ready to go into the coolers. Not sure what she was expecting, Kate was surprised to find the back of the club looking more like a restaurant than anything else.

They passed a dressing room with a bunch of well-lit mirrors and a few girls getting 'dressed' in scandalous outfits that were clearly meant to be removed. The women barely noticed Kate, too busy applying makeup and confirming wardrobe placement before their turn on stage.

Passed the dressing room, Thom went into a small office and gestured for Kate to take a seat. He shut the door, but not completely, leaving a crack through which she could see the outside hallway and hear the music. "Sorry about the rush," he told her with a smile. "I ruptured an eardrum last year and I can barely hear in the main room." He sat down behind a desk that was covered with order forms, catalogs, and other banal trappings of running a business. "Now, what can I do for you?"

"I was hoping I could audition," she told him, trying to seem eager and happy and in no way desperately afraid for her immediate financial future.

"Right," he said, sighing and leaning back a little in his chair. He wiped his mouth as he again looked at Kate's body. "See, here's the thing: we don't do auditions. We have an amateur night and if girls do well there, we'll invite them to come back on one of our slower nights. If they do well on a slower night, we then try them on a more populated night. If they do well, and they like it, then we provide them with the option for a regular schedule." When Kate seemed to struggle to follow that, he explained honestly, "There's no regular job. All our dancers are private contractors, who work on a semi-scheduled basis."

Kate's sinking stomach made her smile fade, but the way Thom kept looking at her, she couldn't give up hope just yet. "Would you stand up for me?" he asked her. She left her bag on the chair and rose. "Turn around," he requested, looking her over. He again wiped his face. "We normally hire from amateur night, but we..." He looked her up and down. "We rarely get talents like you."

Kate laughed happily, then thought about what he'd actually said and couldn't decide if she should be flattered or not.

"So..." he said, mostly to himself. He looked around his tiny office and appraised the space in the room. "Do you have any previous experience?" he asked, though it was clear that he knew the answer. Kate shook her head, but that didn't seem to bother Thom much. "Have you ever given a lap dance, like to a boyfriend or a girlfriend?" Again, Kate shook her head. "Do you have any experience with dancing? Do you go to clubs?"

Kate answered sincerely, "Not really. I haven't been to a club in a while." She laughed nervously, "The cover charges have just gotten too expensive."

Thom smirked and nodded. "For real. Even bars are charging entry fees. I'm like 'I'm already paying eight bucks for a beer!'!" he exclaimed, the two sharing a laugh. Laughing with a guy, especially alone with a guy, caused a pang of paranoia hit Kate. Thoughts of a stairwell and nails being driven into flesh hit her and she had to look away. Her heart began to race and she tried hard to keep from looking panicked.

Thom didn't seem to notice because he was looking at the door, clearly only a focal point for his eyes as he thought. "Look, I know we don't have a lot of space, but show me some moves in here," he asked. Kate's memories took a backseat to the real fear of finally being put on the spot. She pushed the chair to the side, looking at the space she had to work with.

She held her hands in front of her and tried to find a rhythm. The lack of solid music made for a problem, with only rumbling white noise coming through the walls and the crack in the door. Kate swayed her hips, but felt like she wasn't dancing so much as miming being on a boat. She started trying to do what came naturally, but all that came naturally was some kind of bizarre parody of old movies with Ginger Rogers. At a complete loss, she tried to channel her inner Jamie Lee Curtis from True Lies. The way Thom pinched his nose and looked embarrassed on her behalf did not inspire confidence.

Growing more desperate, Kate decided to double-down. She bowed forward and kicked up into a handstand. Her feet wobbled and she nearly fell apart, her ankles and hips teetering. She struggled so much to right her posture, Thom shifted nervously forward to catch her if she fell, to keep her from collapsing onto his desk and breaking her back. She managed to tighten up and perfectly straighten her body. Frantic to make a lasting impression, though, she picked up her left hand. She hovered there on one hand for just a second, and then kicked back down, flipping her hair behind her as she came up. She locked eyes on Thom and smiled, flashing her eyebrows at him as confidently as possible.

He stared at her, clearly scared for her safety and perhaps sanity, and said, "No."

Kate's hopes shattered like a plate dropped from a roof.

"Look, I think—" he started to explain.

"Okay, look, the handstand was rough," Kate stammered quickly, pulling the chair over. "I'm more of a kettlebell person, I know, but I can get a good handstand. I can do all sorts of calisthenics; that was literally the first time I've done a handstand in years. I—"

Thom held out his hand and stopped her. "Learn to dance," he advised constructively but finally. "Go to the club and learn how to move a little more naturally. You've got great proportions." His expression flared at the understatement. "We would be lucky to have you, but I don't want to put you out there," he explained, talking a little louder when she tried to plead her case, "for you to get embarrassed and feel self-conscious. I want to hire you," he tried to salve her, "but it would be irresponsible to put you out there if you don't know what you're doing. It would be bad for us; it would be really bad for you."

He sat back in his chair and checked his watch. Kate expected him to usher her out, but he stayed for a second. He asked almost rhetorically, "Let me guess: bills?"

She saw no reason to hide it at this point. "Yeah."

Thom smiled sympathetically. "Yeah, we get that." It seemed almost remorseful, like it was a burden being so often the resort of the desperate. "The money here's good," he promised her, though with a hedge of uncertainty, underscoring a host of unspoken caveats. "Do you have any experience with working with food? Do you have a bar-tending license?" Kate shook her head. "Because we could put you to work behind the counter or something. We've got more than dancers here."

Kate thought to mention her cosplay experience, but didn't. A fear of that life mixing here, or dancing here becoming common knowledge in her cosplay life, worried her.

"I don't think we can help you right now," Thom told her, standing. He opened the office door for her and said, "If you can get some experience dancing, even if it's just at a club, then come back. Come to an amateur night and give it a try. But..." He shrugged. "You don't want to be trying to give a lap dance if you've never even danced in public."

He gestured subtly and encouraged her as best he could with, "Come back on amateur night."

Come back on amateur night.
Come back on amateur night.
Come back on amateur night.

The words rolled around inside Kate's head as she stared through her reflection on the lonely nighttime bus heading across downtown. Past street lamps and neon business fronts, she kept the idea firmly before her: Amateur.

Also firmly in her mind was every costume she'd ever made, most of which were from scratch. Firmly in her mind was every convention at which she'd ever won an award, every website where she'd graced the front page. Firmly in her mind was every panel she'd ever sat on and even moderated. Firmly in her mind was every poster and print she'd ever sold.

Firmly in her mind was that word: amateur.

In a cold, hopeless numb, she found herself tallying up all the hours she'd sunk into making costumes, finding an average across her efforts. She tallied up all the dollars she'd spent, a few here and there, a lot more often than she wanted to consider, on buttons and embroidery and other pieces that seemed so insignificant to anyone but a connoisseur. The running total in her mind grew quickly.

Amateur.

She didn't do it for the money, but the money mattered. The money mattered because it was what would allow her to keep doing it. The money mattered because it was the only real, tangible proof that what she did was worthwhile. Words might sustain her spirit, Likes on social media might sustain her enthusiasm, but money kept her alive. Money mattered because it was validation that she did it well enough to support herself.

It meant she wasn't an amateur.

Kate pushed the need for support – not validation but support – down deep. If the strip club wouldn't work, she'd go the populace route. She'd buy a web cam and go to one of those sites. They were easy enough, and she wouldn't even have to dance. She just had to discard all thoughts of modesty. She'd changed clothes in enough bathrooms to be comfortable with that. All she needed was a webcam.

And a computer that could properly run those services.

And a clear space to perform.

And a good pseudonym to keep from being discovered as herself.

Kate took out her phone and activated the camera feature and stared up at herself. The angle was unflattering, but she was alone on the nighttime bus. It didn't matter that—

Amateur.

She couldn't get away from that word.

Something dripped onto her camera screen. The crystal droplet ran off the top of the screen and fell onto the dirty bus floor, splattering like a drop of blood. Kate touched her cheek and realized she was crying. Her face was stony and passive, but her tears were running down her cheek and dripping off her chin.

She put the phone away. She wasn't going to set-up a webcam account anywhere. She was going to go home and cry into her pillow and do nothing. She knew it.

Amateur.

CHAPTER SIX

Kate very slowly peeled the wrapper off a tin of biscuits, holding the cylinder farther and farther away the more the wrapper came off. By the time the entire wrapper of the store-brand biscuits peeled off entirely, Kate was holding the tin at full arm's length. She looked warily at the tin for a second, then inspected it. The silvery cylinder in her hand was fully intact and hadn't ruptured explosively like it was supposed to.

Dressed in Legend of Zelda pajamas from bed and her morning kettlebell routine, Kate looked around the kitchen of the small three-bedroom apartment, not sure what to do. She looked at the edge of the counter, looked at the tin, looked at the edge of the counter, and lightly tapped the tin on the edge of the counter.

Kate squealed in shock, recoiling when the cylinder burst at the seams. The biscuit cylinder, torn open with doughy biscuits exposed, flew into the air. Kate realized what her surprise had resulted and leapt for the tin and grabbed for it before it hit the ground. She missed and knocked the tin to the side with her hand, and she grabbed with her left. She juggled the tin with a few different, though equally unsuccessful grabs before she caught it between her knees.

A moment of equal parts panic and surprise passed before she was able to retrieve the ruptured container. She took a breath and then continued unpeeling the tin and laying the biscuits out on the greased baking sheet. Just as she slipped the pan into the oven, Lauren came shuffling out of the master bedroom in a night gown mimicking Chewbacca's bandolier. She grumbled something approaching a greeting and set about making coffee.

"Since I don't have to work today, I thought I'd make biscuits for you and Nana," Kate said cheerful, backing away from the coffee maker to give her mother room. Her mother only grumbled something, one eye more open than the other. Kate watched her spoon granules of black life into the filter and remarked, "I think that's too much coffee."

"No such thing," the older woman growled harmlessly. She fetched water from the sink, the seals dribbling a bit whenever it was turned on too high. She set the coffee pot to brew and went fishing through the cabinet for a coffee mug. Selecting a Yoda mug this time, she set it next to the coffee maker. In a daze, Lauren sat with her hand atop the magic machine that would make her life tolerable. She and Kate shared the kitchen as it warmed from the stove and the coffee maker simultaneously. Facing the opposite direction, Lauren was almost the time-elapsed mirror image of Kate, with similar height, hair, and proportions.

Finally, the coffee was ready and Lauren poured a cup. Cream and sugar were liberally added and she finally took a sip. The result was nothing short of magical because her eyes blinked awake and into intelligence. She looked at Kate and asked, "What was that about biscuits?"

Kate laughed at her mom. "I made some," she said before checking the time on her phone. "They'll be ready in about eight minutes."

Lauren sipped the coffee more. "And what do you want?"

Kate feigned a look of astonishment. "Nothing!" she exclaimed with a laugh, quietly worrying that her mother was telepathic. Lauren wasn't quite awake enough to challenge her. Kate said with some honesty, "I thought biscuits would be a nice surprise is all."

"Uh-huh," her mother teased. She stretched and yawned, then rubbed her eyes. "Is it Saturday yet?" she grumbled as she shuffled back into her room to get dressed.

Kate waited out in the kitchen and prepared the biscuits once they were done. Despite coming from the pre-packaged tin, they gave off a wondrous buttery smell that filled the entire kitchen. Regretting not waiting until cheat day, Kate drank in the scent as best she could, then prepared two biscuits for her grandmother. She drizzled some honey across the golden pair, then headed into the living room.

Watching the news on low volume and playing a crossword puzzle on a cheap tablet computer, Deloris looked surprised when Kate laid down the biscuits for her. "Oh, thank you, baby!" she said with a huge, joyous smile.

"Here ya go, Nana," Kate told her before leaning over to kiss her gray hair. Kate retrieved her water bottle from the kitchen and took one more sniff of the biscuits, then sat down next to her grandmother. To the dulcet tones of the morning news, she began scrolling through her social media feed.

Facebook: thirty-seven messages from strangers, eleven messages from friends and other acquaintances (including Eliot, bragging about how well his costumes were received), over two hundred likes, sixty-seven comments and only forty-something of them were from trolls.

Twitter: Over a thousand likes across various posts and pictures, two hundred retweets, and over a hundred comments. Only seventy of them were sexual propositions or similar harassment.

Tumblr. Pintrest. Instagram. All across the social media network, Kate responded where appropriate and where she was able, while being careful to not feed the trolls. She sent messages, liked comments, responded to (appropriate) question, and spent the morning trying to validate those who validated her.

At ten-thirty, as the second episode of Family Feud was coming on, Kate rose from her seat. "I'm gonna head out in a bit, Nana."

"Oh?" she asked, not quite turning away from Steve Harvey.

"Yeah, I'm heading over to Denise's place," Kate reminded her grandmother. "We're gonna try to plan out the summer conventions."

Her grandmother asked, "Is Denise the little colored girl?"

Kate stopped in her tracks. Halfway through her door, she just stared, wide-eyed in horror. "Uh…"

"I like her, she's so sweet."

"That's Emily," Kate simply said, too mortified to do anything but disappear into her room. She exited ten minutes later, fully dressed and with a backpack full of sketch pads over her shoulders. "I'll be back later, Nana," she told her, kissing her hair again. "Text me if you need anything."

"Okay, baby," said Deloris as Kate disappeared out the door.

It was awkward riding the bus again after last night. While it was a different line with different seats, Kate always rode three-quarters of the way to the back, a habit learned in elementary school and never broken decades later. It was there that the rumble of the wheels always seemed to cancel other out and people passed her a little less frequently. It was also there that she looked out the window at the world passing her by and found a certain kind of melancholy reserved for lonely travel.

The day was overcast, but not too cold. The thick humidity meant that most of the cars on the street had a sheen of condensation. It made the world seem a little newer, which somehow made Kate feel lonelier, like she was the only thing in the world that felt old.

The bus stopped at an apartment complex made up of large, squat buildings that were three-stories tall and lacked even the most basic of decorations. Ugly brick that didn't match, the breezeways in the middle of the buildings were strict wood with metal railings. There was nothing aesthetically pleasing at all about any of it. Kate crossed the chipped and pockmarked parking lot of faded parking spaces and headed towards the rear of the complex. Someone from a window wolf-whistled and called "Mamacita!" but she ignored it without effort.

She ascended the steps to the second floor of building 1216 and went for apartment G. She knocked on the rusted door with chipped paint and waited. She glanced into the distance, well beyond the confines of the complex, to see a trash crane in the scrap yard distributing junk. The metal grinding noise carried across the distance, echoing in the breezeway. Kate heard steps on the other side of the door and the peep hole went dark for a second.   A chain was moved, two locks were undone, and Denise's completely shaved head opened the door.

Gone were the long black locks and instead, she sported a smooth head with a dozen tattoos of various quality, all covered in a sheen of bristling hair stubble. "What happened?!" Kate exclaimed, followed by laughter from inside the apartment.

Emily and Rachael were both inside, laughing hysterically at the reaction. "Knew you'd say it," Rachael all but cheered.

"We don't have any cons coming up and every costume I want to do has a wig, so I thought I'd go natural again," Denise explained for what was clearly not the first time that morning. "Plus, I wanted to remind myself of every bad decision I ever made." She gestured to the violent punk and metal tattoos that encircled her scalp.

"Man, I haven't seen these in forever," Kate said, brushing at the stubble on Denise's scalp to see the tattoos more clearly. "Holy crap, that's the one you got in juvie."

"UGH!" Denise grimaced. "Don't remind me. I still have puncture wounds from getting Golden Staph." She flopped down on the couch with Rachael. "What's up with you?" Kate only shrugged.

"Any news on your car?" asked Emily, sitting on the floor around the coffee table. It and the couch were the only pieces of furniture. Even the TV was set up on a plastic milk crate. Video game systems, a cable box, and a wi-fi router, were all arranged unceremoniously on the ugly, stained carpet, a snake's nest of cables winding along the wall behind them.

"Not yet. I'm waiting to hear from them. They were going to try and...do something," Kate said. She set down her backpack, remarking, "If I don't hear from them by the time we're done, I'm going to head over there." She sat down opposite Emily, her back to the door and exhaled. "God, re-entry has been stupidly rough."

"Tell me about it," Denise concurred with a world-weary shake of her head. She ran her hands over her almost-smooth cranium like she drew strength from being free of the bonds of long hair. "I was legit in tears when the alarm hit Monday morning. Oh my god, I did NOT want to go to work."

"Yeah," agreed Emily. "It's kind of hard to go from the cons, where everybody's all 'hey, I love your costume' and 'you look so great, can I take your picture' to 'yes, I would like fries with that'," she recounted with a condescending imitation. She scoffed and looked away. "Man, I hate real life."

"Yeah, because cons are so great," Kate griped. She looked to Rachael and asked, "So how'd we do?"

Rachael took out her ledger and reported, "We did...okay."

"Did we break even?" Denise asked.

"Right at," Rachael said, handing the ledger to Denise. The bald beauty began to look over the numbers. She didn't seem enthused. "We've got nothing to make new costumes but at least we've zeroed our accounts with the printers." She half-nodded at that not-trivial accomplishment.

"A black zero is still in the black," Emily said, working overtime to sound optimistic, though without her usual smile.

"Looks like we've got $6.42," Denise said as she looked over Rachael's figures. She snickered and suggested, "I say we all go to Wendys and get some Frosty's."

"Here-here," Kate joked, accepting the ledger from Denise. She looked over the somewhat pathetic sales reports and the long list of expenses. She wanted to call this a victory but it simply didn't feel like one.

"So, yeah, that's where we are," Rachael said as Kate handed the ledger across to Emily. "We're broke, but everything's up-to-date and paid off. We've got the website until the end of the year, which is good. We can TRY to get a group credit card, but I'm not too optimistic about how good it would be. Denise's and my credit rating is awful thanks to student loans; Kate, I know yours isn't great. And Emily is still IN school, so hers might be the best of all of ours, which is kind of sad."

"Here-here," Denise agreed cynically, scrutinizing the numbers.

"But, we've got invitations to six cons this summer, starting in May," Rachael added into the plus category. "We've got to decide which ones we want to hit and how we want to do that. Two conflict, so we have to make a decision, and three are back-to-back-to-back. We may want to consider taking off the intervening weeks rather than deal with the travel expenses and strain."

Kate scoffed at the impossibility. "Uh, yeah, no. I can't take that kind of time off."

"Me either," said Denise.

"And one of those cons is nine hours away," Rachael further added. She looked around the table at the others.

The three cosplayers shared glances, as though confused why a con so far away was even a viable candidate. "Is there a chance they'll pay for airfare?" asked Kate.

Rachael shrugged. "I can ask, but since they're only offering one room, I'm kind of doubting it."

"If they can do airfare, then say yes," Denise all but decided for the team. "But if they can't help us with the travel, I don't think we can do it." She got up from the couch and headed into the kitchen that was devoid of all extraneous appliances except for a blender and a microwave. "Anybody want a smoothie?"

Kate's hand shot up. "Yeah, please!"

As Denise began mixing a protein-heavy smoothie with ice and bananas, Emily asked, "Did you guys hear about the meteor?"

"Asteroid," Rachael corrected as she looked over notes.

"What's the difference?" Emily asked a little obtusely.

"An asteroid is in space," Kate explained, having to shout suddenly when Denise started the blender. "A meteor is if it gets burned up in the atmosphere. A meteorite is if it survives to impact."

"Oh," Emily said, a little embarrassed.

"Yeah, they're talking about it getting close enough for…" She stopped and glared back through the kitchen entryway at Denise. The shaven woman kept blending. Rachael took a pillow off the couch and threw it at Denise. Denise half-blocked the thrown pillow and flipped her the bird in response. The two began to play-argue, yelling violent and vulgar things in absolute silence, pretending to be drowned out by the blender. Kate looked across the table at Emily who was trying to pretend like she wasn't entertained by the mock-fight.

Once the grinding was done, Rachael continued with exaggerated exacerbation. "They're talking about it getting close enough to enter the atmosphere."

"Ooh, we should try to do a shoot!" Emily grinned. "We should do a Sailor Moon shoot. Kate can do Sailor Moon, Denise can do Jupiter, and I'll do Mars."

"I'm Mars!" both Denise and Kate claimed quickly.

"We can't have three Sailor Mars...Marses...Marss...Marsi?" Rachael tried to conjugate. "We can't have three of the same character."

"Sure we can," Denise said, bringing over a plastic cup for Kate, full of a beige sludge. "We could do Sailor Mars classic, Sailor Mars celestial from when she was in the Moon Kingdom, and Sailor Mars from the Crystal remake."

"That...might work," Rachael considered. Then reality hit. "But we don't have time to make the costumes." She looked at Emily. "Do we? When's the asteroid supposed to get here?"

Emily shrugged. "I don't remember. I just heard about it while I was waiting on a to-go order."

"Like two or three weeks," said Denise as she returned to the group with two cups, handing one to Kate.

"Yeah, and we'd have to schedule a photographer, and I don't know what the weather will be like, and it may not even be visible," Rachael thought aloud, her eyes bopping around behind her half-glasses. As she talked mostly to herself, Kate tried the smoothie with the consistency of half-dried cement. It tasted like chalky banana, but wasn't nearly as bad as it looked. Never one to turn down a free meal, Kate eagerly drank it up.

The logistics returned Rachael back to the more pressing business. "And this of course, brings us back to the fact that we have no money currently in our coffers. Everything's paid up, everything's good, but there's no group money. That means we have to A) stick to current costumes, B) pay for new costumes out of our own pockets, or C) we afford some new materials by selling some of our costumes." Kate blanched at the notion. She tried to imagine parting with any of her work, especially the projects she'd made by hand. A tightness gripped her in the chest as she even entertained the idea of an empty closet.

"What costumes?" Denise asked as she guzzled the smoothie from a rinsed-out gas station Big Gulp cup.

"To sell or to make?" Kate asked. She couldn't think of a single costume she'd made that she was ready to part with.

"Either," Denise said, wiping her mouth. "What costumes do we want to make?" She looked at Emily and Rachael. "I mean, I haven't watched any new anime in, like, six months. I've mostly been watching Afro Samurai again, and Robotech."

Kate teased her with the correction, "Macross."

"Shut up, elitist," Denise snapped jokingly. "Besides, Dana Sterling's my patronus." She took another sip of her fruit-flavored sludge. "But yeah, and any new video games?" She gestured at the game systems on her floor. "I don't even own a current-gen console. Not like I could afford a new game, either. Or have time to play an 80-hour game."

"Yeah," Emily lamented.

"What if we did some gender-swap stuff?" Kate suggested. "Maybe some Bombshell superhero stuff? Bombshell Iron Man, Bombshell Captain America?"

"Expensive," Denise asserted. "If we do popular characters like that, we got to get the details solid." She ran her hands over her head yet again, an act which sounded like rubbing sandpaper. "I mean, if we had a red wig, maybe one of us could do a Mary Jane thing from Spider-Man. We've got blonde," she said with a nod at Kate, "we could do Gwen Stacy."

"I'd like to do Spider-Man," Emily said with a smile, raising her hand like she was in class.

"Yeah, but Gwen and Mary Jane both wear regular clothes," Kate told the youngest of their group. "We could make their costumes with little work. A good Spider-Man outfit—"

"And it HAS to be good," Denise inserted, Rachael nodding.

"A good Spider-Man would be expensive to do," Kate said, agreeing as well with Denise. She addressed Rachael. "I think a Gwen/Mary Jane shoot could be—"

"Dammit, in a MINUTE!" came a shout from upstairs.

The four women fell instantly silent as they looked as one up at the ceiling. They listened, hearing talking but no further distinct words.

"They're at it again, huh?" asked Rachael.

"Yeah, she's back with that asshole," Denise griped. She finished off her smoothie. "I keep waiting to hear him hit her. Like, for certain." She looked into her cup. "Not sure what good it would do, though. I've called the cops on him, like, four times. I'm not sure they'd even come out again."

The four were quiet, listening. They tried to hear the telltale sounds of crying that they'd all heard in the past, but all that came from above was an eerie quiet.

"Has he hit her?" Rachael asked, whispering as they all listened.

"I'm sure he has, but I can't tell for sure," Denise told her, staring up. "If I for real know he has, like if I hear him making impact or something, I'm going up there."

"That might make things worse," Kate warned her.

"No, it can't," Denise told her adamantly. "It can't make things worse than her already getting beaten by that jackass."

"Yeah, it can," Rachael told Denise. "She can survive the beating." She let the rest of her point go unstated.

Denise didn't take the implication well and snapped back at her, "I'm not going to stand by while he hits her."

"What's happened when the cops show up?" Emily asked, both curious and trying to keep Denise and Rachael from arguing.

Denise shrugged aggressively. "Nothing that I can tell. They talk to the guy, ask if things are okay, and then they leave. Last time they were here, they weren't at the door for a full minute."

"Jesus," was the only thing Kate could say as she shook her head.

They listened for a moment more but heard nothing more from upstairs. Slowly, their eyes drifted back down to their own conversation. "What if instead of comics we did some boudoir shoots?" Rachael suggested. "Get some lacy stuff and do some shoots? We don't have to go full-nudity, but it will help us move prints."

"We could even do it as a fundraiser," Emily said eagerly.

"I don't like the idea of doing that," Denise hedged. "I legit don't have a problem with others doing it, but I just...I don't want to be flashing my cleavage just to..." Her words, like her gaze, drifted into her empty cup.

"Just to what, pay the bills?" Kate said a little harshly. Denise looked like she'd genuinely hurt her. "I don't want to do that either. I'm not a model, I'm a cosplayer, but..." Kate found herself choking up. She looked down into her cup, knowing it was empty. "But I—" She fell into embarrassed silence when her stomach growled.

"Jesus, was that a tiger?" Rachael exclaimed. Kate averted her eyes, trying not to cry in front of her friends. Rachael's humor drew tight. "What's going on, honey?" Rachael whispered at Kate.

Kate laughed, growing mad at herself for, among other reasons, being unable to keep from bringing these issues to her friends. "It's just...it's been tight," she understated. "I'm actually in the hole for this whole—" Her phone began to ring. She checked the caller ID and laughed. "Speak of the devil." She got up and paced into the hallway towards the back of the apartment. "Hello?"

"Ms. Harbough? It's Jake," said the friendly mechanic from the auto-shop. "We've finished the full evaluation of your vehicle. I've contacted a bunch of different parts dealers in the area. Is there any chance you can come by? There's, huh," he gave a chuckle, "there's a bit to go over."

Kate happened to glance out the window of Denise's bedroom and saw the warm sunlight coming through the clouds of the otherwise chilly day. She turned to the others and called, "Any of you guys feel up to a walk?"

The four women walked along the side of the road like the boys out of Stand By Me. Kate walked at the front, swaying her long legs a little as she walked. Her hands in her jacket pockets, she looked down at the sidewalk. Behind her, Denise and Emily walked with Rachael, continuing to argue about the practicality of doing a cosplay shoot with a meteor in the background.

The route from Denise's apartment to the shopping center in question passed along a stretch of a forgotten two-lane road. Beneath it, a small junk yard was dotted with tiny sprouts of young trees among the broken cars and metallic refuse. Along the sun-faded pavement that through the hills, patches of flat land circled the area. Forgotten structures that never got off the first stages of construction along with a few abandoned buildings that had once been standing businesses. The smell of iron and rust wafted through the air, along with the ripe scent of mold and overgrowth.

Kate led the way to a deep ravine that had once been a train track. The mounds of rocks at the base were overgrown with green spots of vegetation and the tracks were rusted to a dark, ugly color of brown. Rather than cross at the street bridge, Kate detoured off the sidewalk and into the grassy, litter-filled field that headed towards the ravine. Stretching at a slight diagonal across the ravine was a walking bridge made of wooden planks across metal wires. Kate headed across the bridge, the others following.

"Who makes stuff like this?" Emily asked with a laugh, looking over the side halfway across.

"Some Boy Scouts, like, a dozen years ago," Denise told her, the rest of the group clumping together around her. "It was part of some kind of civic project or something. It was in the newspaper."

"Back when we had newspapers," Rachael joked.

"It was kind of a tourist attraction for, like, a week," Denise went on. She looked over the side as well. "We should do a shoot on here. Like, a gender-bent Indiana Jones shoot, out of Temple of Doom." She quickly claimed, "Dibs on Indy!"

"Billy," Kate added right after.

Emily rolled her eyes. "Great, I'm either Mola Ram or Shortround."

"That could work," suggested Rachael, looking up and down the bridge. "Although Kate needs to be Indy. She's taller." Kate looked at Denise and stuck her tongue out at her. Denise shoved Kate, making the bridge sway a little.

Laughter subsided and the walk resumed. They cut through the woods past the bridge and headed down a steep tree-covered slope into the forgotten shopping center. They had to go around the grocery store that was the main site of the center, then headed to the far end where the auto shop waited. Kate wasn't encouraged to see her car in the parking lot, two plastic trash bags duct-taped over the missing door.

The auto-shop smelled of motor oil and grease. Four computer stations were setup on kiosks at the far end, while a circle of mismatched couches was focused on an analog TV in the corner, the fuzzy image switching from the schedule of an upcoming art festival to speculation on the best site for meteor viewing. At the back of the waiting room, a broad-shouldered, big-bellied man with a shaved head and a long beard was typing at the computer. "What's happening, Ms. Harbough?" he cheerfully called as the four women entered.

"Hey, Jake," Kate said as she left the others by the TV. "Please tell me you've got some good news."

Jake snickered. With caricature of contrition, he said, "Well, depends on what you call good news."

"That you can fix my car completely for six dollars and ninety-three cents?" Kate asked with a hopeful smile.

Again, Jake snickered. "That'd be a no," he said emphatically. He punched a few keys on the keyboard and gestured for Kate to take a look. She leaned around the kiosk and studied the long list of repairs with eyes that grew swollen in horror. "So, here's the thing: the car wasn't in good shape before the damage to the door. Now that the door's been ripped off – which I still want to know how that happened – the entire chassis is compromised."

"Compromised?" Emily half-exclaimed from the other side of the shop.

"Yeah," Jake told her with an astonished laugh. Speaking mostly to Kate, he explained, "The car isn't street-legal at this point. And it will never pass inspection."

Kate only knew to push the one issue that truly mattered. "Can it be fixed?"

"No," he said just as emphatically as before, but without the humor. "I mean, yes, technically, we could completely dismantle the car and go in on it with hammers and a torch to work out all the kinks, but you're talking about way more bodywork than that car is worth. Way more. We're talking five digits of body work." Kate's jaw dropped.

"Yeah," he said, not at all surprised by her reaction. "And even if the chassis wasn't compromised, the damage to the door is still significant. We can't just hang a new door on there; we'd have to remove the warped hinges and then install new ones. And then there's all the little, related stuff like the locks and things. You'd be looking at four digits of work, even without the chassis issue."

Kate's hands were shaking. She couldn't feel her legs.

Sensitive to Kate's state, Jake pointed to the screen. "We can make this offer on the car, as parts." Kate looked at the pittance and felt like she was going to fall over. "I mean, you can try to take it somewhere else. Maybe you can get a better deal, but I'm gonna be honest with you, I kind of doubt it. I know CarMax won't even buy a car in this condition. If you want, I can give you some numbers for some junk shops and see what you can get." He laughed with nervous sympathy. "You're a bit cuter than me. They might cut a better deal for you."

The others came to Kate's side as she stared at the number. She had to lean on the counter of the kiosk to steady herself. Rachael looked at the screen and saw what they were looking at and closed her eyes. "Oh honey," she told Kate, brushing her back. Denise caught a glimpse and swore quietly.

Kate stared at the wide pixels of the screen and wanted to die. Her hands had stopped shaking but the shock was still intense. She swallowed and felt like she'd break down. Jake clicked his tongue nervously and looked at the three women by Kate, no one sure how exactly to proceed through the moment. Jake finally offered weakly, "If you want, you can call your--"

"I-I'll take it," Kate said, her voice hoarse. She looked to Jake and repeated with tears in her eyes, "I'll take it. That'll be fine."

For the first time, Jake seemed surprised. He glanced away from Kate and stammered a little unevenly, "I'll...let me...I'll go let the manager know and we'll draw up the paperwork," he said. "Think you can come back tomorrow with the title?"

Kate was staring at the screen, at the tiny pittance of money her car was worth. "The title's in the glovebox." She didn't answer; the answer just came out while she stared at the money.

Jake started to protest about how that wasn't a good place for such an important document, but stopped himself. "I'll go find Dale," he said and excused himself.

Denise, Rachael, and Emily all crowded together in support as Kate stared into the distance. "I want to go home," she whispered to herself.

The four exited the auto shop half an hour later and started out of the shopping center. They headed towards an overgrown median dividing the parking lot right in front of the beauty supply shop when Kate abruptly detoured without any warning or signal. The others stalled in surprise and turned as she abandoned the return route to go storming into the grocery store.

As the others rushed to catch up with her, Kate plowed through the midday void of customers and went right for the cereal and snacks aisle of the off-brand, third-tier grocery store. Snatching a box of superhero-shaped fruit snacks off the shelf, Kate walked right back by her friends without saying a word.

She tossed the box of fruit snacks down on the conveyor belt at the register and stared aimlessly. "Will this be all?" asked the middle-aged woman that rang her up without paying a lick of attention.

"Do I look like I can afford—" Kate started to snap, when she caught herself. She looked at the woman, clearly old enough to have grandkids, and saw herself. Kate saw her very visage behind the register, wearing the apron and sensible shoes and still waiting to 'make it' in cosplay.

Kate swallowed and hated herself; hated herself for hating this woman's life, hated herself for looking down on her, and hated herself for fearing the inevitable of ending up like here. "Yeah, that's all," Kate surrendered, paying quickly and leaving even quicker.

Once outside, Kate simply sat down on the curb in front of the grocery store, plopping down with indifference usually reserved for ornery teenagers. She tore open the box of fruit snacks and pulled out a pouch. Ripping it open, she poured all the neon-colored fruit-flavored jellies into her mouth. The others cloistered around her, not sure what to say.

As Kate ripped open a second pouch, she looked at the edible treat for a second. "I wonder if these are even technically food? Or are they, like, a food-like product, like cheese singles?"

Rachael sat down on the curb with her and took the box. She turned it around and read, "Made with less than 10% fruit juice." She kept studying the box. "I don't know."

Kate was a little slower with the second pouch, eating the pieces by flavor. "I bet Yaya Han binges on, like, expensive French chocolate or something. And Kato has, like, a filet mignon and champagne." Kate looked at the orange-flavored piece of jelly. "I eat Batman-shaped fruit snacks." Emily and Denise both sat down with her. Kate tore open a third pouch and shared with her friends, none of whom refused.

The walk back to Denise's apartment was a lot slower than the walk to the auto-shop. All of the women felt despondent in the face of Kate's situation, like it was a harbinger of what they all would eventually face. Emily, walking ahead of the others up the earthen hill covered with trees, turned around and walked backwards as she said, "Kate I'm so sorry." Kate just nodded, her eyes cast down as she looked for spare change and hope.

"Think you can get a new car?" asked Denise from the rear of their procession, helping Rachael navigate the steep incline.

Kate scoffed. "Not a chance. The money they gave me for it will barely cover what I was short this month as it is."

Rachael, desperate for something to suggest, proposed, "Well, at least you can cancel your car insurance." Something about that prospect made Kate tear up. "Oh honey, I'm sorry," Rachael said, going into full den-mother mode. The attention and support did little to stem the tide, however.

"I've just about had it," Kate choked up, her chin shaking and her eyes welling up. She stepped around Rachael and stormed ahead. "I don't think I can take much more. I've been at this for almost fifteen years!" She stopped walking and succumbed, beginning to cry. "I thought at some point, I'd...I'd get a break. I'd get...I thought if you worked hard, that was..." She shook it off in a fury and stormed ahead of the others.

Rachael and Denise looked to each other, worried of the direction this was going, and chased after her. Emily, in a fog of clueless disorientation, could only follow. The trio followed as best they could but fell behind as Kate all but burst out from the trees into the field with the wire bridge. "I just...I just don't get it!" she sobbed, wiping her tears from her eyes, only for them to be replaced. "What do I have to do to make it?" She found herself approaching the ravine, the swaying bridge the only immediate option to cross it. Rather than approach the bridge, she walked to the edge of the ravine itself and looked down at the tracks. The metal bands were overgrown, rusted and desolate-looking. She could feel the heat coming off the grass-dotted path of rocks.

A hard thought entered Kate's mind and she realized as she was staring directly down into the train tracks, she was wondering about a landing. She wondered what it would be like to feel free of the ground and to feel herself fall. She fantasized about the sense of relief she'd feel if it was all to just end, to know the serenity of endless blackness.

The thoughts warped and she imagined a funeral. In the blink of an eye, she fantasized about cosplayers paying tribute to her and her name in lights at a convention, posthumously honoring her hard work. But the dream was dashed when she realized she wouldn't be around to see it. Slowly, she accepted that if she died, it was likely other cosplayers wouldn't even notice. She'd be relegated to a few asking 'hey, what happened to that one girl who was here last year'. The following year, she wouldn't even be remembered.

Kate felt silly. Staring down at the train tracks, she internally chastised herself for her childishness. "How silly is it to fantasize about death, just so you can be recognized?" she whispered at herself. She laughed at herself, desperate, and wiped her tears away with her hands. "I'm sorry, guys," she sobbed as turmoil and shame compounded. The crying got worse and she whimpered, "I want to go home."

"Kate...honey...?" said Rachael in a slow, distant tone.

Kate felt more ashamed by the second. She turned back towards her friends, ashamed of feeling undeserving of their support and quietly terrified that their support would be withdrawn. They had to be sick of her melancholy, sick of the emotional strain she placed on them.

Instead, Denise, Emily, and Rachael were all terrified.

The three women stood at the mouth of the bridge, staring slack-jawed with huge eyes. Their gaze was locked just beyond Kate, just below her. "What?" she asked, sniffing unseemly. She wiped her nose for fear of a giant snot bubble, then turned to the far side of the bridge behind her. She didn't see a bear or a wolf or anything in the field beyond. She looked back at her friends. "Guys, what is it?" she practically demanded, transitioning from confused to scared.

With a trembling hand, Rachael pointed at Kate's feet.

Kate glanced down at the wires of the bridge that formed the basis for the slats to walk across. It took her a second to realize that the slats were on the wrong side of the wire. She was confused and looked for what they were attached to, seeing another set of wires passed them. "Did they add another bridge?" she asked, confused. She looked down at her own feet and saw only the train tracks beneath the soles of her sneakers. Far beneath the soles of her sneakers.

Kate looked to her friends for help understanding because she wasn't quite processing what was going on. She looked down again at the train tracks directly beneath her feet. She could tell something was wrong but couldn't quite place it. She had been walking across the bridge...

Like a punch to the gut, Kate suddenly realized she was standing in thin air, hovering over the tracks and next to the bridge.

Dawning terror like she'd done something horribly, horribly wrong crept across Kate's mind as it hit her that she'd never actually stepped on the bridge. She'd been on the edge next to the bridge and gotten transfixed by the train tracks. She remembered the tracks looming more prominently but she never stepped out onto the bridge itself.

Kate looked again at the bridge only a few steps to her left, then down at her feet that were a few dozen feet above the rusted train tracks. She very slowly and very fearfully extended her left toe a bit and tapped at where she felt like the ground should have been. The toe of her sneaker met nothing, just swished awkwardly through the air.

Kate nodded very slowly for a second, on the verge of total hysteria. She turned around a bit, beginning to grasp that there was no ground beneath her and she was simply standing in the air. She looked to her friends, like she was afraid she was going to get into trouble for being on the wrong side of the metal ropes. The three were just staring, every bit as shocked as she. Kate's heart began to race and she whispered fearfully, "Guys, what's happening?"

"Kate, honey," Rachael whispered, "why are you flying?"

Kate looked at the ground too far beneath her feet. "I don't know."

"HOW are you flying?" asked Denise.

"I don't know!" Kate whimpered, afraid. She looked to the bridge and reached out for it. She grabbed the wire hand-railing and yanked herself over to the bridge. Her toes dangling on the side of the slats, she clung suddenly to the railing, afraid of falling over the side.

The others rushed onto the bridge with her, the flimsy structure swaying unsettlingly. They crowded around her as she clung to the side of the bridge, mildly hysterical with relief. Kate looked over the side of the bridge, down at the tracks that had seemed so innocent a moment ago. "How did you do that?" Denise asked, terrified.

"I don't know!" Kate all but shrieked. She looked to her friends with eyes hungry for comfort.

Now that she was back on the bridge, her feet on the wooden slats where they belonged, the four women took a collective breath of relief. A few nervous laughs were shared. After that moment of relief passed, Denise's lips curled slowly into a mischievous grin as she asked, "Can you do it again?"

CHAPTER SEVEN

Denise swept her hand along the floor, her palms gently ruffling the cheap, faded carpet. She made a fist and repeated the sweep, the top of her knuckles rubbing against the soles of Kate's sneakers. "I just...how are you doing it?" she asked, looking up at Kate.

Hovering a few inches off the ground, Kate stood suspended in the air as casually as if she was standing on the floor. Denise stood, leaving Emily on the floor to pass her hands under Kate's feet, giggling to herself the whole time. Kate was chewing on her thumbnail, her right toe vibrating from time to time as if she was nervous to tap the floor. "What's it feel like?" Denise asked. Kate shrugged distantly. "Come on, think."

"I don't know," Kate exclaimed with a laugh that was clearly more nervousness than humor. "It feels like...I don't know."

"Do you just not feel gravity?" asked Emily, sliding a notepad under Kate's feet.

"No, I feel gravity...I guess...I mean, I think I do," Kate said, looking down. She bent farther forward and brushed her hair out of her face so she could see the cell phone Emily was now waving under her feet. "I just..." She snapped her fingers suddenly. "It's like standing in the ocean. Or, like, a river or something. And you kind of stand against the current. That's what it feels like. It feels like I'm standing against a current." She looked over to the couch where Rachael was reading on her cell phone. "Any ideas?"

"No," Rachael said, shifting one leg out from underneath her and replacing it with the other. She looked displeased. "Nothing that seems even remotely useful. I checked how Superman flies, how Rogue flies, how Wonder Woman flies. Every explanation is basically some drummed-up version of 'magic'."

"Great," Kate said, looking down at her feet as Emily passed a couch pillow beneath her feet. "Okay, that's enough," she declared, lowering back down. She touched down and looked unhappy. "Guys, what is this?"

"Cool is what it is," Emily giggled, standing.

"Yeah, it kind of is," Denise agreed.

"I'm scared," Kate half-exclaimed.

"Honey, would you let those of us who aren't you enjoy this?" Rachael said as she searched.

"Ooh, carry me again," Emily said, holding out her hands like she was an infant demanding to be picked up by a parent. Kate sighed and picked her up. Holding Emily in the classic superhero-carrying-the-damsel-in-distress pose, Kate rose off the carpet about two inches. Emily shouted excitedly. "Ooh! Fly around! Fly around!"

Even Kate couldn't quell her smile as she began to hover slowly around the room. Emily began squealing like a child, practically shaking with excitement in Kate's arms. "This is so cool!"

"I want a turn," Denise said after Kate had finished one rotation around the couch. Kate was laughing as she set Emily down and, without returning to the ground, scooped up Denise. Carrying Denise in her arms, she began to slowly circle the couch again. "Can you read my mind?" Denise asked after just a second, batting her eyelashes sarcastically. Kate looked at her, confused. "Do you know what it is that you do to me?" Denise kept on. Recognition made Rachael roll her eyes. "I don't know who you are. Just a friend from another star." Kate and Emily got the reference simultaneously. As Emily laughed and rolled her eyes, Kate's expression comically soured and she removed her supporting arms from beneath Denise, letting her fall onto the couch next to Rachael.

As the others laughed, the biggest of the four women got up and said, "Okay, I want a turn."

"Whoa, I'm not sure…" Emily began to protest but stopped when she wasn't sure how to phrase it without sounding mean.

"Kate's buff; she can carry me," Rachael said certainly.

Kate looked trepidatious but she lowered down to the floor and put her arms at Rachael's legs and shoulder. "Ready? Sit back," she told Rachael. Rachael leaned back very slowly and Kate picked her up with surprising ease. She began to lift up off the carpet, making the usually nonplussed Rachael shriek and grab onto her. "Fun, isn't it?" Kate asked Rachael.

"OhmygodohmygodOHMYGOD!" Rachael repeated in an ecstatic panic.

Kate encircled the couch and slowly set Rachael back down to the floor without trouble. The Rubenesque woman backed away with a nervous laugh and brushed her hair back from her glasses. "Wow, that's…" She giggled into a snort that caused her to fall silent, then laugh louder.

"Is it any harder carrying somebody? Like, harder to fly?" Denise asked Kate. Kate just shook her head, not having even thought about it enough to notice. "I wonder how much you can carry like that,"

"I wonder how fast you can go," asked Emily.

The three non-flying women all looked at each other with the same look. They turned to Kate and slowly, their knowing grins spread into toothy smiles.

"Three," Rachael yelled. "Two…one…GO!" She hit the button on her cell phone screen, the stopwatch feature counting furiously.

Above head-height, Kate flew through the air, zipping along the street, tracking along the edge of the pavement. Rushing along the backstreet behind the shopping center, near the very bridge where her flying had been discovered, Kate soared from one segment of trees to the other and slowed to a stop. She lowered to the pavement and jogged back.

"Same time," Rachael called to the approaching Kate, Emily and Denise reading the stopwatch over her shoulder.

"Actually, three-tenths slower," Emily added cheerfully, trying to be helpful and failing.

"So it looks like you can fly at about the same speed you can run at," Rachael decided, recording the flight time in her phone.

"How do you feel?" asked Denise, looking at Kate, one eye shut in the sharp afternoon daylight. "Are you tired?"

Kate had no appreciable answer to offer, barely even breathing hard. "Yeah, kind of. I don't feel gassed or anything, but I feel like I've been running sprints."

"You kind of have, I guess," said Rachael. She looked up, then around at the empty and silent street running behind a larger but still insignificant backstreet. "I wonder how high you can go?"

Kate barely gave it any thought and began to rise straight up. "Uh…" Denise said, unsure what to actually say.

Kate lifted above the trees and into the sky over the city. She saw how it stretched out in all directions as she continued to go up. A giant smile spread across her lips as she kept rising. She looked up and saw a white cloud and began to head towards it. Long before she reached the cloud, however, she realized she was panting a little. A stark chill shot through her and she stopped rising.

She stayed aloft for a moment, effortlessly floating in the sky. She looked out at the silent world around her. Besides the blustering wind that chilled her to the bone and set her shivering, there was not a single sound. No cars or traffic, no hum of electric power or even a single chirp of a solitary bird. Nothing but pure silence. She looked down at her feet and saw her city far beneath her. She smiled at the magnificent sight, but a whirling sense of vertigo overtook her. Her stomach rebelled and threatened total upheaval. She quickly began to descend.

It was disconcerting to descend from the heavens because she saw all the cars in the distance and worried someone might see her. She lowered quicker to try and avoid being noticed. Once she reached the treetops, she decided to try a crazy idea.

Kate stopped flying.

Just above the trees, she dropped abruptly. Rachael, Denise, and Emily all panicked, but Kate caught herself before she hit the ground and landed in a crouch like a parkour traceur. "Huh," Kate said as the others approached. She checked her hands, the tips red from cold exposure.

"What happened?" asked Rachael, worried.

"Nothing," responded Kate with a thoughtful look at her landing spot. "I wondered what was different between flying down and falling."

"What is the difference?" Emily asked.

"I don't know," said Kate. "But there is one."

"We could tell," Denise told Kate with a rare maternal tone. "Don't do that again, okay?" She glanced down and smirked, asking, "Was it the cold that sent you back down?"

"Actually, yeah, it--" Kate looked down and saw her t-shirt pointed outward. She made a snarky face at Denise, who made one back.

"Any idea how high up you went?" Rachael asked but Kate shook her head. She looked thoughtful for a second. "Was that landing rough at all?"

Kate looked back where she'd touched down by the street. She shook her head. "No, why?"

"Because you fell two or three stories," Rachael noticed, looking at the height of the trees. "Even curving back up or whatever that little move was, you came down with some force." She smiled with mischievous delight at Kate and said, "Let's try something else."

Kate wrapped her hand around the metal bar and tested her grip. The metal was heavily rusted, and so thick that her fingers couldn't entirely close around it. She planted her feet unevenly on debris in the junk yard, then checked her form. Back straight. Knees bent but poised. Hips coiled like a spring. She took a few readying breaths, then ripped the bar into the air. She hoisted it overhead in a single snap, one hand extended overhead, supporting the bar at the very center.

She held the weight aloft for a solid breath and stepped forward from underneath it, letting the heavy eighteen-wheeler tire axel slam onto the junk. Kate turned and staggered a little away from the tire axel, panting and stunned. She looked back at the others who were all applauding.

As dusk set around them in the junk yard, the smell of rust, iron, and mildew heavy in the cooling air, the four women gathered. "That's, like…a lot," Emily said of the truck part. "And one-handed, too!" Kate nodded, amazed at her own feat of strength. It was less a look of pride and more displaced worry.

"Do they make kettlebells that heavy?" Denise teased.

"What else can we try?" asked Rachael, looking around.

"There's got to be a refrigerator or a dryer or something around here," Denise said, eager to keep the experiment going.

"Guys, can we go home?" Kate said, holding her stomach. "The smell's getting to—" Her stomach let out a loud, displeased gurgle.

"What the hell was that?!" Denise exclaimed.

"I'm hungry!" Kate laughed, embarrassed. "I've been running sprints and lifting crap for the last two hours."

"Yeah, we do kinda need to go," agreed Rachael, looking out over the trash dump next to the junk yard. With a gesture to the others, she led the way down the heap of metal junk, towards the chain link fence they'd slipped through. Rachael went through the torn metal fence first, then held it for Emily and Denise. She began to hold it for Kate when she realized, "Why don't you fly over?"

Kate looked at the tall fence with barbed wire strung along the top, then at Rachael. A strange look of panic came over her. She said nothing, but just ducked through the fence hole. They exited out into a wooded area and started through the trees back towards Denise's apartment.

"I think I know what we should do," Rachael decided as they walked, using her cell phone's flashlight option to illuminate the darkening woods. She shone the light at Kate and said, "We're going to do a photoshoot." Emily and Kate shared glances of worry over Rachael's epiphany.

"Okay, of what?" asked Denise.

Rachael smiled, super-eager. "Denise and Emily, you'll be crooks. Kate, you're going to be Supergirl."

Kate paced uncomfortably, struggling with the knee-high red boots with pronounced heels. She kept brushing her long blonde hair, going over, then under, trying to give it as much volume as possible. She wore a blue and red Supergirl costume that was clearly intended for someone smaller than her. The skirt rode up her hips, revealing the bloomers beneath while the halter top was rendered into essentially a sports bra with the red and yellow S stretched between her breasts. On the couch, Rachael was looking through the four women's cell phones, considering the quality of each. "Why did Denise have to make this one with heels?"

"She likes heels, honey," Rachael said as she held two cell phones up and aimed them at Kate, comparing the visuals with an unimpressed sneer.

Kate flipped her hair to the other shoulder and kept brushing. "Only people who are gluttons for punishment like heels," Kate griped.

"Prosecution rests, your honor," Rachael agreed just before the bedroom door opened.

Denise and Emily exited from the rear of Denise's apartment, wearing black pants and black-and-white striped shirts. They were both eyes sporting masks made up of long black socks with eye-holes cut in them. Denise was carrying with her a large bag that she had hastily spray-painted with a green dollar sign and was stuffed with pillows. She was also wearing a huge, stupid grin. "Well," she asked, "how do we look?"

Kate's awed look said it all, but Rachael added, "Not bad." She rose from the couch and studied the mask that Emily wore. "I think it looks better against your skin than Pasty McGee's," she said.

"Hey, we prefer Melatonin-challenged," Denise snapped back sarcastically.

"Melanin," Emily corrected absently like she'd been called upon in class. Rachael turned her around and studied the quick job of the costume. "Melatonin's a neurotransmitter." Denise made a face at Kate, causing her to snicker.

"Okay, good job," Rachael declared. She snatched up her preferred phone and said, "Let's make some magic." She started for the apartment door.

"Wait, what are you doing?" Kate half-shrieked with a laugh.

Rachael froze, a little surprised. She turned to the door, then back to Kate. "Going…outside?"

"What if someone sees us?" Emily asked with a laugh.

"We're doing a photoshoot," Denise told Emily, as if reminding her. "That's kinda the point."

"Yeah, but that's see us in there," Emily argued, waving her hands at the phones. "I mean out there. See us out there." Denise teased Emily by mirroring her hand gestures.

"Guys, we NEED to generate some revenue," Rachael pushed. "We'll take some prelim shots, post them online as part of a crowd-funding thing, and then take it from there. Action shots are actually kind of rare in cosplay, so if we can post pictures of someone actually flying, they'll generate real interest."

"I just don't want the neighbors to see," Kate said, covering her midsection like her skin was what she was afraid of being revealed.

"Shut up, Ms. Six-pack," Denise grouched at her.

"It's dark, it'll be fine," Rachael assured her with absolute certainty, already heading out. Emily's phone in hand, Rachael headed down the steps. She looked out over the parking lot and considered different locales. "Let's do it over there." She pointed to a corner of the apartment complex, not so much isolated as simply easy to overlook. The tree line would box them in between the windowless sides of two of the giant buildings. Bright lights on the sides of the buildings cast intense light, but were washed out by the dimmer yet more prevalent street lamps that dotted the parking lot.

Tugging self-consciously at the mini-skirt that was more of a thick belt, Kate followed, with Denise and Emily at the rear. They arrived at the corner locale and Kate considered the space. The whole slapdash complex was made up of big ugly bricks of low-income housing that were haphazardly arranged, with a parking lot poured more than planned between them. The late-winter was quiet except for the buzzing of long-neglected street lamps. She finally asked, "Okay, so how do you want to do this?"

Going into improvised photographer mode, Rachael began to play with the settings on the phone's camera options. "Well, let's start with just getting a couple of you in the air," she proposed, refamiliarizing herself with the interface of Emily's camera phone. Kate looked nervously passed Rachael but consoled herself that not only did the parking lot look empty, but so did most of the apartments. In the chilly night air, she lifted up about a foot off the ground.

"I don't think that will ever get old," Emily giggled from next to Denise.

"Okay, start striking some poses," Rachael said as she began to circle around Kate. Kate nervously brushed back her blonde hair, then struck a classic Supergirl flying pose. She let Rachael take a few digital stills, then took up a classic power pose, her hands at her sides and her head turned out slightly. She channeled her best Melissa Benoist and flexed her arms, her shoulders and fists turning hard. Her joints popped and the gently reflective blue fabric announced it was stretched to its limit, so Kate pushed it no further.

A dozen poses and many dozens of pictures later, Rachael said, "Okay, guys, look like you're sneaking and Kate's just lowered down behind you." Denise and Emily both took on sneaking poses straight from an episode of Scooby-Doo while Kate played her role above and behind them.

For over twenty minutes, they tried various poses and angles, with Rachael playing amateur photographer. Eventually, Kate griped, "Can we call it? I'm seriously cold." She continued to tug down the halter top that kept riding up.

"Yeah, yeah, just a second," Rachael assured her distantly as she and Emily looked at some of the pictures. Rachael checked up into the air, then at Kate. "Think you can hold me on your back?"

Kate looked worried. "Why?"

"I want to do an over-the-shoulder shot of you looking down on the crooks," said Rachael. Kate couldn't think of a single reason to say no and turned her back to Rachael. She squatted low and Rachael stepped on her thigh to climb onto and cling to her back.

Rachael's legs wrapped around her waist and one-arm looped over her shoulder, Kate lifted up into the air. She turned around and floated about a story above Denise and Emily. "Now look like you're sneaking," Rachael yelled passed Kate's ear. She leaned very carefully back from Kate so that she could position the shot. She adjusted Kate's hair a bit and then began taking pictures. "Now you see Supergirl," Rachael directed. Both women turned to look over their shoulder and looked shocked.

"O....kay!" Rachael declared as the camera's simulated shutter chimed again and again. "I think that will do." Kate lowered back to the soft half-dead grass of the complex and Rachael hopped off. "I think that does it," Rachael said with a big smile. She was already sorting through the pictures in her mind as she reviewed the images on the cell phone's screen. "We'll pick two or three and post them online tonight to solicit donations to pull off a real shoot."

"Sounds good," Emily said happily, but with a yawn as they started back towards the apartment.

On their way, Denise looked at her costume on Kate's body and asked, "Did the collar rip?"

"I don't think so," Kate answered just before a loud rip followed with a step. Kate blushed and smiled harmlessly at Denise who glowered at her.

With a heavy brow, Y'dosh covered his mouth. "There it is again," the male observed with a curious, confused look. He studied the readout on his left forearm, the multi-colored symbols imbedded in his bodysuit. Scratchy hair rustled in the nighttime wind as eyes devoid of irises were fixed on the display.

Y'marda turned to him. Standing atop the building, she was a silhouette thanks to the nighttime lights of the cityscape that stretched to the horizon and seemed to melt with the stars in the sky. "There what is?" she asked. Her hair, as short as his but much finer, blew in the night wind. She left the edge of the rooftop and joined him by the doorway access. She leaned over his shoulder, the glow of the screen illuminating a face that was almost human. Eyes danced over the readout for a moment as a grin slowly spread. "This is perfect," she remarked with relieved pride. "The amount of potential necrotic energy is--"

"No, not that," Y'dosh told her, his words distant with thought. He pointed to a single indicator in the left corner of the display. "There."

Y'marda leaned close, her smile fading. For a brief second, worry crossed her eyes and she pulled Y'dosh's forearm closer to her, causing him to groan in surprise pain. Confirming the readout wasn't her misreading, she released him. "It's an anomaly," she declared with absolute, almost hysterical, insistence. "Standard deviation. Or, or background interference. It's statistically insignificant, whatever it is."

"Just because it's minute doesn't mean it's insignificant," Y'dosh cautioned her. He rolled his shoulder, confused by the pain. He began to speak when a hot gust of exhaust-tainted wind blew up on them from the road below. "It may be nothing," he allowed eagerly. "But it may not." Y'marda consulted her own display on her left forearm. With his counsel in mind, she grew increasingly worried. "I want to use the collectors to triangulate this signal, whatever it is. Once we have over half of the array set, we will be able to far better identify the anomaly."

"How many collectors have we to set?" asked Y'marda.

"One hundred and twenty-eight," he said. As if to make his point, he tapped his shoulder and his hand began to hum. He reached into thin air, his hand disappearing beyond a seeming arbitrary point. He withdrew from nothing a small oblong device like a steel bowling pin. "The array will need to be asymmetrical as well. It will take me time to even formulate the optimal placement. And they each individually will need to be placed. Meticulously."

Whether Y'marda didn't hear him or had nothing to say, she remained silent, focused on the worrisome display Y'dosh had brought to her attention. Y'dosh waited for a response but getting none, he set about the task at hand. He ran his hand over the narrower end of the collector and it bloomed like an artificial flower. Within the metal petals sparked green crystals that shimmered in the nighttime light.

The rooftop access door opened and a woman in a blue security uniform stepped out. She took a quick sweep of the rooftop, spotting the two strangers immediately. "Hey!" she called with a cigarette-stained voice. She shined a baton flashlight at the two strangers in odd, dark gray attire. "You two!"

Y'dosh looked back into her flashlight, totally nonplussed. He didn't even blink. "We have an intruder," he told Y'marda as if he was being sarcastic.

Y'madra barely even acknowledged the guard's presence, or even her existence. "Deal with the thing," she said, still scouring over the readings as she paced towards the edge of the building.

"I said you two!" called the guard as she moved at Y'madra. "You two can't be up here."

"Sorry for the confusion," Y'dosh quickly told the guard as she neared. He set the collector very carefully on the rooftop gravel. "We were…" He glanced around and saw nearby rooftops of adjacent buildings. "We hopped the ledge for the view."

The guard looked at the alley leap and realized how far it was. She approached the man and explained, "Listen, I—"

He grabbed her by the back of the head and punched her hard enough to crack her skull. The resounding impact, along with the hollow break, passed loudly through the air and urban silence resumed. The guard wobbled in Y'dosh's grasp and he shoved her down onto the rooftop, caving in the back of her skull. The crystals in the collector sparked with a brief but intense burst of light.

Y'dosh stood slowly and took a long breath that was uneasy. He put his hand to his chest and felt his racing heart with a confused look. "I don't like having to do that," he remarked. His words were jagged. His eyes treacherously turned to Y'marda. His superior was only a silhouette against the city lights, but her gaze was aimed back at him. Y'dosh snatched up the collector. "It seems a waste," he said with forced callousness.

Y'marda watched him for a long moment, then turned into the city. "One pales compared to tens of thousands," she told him. Her eyes lit up, glowing in the soft illumination of tens of thousands. She turned and approached Y'dosh. "Monitor for any future anomalies but for now, I see no reason to deviate from our plans." She stepped over the motionless body of the dead guard. "Let's be on our way. We've many more sites to confirm before we can even begin setting the collectors." The two left the building, leaving the corpse of the security guard unmoving atop the building.

Kate opened the front door to the sound of video games.

Lauren sat in one recliner, Deloris in the opposite chair, both of them on their iPads. The TV was on but the volume turned low as a sitcom nobody liked played out on the screen. As Kate entered, her grandmother perked up and said, "Welcome home, baby!" She held her hand over the head of her chair and Kate gave it a squeeze.

"The auto shop called," said Lauren, putting her game aside and putting a chill in Kate's soul.

"Yeah," Kate said with a nod, coming to sit in the recliner between the two. She grabbed up the remote and muted the TV, ending the noise that was only audible enough to be a distraction. "The car's...it's essentially totaled."

"Oh honey," Deloris cooed sadly.

Lauren sat forward, worry in a thousand different forms coming over her face. In sweat pants and a baggy Starblazers T-shirt off one shoulder reminiscent of 80s style, she immediately went into damage control mode. "What happened?"

"The door?" Kate prompted, unsure what the question was about. Her mother stared blankly. It was clear she remembered, but could place no details. "The rear driver-side door got yanked off," Kate reminded her. "And it damaged the whole—"

"How did that happen?" exclaimed Lauren, as if this was the first she'd heard of it.

"We..." Kate began but then decided not to bother. "We went over this mom," she reminded Lauren in an even tone. "The door's been wiggling for a little while now." The lie felt more comfortable with repetition. "At the con, it was stuck because of the cold I guess. I gave it a pull and..." She offered nothing more.

Her mother's expression was one of confusion. She recalled every last word, but as if it was something she hadn't thought about in a year. She put her hands on the top of her head, golden hair like Kate's flattening as she tried to grasp the magnitude of the loss of the car. "No-no one...did anything? I thought you said...the hotel...or, or one of your little convention friends..."

Kate decided not to let the convention friend comment get under her skin. "We found it like that when we left on Sunday," Kate said simply. Knowing what was coming, she added, "The convention hotel had a strict and obvious 'not responsible for parked vehicles' sign."

Lauren's voice was shaking, as were her hands atop her head. "I thought you said somebody did a prank or something?" Kate didn't know what to say. She was resolved to not deny anything, for fear of leaving herself with some possible explanation down the road. "Did you fill out a police report?" her mom asked.

Kate balked. She quickly tried to think of an explanation for why she wouldn't have. "We...weren't sure if we should. Nothing seemed to be taken. It seemed more likely that it was, like, the weather or something." She repeated what she'd said in her head and decided it sounded plausible-ish. "If it was a prank, it probably wasn't meant as anything mean."

"Mean or no, it's still vandalism," Lauren insisted with her voice raising. "Vehicular vandalism is a felony." Kate tried to hide her sudden fear of being implicated in vandalizing her own car. Her mother cupped her hands in front of her face, obscuring her nose and mouth. She took a deep breath, as if breathing through a mask made of her hands. "What did the auto-shop say?" she asked, transitioning to the present. She grabbed the armrests of her recliner like she was a captain retaking command. "Can they fix it?"

Kate felt the pit of her stomach begin to burn. "No," she said simply and clearly. "They offered to buy it for scrap." She hesitantly added, "I already accepted." She took from her purse the check and handed it to her mom. "Here's my portion of the bills for this month."

For a terrifying moment, Kate's mother was totally still. She just stared at the check in the electronic silence of the apartment. Her lips parted to speak, but she stopped. Her face was flushed but her expression was placid. Instead of speaking, she very hesitantly accepted the check and looked at the number it held. She swallowed tensely. "This is all they offered?" Her voice was cold. Kate didn't bother answering.

Lauren closed eyes that felt older by the second. She finally just sighed as she accepted yet another blow of fate. "I'll take you off the insurance in the morning." Leaving the check on the TV tray between their recliners, Lauren rose and collected her iPad and her Star Trek mug full of tea. "I'm going to call it a night." She headed into her room at the back of the apartment, calling without turning back, "Goodnight, mom."

"Goodnight, baby," Deloris told Lauren.

Kate watched her mom disappear into the master bedroom, until the door shut. Once it did, she slumped into her own recliner and felt saturated by her sense of failure. Her eyes fell to the check and the numbers on it, so little and so much at the same time. Her head fell into one hand as she stared at the soundless TV. She didn't even whisper, only mouthed, "I want to go home."

Kate's grandmother said, "I'm sorry about your car, baby." Kate only smiled morosely, her vision splitting from tears. "Aside from that, did you have a good day?"

Staring into the distance, Kate tried to figure out how to sum up a million different emotions that she carried inside of her from day to day. She resolved to admit to her grandmother her dread and disappointment. But turning to the kindly old woman's face and Kate only smiled, albeit sadly. "Yeah," she told her grandmother. "It was…" She tried to figure out how to encapsulate the day quickly. "It had a lot of ups and downs, but…" She smiled at herself, thinking about flying and proud of her pun. "But…but yeah." She nodded, surprised to admit, "I think, maybe, all told, it was a good day."

"Good," Deloris said with a happy smile.

"Yeah, we ended up doing a photo shoot after all," Kate said shared, almost like it was another lifetime ago. She turned in the recliner, one leg up on the seat as she faced her grandmother. "It was just kind of a rough one. Sort of a trial shoot, to, uh, to try out something new." Kate smiled and found a strange sense of optimism and admitted, "I think, maybe, this is what might get my career going again." Kate paused, trying to remember when it had been going.

"Good, baby," her grandmother all but beamed at her.

Smiling, Kate felt like crying. "It's kind of scary," she sort of blubbered. "I'm, like, genuinely not used to feeling hopeful." She took a

133

deep breath and told her grandmother, "I really think this could be it." She got up from her chair and kissed her grandmother on the head. "Don't stay up too late, Nana."

"Oh, I won't," said Deloris with playful indignance. Kate retired to her room, drinking in the feeling of optimism.

CHAPTER EIGHT

Fake.

That was the most frequent word used throughout the reviews.

Three days after the shoot, Kate sat on the floor in Denise's apartment, scrolling through the reviews online. Across six different social media outlets, Rachael had posted some of the pictures with links to their crowdfunding account, hoping to solicit support. While some people were engaged and positive, the overwhelming majority were clear at how low they thought of the production. Fake was the most common word used, and often the nicest.

"'Maybe if she'd done Power Girl, this might be worthwhile'," Kate read to Denise on the couch, who was similarly scrolling through responses, her lip turned up in a sneer. Kate looked at her friend and said, "So a midriff isn't sexy enough? They need the boob window?"

"Pervs," Denise griped indifferently as she lay across her couch, her feet up on the armrest. "I swear, half of the cosplay scene is just lonely dudes cruising for hot girls in revealing costumes."

"'I've seen some fake-ass photoshops in my time, but whoever did this should kill himself'," Kate read off another comment. She exclaimed, "I was flying for real and they think it was trick photography! They're SURE it was trick photography! And not just trick photography, but BAD trick photography!"

"'Why are the lady crooks wearing pants?'" Denise read to Kate. "'Get some booty shorts and they might be in business'." She looked up from her tablet. "That got the most likes of all the comments."

"'Why does she got to wear that diaper," Kate read, "if you're gonna show up the skirt, she should wear a thong or better yet nothing'. Jesus, you asses, they're bloomers!" She nearly threw the tablet across the room. She dropped it instead and grabbed her head to keep from screaming. "Oh my god, I hate everyone."

"We've got sixteen supporters on the crowdfunding," Denise suggested with a sour, unenthusiastic look. "That's something. Two of them even ponied up the five-dollar support level."

"Twenty-four bucks on a project that's gonna cost hundreds," Kate griped. She leaned back against the wall, banging it slightly with her head. She felt vile, furious that her hope from a few days ago hadn't just been taken from her, but been replaced by belittlement and objectification.

The door opened and Rachael and Emily came in, carrying a few bags of fast food. "So what's the news?" asked eagerly the team's leader.

"Whatever do you mean?" Denise asked innocently. "We promised we'd wait for you before we read the comments sites."

"Right," Emily said sarcastically.

"Did you?" asked Rachael.

Denise looked over at Kate, then said, "It's about what we expected."

"Alright!" Rachael said as she traded the bags for the tablet.

"Wrong expectation," Kate corrected glumly as Rachael sat where Denise's feet had been.

"Today's word of the day, kids, is fake," Denise proclaimed in an announcer's voice as she handed over her tablet. "Or amateur. Or worthless basement-dwelling loser. Take your pick."

Rachael handed the bag to Kate as she began to scroll through the comments. The other three women were able to tell which comment she was on by the way the light died from her eyes and her face tightened. Each time her eyes darted to the next comment, her smile faded a little more until it was replaced with an angry scowl. When she'd had enough, she didn't say anything. She just handed the tablet back to Denise.

In a desperate attempt to salvage the afternoon, Emily asked, "Did anyone sign up for the donation set?"

"Sixteen people," said Kate.

"That's good," the youngest said eagerly.

"Fourteen are one-dollar donations," Denise clarified.

"Oh," the youngest said less eagerly.

"Yeah, I particularly like 'maybe the asteroid will hit them before they make any more stupid, second-rate sets'," Kate share with faux-idealism. She accepted the pack of tacos that Rachael passed out half-heartedly. "Guys, this is ridiculous." She halfway unwrapped the first taco before exclaiming, "I can't believe how angry some of these people are. It's like they're somehow offended that we're trying to do something cool."

"That's probably exactly it," said Denise, already halfway into wolfing down lunch. "These pathetic losers don't have anything going on, so if we do anything to try and break the mold a little, they got to attack it because otherwise, they're confronted with how pathetic they are." She scarfed down the rest of the taco like a snake swallowing prey. She chewed hostilely, glaring at all she hated.

"I was all excited," Kate admitted. She felt like she was going to throw up or cry, she didn't know which. "I mean, having to sell my car sucks, but I've got a little bit of money left. I was hoping if we got something going, then maybe we could use it to really buy some good fabric and some good costumes and..." She turned away and stared at the carpet to try and calm herself down.

"Honey, I think maybe you should just save whatever you've got left," Rachael told Kate. She had joined Denise on the couch, Emily sitting on the floor between their legs. "I mean, you're not getting all that many hours right now. Next month, you'll be in this same position all over again."

"Yeah," Kate said distantly. She thought about the twenty dollars her grandmother had given her, and how that had ended up spent immediately. "I just want some costumes," she whispered, almost entirely to herself. "And, I mean, it's gotta happen eventually, right?"

"What?" Denise asked, not hearing.

Kate dismissed it all with a futile shake of her head, her expression shifted from sad to morosely placid. She looked down at the tacos in her lap and felt a pang of guilt at splurging on food. In her mind, she tallied up the constituent parts that went into it – the meats, the shells, the vegetables, the sauce, the cheese – all of which could have been bought at a grocery store for less, or for the same but for more food. She felt incredibly wasteful for having bought it all. Eating a cheap meal wasn't an indulgence; it was a genuine luxury. She felt like crying as she thought, "I want to go home."

"Shut up!"

The attention of all four women snapped upwards, to the roof. "Great," grumbled Dense. "Craphole is at it again."

"What are they fighting about?" asked Emily.

"What are they ever fighting about?" Rachael answered.

"I don't know," Denise answered, too focused on above to realize the question was rhetorical. "I've never been able to figure it out. I think she's—"

A loud thud from overhead silenced the room. It was followed quickly by sobbing. "I said, shut up!" yelled the man from upstairs. All four women were perfectly quiet, perfectly still, perfectly focused. The voice yelled, "You don't shut up, I'm going to make you shut up!"

Denise's furious glare lowered from the ceiling and set on the door. Her eyes burned with true intensity, her jaw clinched tight. She burst up from the couch and threw open the door. "Denise!" Rachael warned, trying and failing to catch. Emily and Kate both jumped to their feet as Denise stormed out, neither sure what was about to happen.

In the breezeway at the center of the ugly apartment buildings, Denise rushed up the stairs, the cement steps and the metal railing rattling as she ran to the third floor. "Denise!" Rachael warned as she came up last.

Denise banged on the door over the apartment over hers, barely giving anyone a chance to answer. She slammed it with her open palm a second time. A voice came from behind the door. "The fuck you want?" bellowed a male voice.

"I want you to stop hitting her, you dumb shit!" Denise yelled through the door.

The door pulled opened and a middle-aged man in a white t-shirt looked down on Denise in every sense. A scruffy beard and the smell of alcohol accompanied the sound of a televised boxing match. Behind him, the four women could see the upstairs neighbor getting up off the floor, blood dribbling out of her mouth. Her left eye was swelling up, her black skin doing little to hide the gross bruise spreading from her puffy eyelid. "Bitch, you need to get the fuck out of here," the man said, pointing.

"You're not hitting her anymore," Denise told the much bigger man.

"Fuck off before I dick-start that mouth of yours," he told her.

"We're gonna call the cops," Rachael told the guy from the back of the quartet.

"Bitch, you call the cops, I'm going to fuck you up," he threatened, pointing a single finger right at Rachael.

Denise jumped in front of his finger. "Don't fucking threaten her, you son of a bitch!"

The man smacked Denise to the ground with a sudden backhand. Denise completely crumpled to the ground, her cheek split open. She dabbed at it with her hand, shocked to have so easily been taken off her feet. Disbelief in her eyes was beginning to stir into a smile as the hounds of war were about to be set free. The man, almost twice her size, stepped towards her, yelling, "Now you shut your cunt mouth before I—"

Kate stepped between him and Denise. Arms locked across her head as she turtled defensively, she did little more than press straight into his chest with her forearms. Only a quick pop in a defensive effort, she just meant to keep the bigger man from striking the downed Denise a second time. Rather than disrupt the hit, rather than stymie him or even force him back half-a-step, Kate knocked him off his feet and slammed him hard into the doorway.

The bulb in the doorway light burst in a shower of glass as a loud crack came from his body. He shouted and slumped to the ground. Moaning in pain, he fell onto his side, holding his chest. "You fucking bitch!" he squealed in pain. He tried to cough but that seemed to only cause him to wheeze and gasp for air.

Kate backed away from the guy, truly stunned. She looked at her friends, then inside at the neighbor who was every bit as surprised as the rest of them. Kate backed further away, then turned and darted down the stairs, running as if for her life.

"It's back," Y'dosh said suddenly. He stopped walking abruptly, causing the older couple strolling behind him on the sidewalk to detour vocally.

As indifferent to the pair as Y'dosh, Y'marda turned back and looked at the screen on the forearm display of his bodysuit. "The deviation," he told his superior. Y'marda studied the complicated, three-dimensional visuals before summoning the same readout on her suit. She began to turn the displays, gleaning additional details from the changing information.

As Y'marda read the results, Y'dosh checked their surroundings. The pair looked less out of place in the art fair. A large celebration, the multi-block street festival was full of people dressed more elaborately than they. Many of the patrons of the festival were wearing makeup which only further lessened Y'marda and Y'dosh's subtle-but-unusual appearance. Local bands played at booths while craft breweries and local farm associates sold hand-made products. Children played in bouncy castles while kiosks and tents were set up, showing off a vast array of local arts and crafts. "Amazing," said Y'dosh with a smile.

Y'marda didn't look up from the display. "What is?"

"We are dressed as we are, looking as we are," he said. "None of the natives seem to pay us much attention." He caught his reflection in a bank display window and could tell his appearance was different in almost imperceptible ways from the locals.

"We're not dressed that unusually," said Y'marda, glancing up only briefly. She saw Y'dosh changing his expression, experimenting with the movement possibilities of his face. She dismissed it with a disapproving shake of her head. "We're in human-shaped bodies too."

"Still seems that they're curiously inobservant," Y'dosh smiled. He saw a small girl walking hand-in-hand with her infant brother, the pair ahead of their parents. Y'dosh smiled slowly, then a pang of conscience struck him. His amused, even delighted, smile very quickly drained. He swallowed hard and had to look away.

Y'marda sighed and just closed the display. "Half of these creatures – I wouldn't even call them beings – they are on their own devices anyway. Why should they notice us?" She nodded at the cell phones and tablets, strangely bitter as she turned to the smaller male. "As for the anomaly, once we've finished setting up the rebound vectors, we need to identify the source and origin."

Y'dosh nodded obediently but couldn't hide his concern. He brought up a different readout on his forearm and turned a bit, re-orientating. "We've still some distance to go to the next site we need to confirm for the collectors." He spoke quickly, needing to focus on the task ahead of them and not the people around them.

"We've time," Y'marda assured him. "My primary concern now is that we may not be alone," she told him. Anger crept into her gaze and she looked again at the people like she was looking at unruly cattle. "If this anomaly is...we can't afford a third." She resumed walking along their chosen route.

"I concur," Y'dosh said sadly. He looked again at the children and their chalk drawings on the pavement. "That would be a waste." He rushed to keep up, to not be slowed down by his growing guilt.

"You should totally be a superhero," decided Denise loudly over the roaring blender. Once her smoothie was complete, she poured the fruit-smelling sludge into a large Taco Bell cup from a promotion a year ago. "Like, we should make you a costume and stuff and you can fight crime."

"What crime?" asked Kate as she sat with Emily on the couch. "Like, street crime? Great, I get shot. And how do I even find it? This isn't Gotham City. There isn't crime on every street corner."

"If you got shot, would it hurt you?" Emily asked curiously.

"Yes!" Kate exclaimed, terrified the question was even being posited. "Why wouldn't it?"

Emily sort of shrugged and accepted her assumption. Denise didn't. She disappeared with her smoothie down the hall into her bedroom. She returned with a cardboard box with faded labels. Sitting down between Kate and Emily and handing her smoothie to Rachael sitting across from her on the floor, Denise produced from the case a long knife. "What are you doing?" asked Kate just before Denise took her hand.

"Testing a theory," Denise told her. She lightly drew the blade across Kate's thumb.

"Ow!" Kate shrieked and jerked her hand away. "What the hell?"

"Are you bleeding?" Emily asked, almost hopefully.

Kate checked her thumb to find it devoid of any blood. "No," she admitted very skeptically. "But it hurt."

"Gimme," said Denise, raising the knife and gesturing for Kate's hand.

"What the hell, no!" Kate exclaimed, starting to crawl at Emily for defense. Emily nearly dove off the couch and crawled at Rachael for defense. Rachael helped herself to some of Denise's smoothie. She crinkled her nose in disapproval at the taste but that didn't stop her from having more.

"Pain without injury is just another sensation," promised the woman with multiple tattoos on her scalp. She summoned Kate with her hand. With great hesitancy, Kate surrendered her palm. Again, Denise sliced at her, this time across Kate's palm. Kate tried to endure the pain as long as possible but jerked her hand away with a seething shout. When the burning pain subsided, though, she checked her hand and found her palm without the slightest mark.

Denise returned the knife to the box, saying, "So you're just as sensitive, maybe even more so," she added with a sidelong look that made Kate glare, "but nothing breaks the--" She fell silent when she realized Rachael was drinking more of her smoothie. Now she glared at Rachael who smiled sweetly.

"Getting a piercing's gonna suck," Emily observed, watching this all intently.

Denise continued to glare at Rachael, who nonchalantly had some more of the smoothie in front of its intended owner, then complimented her with a nice burp. Denise succumbed to Rachael's superior don't-give-a-fuck-isma and went back to her room. Rachael upended the Taco Bell cup and patted the bottom, letting the food-ish contents plop into her mouth.

Denise returned with a riding crop, making Kate and Emily both go pale. "Don't give me that," Denise scowled at them, again summoning Kate's hand. Kate very fearfully handed over her arm and Denise immediately smacked her on the thick of the forearm. For a second, Kate was confused until a subtle pain appeared. It grew fast and Kate jerked her hand away, cradling it as she rocked back and forth, trying to keep from screaming to the heavens.

"Show me your hand," ordered Denise in a tone befitting a woman holding a riding crop. Kate did as she was told, revealing her bare skin. "No bruising," Denise reported, inspecting Kate's forearm before turning it so Rachael could see. "I think you might be as invulnerable as you are strong, but you've got the same sensitivity and stuff."

"Great, so what?" said Kate, feelingly physically abused.

"So...Emily's idea might not be invalid," Rachael said, handing Denise the cup with a delightful smile like she was requesting a refill. "Maybe you could be a superhero."

"Getting sliced with a knife is one thing," said Kate as Denise smacked Rachael with the riding crop. "Getting shot is another. Besides, how do I even know where to stop crime? Or where the crime is? Or what good it will do? If I beat up some mugger, so what? He'll just mug some guy tomorrow night."

"Maybe you could, I don't know, join the marines or something?" suggested Emily academically rather than seriously, stepping aside as Rachael evaded further strikes from Denise. "Go to the Middle East and fight ISIS or Boko Haram or something."

Kate looked uneasy with having no clear counter to that suggestion. "I don't know. I just...I don't see how being stronger and stuff can really make that big of a difference. Even in Superman, the world's not a utopia. I just, what can it accomplish?" she asked mostly to Emily. "What kind of a difference is there really to be made?"

Emily only shrugged, only able to offer, "Maybe a big difference, at least to the person getting mugged."

CHAPTER NINE

The echo of the bone-crunching crack still rung in Kate's ears days later.

Riding the night bus from work, Kate sat over the rear wheel, her head down and in her hands. She slowly rubbed her fingertips from the bridge of her nose around her cheeks, to her temples, and then over her eyelashes to the bridge of her nose again. She tried to focus on those motions and the movement of the bus and not thinking about ribs cracking. At least, she hoped they were ribs.

The bus finally stopped with a loud hiss and the doors opened. The running lights brightened and Kate stood. She swung off through the back door, using the guard rail like a stripper's pole. Recalling her failed attempting at stripping made her smirk cynically and she started through the parking lot of Denise's complex. She sent a text to her mom as she walked, saying "At Denise's. May spend the night."

She headed across the bridge to the thoroughfare that divided the large buildings. She glanced up the stairs at the apartment over Denise's, at the doorframe against which she may have killed a man. Her heart raced at the sight and she stopped, staring. She looked over her shoulder, certain the police were going to appear, arrest her for returning to the scene of the crime. Instead, with a trembling hand, she knocked on Denise's door.

It was Emily who opened the door. She seemed immune to Kate's worry and waved her in with a huge smile. "You're never going to believe it," she squealed with eagerness usually reserved for a child on Christmas morning.

Emily's enthusiasm as infectious as ever, Kate still couldn't help be more nervous than hopeful. She entered cautiously, asking, "What is it?"

"We finished it!" Emily grinned as she threw her hands wide at the hallway. Kate looked, then waited, then looked again at Emily. "We finished it!" she called again with the same ta-da gesture. "Guys!" she yelled to the back of the apartment, like they were ruining her magic trick.

Out from the hallway came Rachael and Denise, the pair carrying a dark blue one-piece outfit like they were carrying a golden god. "Here we go!" Rachael said happily. With a bit of a whip, she laid the suit down on the threadbare couch. Made of a heavy-grade material, it was a stark dark blue like the night sky on a full moon. Matte black snaps ran along the forearms and the shins as well as around the neck. There was a hint of a design but it was mostly reinforced seams running along the lateral edges of the body. Rachael smiled like a shyster and asked, "What do you think?" She flashed her eyebrows. "Eh? Eh?"

"How did you guys..." Kate marveled, feeling the fabric. "It's been three days!"

Rachael waved off such trivialities. "Pssh. It was a piece of cake." Denise and Emily both looked at each other, appalled at the dismissal of the effort. "If I can make a steampunk Rescue Armor from Iron Man 3 in two days before Dragon*Con – and that was back in school AND I had a job – I can make this, no problem."

"I?" Emily repeated incredulously.

"What the hell?" Denise challenged. "It was a team effort." Rachael dismissed their protests just as readily.

"Wow," was all Kate could say as she scrutinized the outfit further. The suit was smooth and flexible, with long sleeves that came to the wrists and ankles in seemingly seamless construction. From about the collar to the waist was a ribbed padding that gave the impression of armor. Similar patches of ribbing dotted the limbs strategically, especially the forearms and the shins. There was a gap between the abdomen and the pelvis, perfectly spaced for a low-riding belt.

Kate was simply dumbfounded by the outfit but her attention was detoured when she noticed a helmet at the base of the couch. Identical in color to the outfit, she picked it up and laughed in both delight and awe. She turned it to Rachael. "What's this?"

"My idea," said Denise before Rachael could claim co- or even total credit. She glared at Rachael, who smiled sweetly at her again. "We don't know how high you can go," Denise explained, back to the briefing, "and if it's at all high up, the air may thin, which could prove a problem."

"Plus, this will hide your true identity if you get spotted," Emily added, munching on a slice of pizza from the single giant box in the kitchenette.

"We made it from Emily's Power Rangers costume from a couple of years ago," Rachael explained. "I added a gas mask filtration system from one of our spraypaint masks. It's a little lopsided and it won't help in, like, a total vacuum, but I think it'll help."

"Cool," Kate decided, opening the helmet laterally. She tried it on but it wiggled a little. "We'll need to pad it, but..." She turned her head, surprised by the range of motion the sentai helmet provided. She took off the mask and sighed. "Guys, have you heard anything?" The three others looked at one another, confused. "About the guy, from upstairs."

"Oh, god, Kate," Denise laughed, making Kate angry. "He's fine." Kate wanted to throw the helmet at her for mocking her concern. "Like, really. He came by this morning and got his stuff. His girlfriend—"

"Ex-girlfriend, thankfully," Rachael half-celebrated.

"Yeah, ex-girlfriend came down and talked to me," Denise further explained. "She's super-grateful." She pointed up at the ceiling. "You want to go talk to her? She's probably still up."

"Doubt it," Emily added as she sawed through a string of cheese stretched nearly a foot between her mouth and the pizza slice.

Kate nearly fainted. She slumped against the wall, wiping her face down to her jaw. "Oh my god," she gasped, about to fall apart with the relief. "I was so worried. I was sure that…" She laughed, tears on her cheeks. "I haven't slept since that happened."

"Why?" all three asked in unison.

"Because!" Kate searched their faces for some sign that they empathize but all three seemed completely comfortable with what had happened. "What if I'd broken his back?"

Denise shrugged. "Fuck him." Rachael and Emily both nodded.

Kate looked disappointed at her. "You know how hard it is to cosplay from jail?" That reality seemed to enter Denise and Emily's thinking and both dulled their enthusiasm.

Rachael, however, was nonplussed. "Self-defense. You were protecting your friend," she told Kate. "It was justified. You would have been fine."

"Yeah, but assuming I didn't lose my job because I missed a shift because I got arrested," Kate argued, academically and hysterically. "What if they wanted, like, a thousand bucks for bail? My mom couldn't pay that. I'd sit in jail until my trial, which could have been a year from now. My mom and na—grandmother would have gotten evicted. Even if I got acquitted, everything would have been destroyed."

Rather than argue, or let the somber reality affect the evening any further, Rachael went quickly back to the costume. "So, we insulated it," she said, trying to affect a tone like they had only momentarily deviated from the topic of the costume. "You said it got cold way up high. This should offset that, but it also means that the suit can get pretty hot kind of quick, but if you fly up, you'll cool off fast."

Kate embraced the chance to speak on happier matters and sat on the edge of the couch cushions and studied the construct. "We added padded plates around the joints, similar to motorcycle attire," Rachael went on. "I also looked at martial arts sparring gear to try to get an idea of what needs to be protected in a fight. We added some padding to the limbs as well." She held up the sleeve and pulled open some of the snaps, showing the internal padding.

Kate took the sleeve and noticed the tight Velcro in addition to the snaps. "To help with flying," Rachael said. "The snaps also double to connect with the gloves." She pushed the costume over a bit to reveal that it laid on a cape of textured color. From within the cape, she produced two gloves.

"You went with the cape?" Kate remarked, pulling the costume farther over. She looked at Denise and Emily. "I thought we agreed with Edna from the Incredibles: no capes."

"Edna didn't know what she was talking about," Denise assured Kate with absolute certainty.

Rachael explained, "Edna thought capes were just a fashion accessory but they have uses." She held up the cape to show Kate the two sides. "It's reversible so that you can hide." She held the dark color towards Kate, which matched the rest of the costume. "Nighttime, which is when we think you'll be most active." Rachael reversed her hands to show a lighter color, textured and passively dynamic. "It's an urban deco that will help give you some camouflage."

"It looks like..." Kate suggested, snapping her fingers.

"We made it from the ream of fabric we had left over from when we took that Star Trek commission," Emily told Kate. "Remember, when we made that dude the MACO suit from Star Trek Enterprise?"

"We want to try making a second urban costume, but we didn't have enough fabric left," Denise explained. "We thought about trying to get more but it would cost too much." Emily and Rachael both glared her into silence.

Kate heard Denise but didn't process what she'd said, too entranced by the outfit. She stood and took the cape from Rachael and held it up to study it. She looked at the double-clasps on the shoulder-straps and neck of the cape. She picked up the costume and affixed the right shoulder of the cape, studying the way the clasps secured it to the outfit. "Clever," she decided.

"The one problem is shoes," Rachael said. "We couldn't figure out a good way to affix any shoes, so for tonight, you'll need to wear Denise's ass-kickers."

On cue, Denise held up knee-high boots with buckles running from the instep all the way up the knee. "Not the most aerodynamic but we'll figure it out."

Kate's smile grew infectious and she looked at the others. "Alright, let's do this!" she exclaimed before gathering up the costume.

Ten minutes later, the door to Denise's apartment opened up and out stepped Kate. Dressed in the dark blue superhero costume that covered her from neck to knees, she walked on the thick soles of punk boots with the cape swaying at her ankles behind her. Under her right arm, she carried the matching helmet. Her blonde hair in a tight bun, she walked out onto the walkway of the building and turned.

Her three friends stood in a tight, anxious group, a cluster of bubbling excitement. They were practically laughing in delight to see the costume in full effect. Kate looked at them, nodded, and put the helmet on. She snapped it in place and lifted up off the landing and floated out into the air beyond. With a deep, calming inhale, she began to lift up into the sky. Denise, Rachael, and Emily all ran up under her, watching her lift into the black nighttime.

Up in the sky, things were clear. Rising above the treetops, the dark world below lit by the gathered light of homes and streets, like luminescent algae at the bottom of the sea. Shadowed spots of forest and suburban patches dotted the world beneath her as she flew along. Her cape waved lightly behind her, not even flapping at that speed.

Kate bent forward and began to accelerate. She tilted down and found it easier to move, watching the world pass beneath her. She peeked up through the forward visor of her helmet and set her course merely by the horizon. "Jarvis," Kate said aloud, "Call Rachael."

The Blu-tooth headpiece connected to her phone activated at the familiar name and Kate heard ringing. A second later, Rachael asked excitedly, "Kate? How's it going, super girl?"

Kate laughed, sweeping slightly from side to side in the air, not quite able to grasp how easy it was to move. "Not too bad, I think."

"How high up are you?" Emily asked, crowding around Rachael on the couch, Denise across the phone from her.

"I dunno," she said. "High? I'm…" Kate craned her head to look up at the clouds, then suddenly shook. "Oh god!" she exclaimed and laid flat again. "Geez."

"What's wrong?" Rachael asked, worried.

"I just looked up," she said. "You ever lie down on the grass and look up at the sky and think about falling up? And you get that vertigo? Or like when you're standing right up against a really tall building and you look up?" Kate shook her head. "It's like that."

Denise wasn't interested. "Yeah, sounds disorientating. How fast can you go?"

"Yeah, are you over downtown yet?" Emily jumped in.

"Guys, I'm not even out of the complex," Kate said with a laugh. "We checked this, remember? I fly about as fast as I can jog."

"Try going faster," Denise encouraged. Rachael tried to quietly get her to stop but Denise just smiled through it. "Like, really try to open her up."

Kate put her fists forward and tightened up. She focused on the horizon and locked onto it with all her mind. The sense of velocity increased and Kate felt like she was tearing through the sky at the speed of sound. The air whipped around her helmet and her cape flapped so violently at her heels, it practically vibrated.

Scared at being heard from the roaring of her own speed, Kate risked looking down and saw the lights of the city passing by. While it was clear she was moving at a greater speed, the sound barrier was clearly quite safe. In fact, cars beneath her were driving on the street faster than she was flying above them. It was humbling to realize that some bicyclists were probably faster.

Zipping along through the cold night air, Kate began to weave this way and that, exploring her ability to move freely in space, as if gravity had ceased to be a concern for her. "One less thing," she remarked with a bit of a giggle.

She flew over a dark spot in the city and slowed, trying to perceive what she saw. With the roadways lit by headlamps and street lights, they looked like golden veins and arteries. Whole segments of the city glowed like phosphorescent organs inside some great sleeping giant. Yet also, whole patches of the city were pristine and dark, undefined by illumination.

Kate slowed and began to lower until she realized she was just above some treetops. She looked up into the sky, having to crane her neck some to see, thanks to the helmet. The white moon was half-hidden behind sparse but thick clouds of blackness more absolute than the night. The amorphous shapes were only clear in relief to the starry sky and the silver edges created by the moon's light. The wind blew constantly at that height and her cape flipped about to her right. Kate looked around and then lowered down to a treetop and stood atop it with barely an ounce of pressure. She crossed her arms and stood tall, doing her best Magneto pose from the X-men comics. She laughed, overcome by the sheer joy of her freedom.

Then she spotted the two kids.

A girl and a boy, each no older than ten, were on a balcony in a house hidden behind the trees. Kate's eyes adjusting to the dark, she could see the sleepy neighborhood through the trees and, more specifically, see the two kids on the balcony. They were taking turns looking through a telescope, aimed in Kate's direction. Panic overtook her and Kate dropped off the tree, descending among the branches. A strange fear filled her, like she might get caught and get into trouble for flying, even while she was consciously aware of how ridiculous the fear was.

"What's happening?" asked Emily over the phone.

Kate looked around the forest in the night. Beneath her, she saw several deer nibbling on a bush. "Nothing," she whispered. A buck looked up at her and let out a startled bleat. The other deer scattered in every direction, evacuating the spot in the blink of an eye. Kate felt self-conscious about startling the deer, but lowered a bit more until she hovered just about a story off the ground. "Some kids…I think maybe saw me. I don't know. They had a telescope."

"A telescope?" repeated Emily. She looked at her friends incredulously.

"Yeah, I know!" Kate exclaimed. "What kind of kid plays with a telescope? Don't they know about video games?"

"Are you near downtown?" Denise urged.

Kate sighed and looked around. "I…I honestly don't know." She rose up through the branches, dancing in the air to get around them without disturbing a leaf. Back above the treetops, Kate turned around, unsure which bright glowing light in the distance was downtown. "I'm going to head for the nearest shopping center," she told the others.

She lifted into the air above the trees and began to fly towards the nearest glowing spot. "Seriously, though a telescope," she continued to gripe.

"Those kids will probably grow up to be scientists, making more than you, honey," Rachael told Kate.

"Scientists don't make that much," she argued.

"It's still more than you," Denise tossed in.

Kate came to the edge of the shopping center and realized aloud, "It's our place, with the garage and that cheap-ass grocery store."

"Alright, sweet, that place is plenty seedy," Denise said way too eagerly. She adjusted her seat on the couch, getting ready to enjoy what she could already see in her mind. "There should be somebody who needs some help."

"For real," Kate said as she slipped across the parking lot and landed on the roof of the grocery store. Her boots touched down and the roof bowed a little, the soft surface covered in light gravel surprising her at its give. She carefully took a few steps and stayed near the edge, for fear of falling through the roof. She knelt down and looked over the parking lot with a handful of cars sprinkled about. "And now we wait," she said certainly.

"And now we wait," she said sometime later, still as certain, but less enthusiastic.

"And now we wait," she said sometime later still, her head resting in her hand.

"And now we wait," she said sometime after that, her helmet off as she looked at the parking lot. With the exception of the 24-hour grocery store, every other store was closed. The parking lot was completely empty except for the cars of the workers inside. Irritated, Kate put her helmet back on and activated the blu-tooth headset again. "Guys, what time is it?" she asked. A second passed. "Guys!"

"Yeah, hey, what's up?" said Rachael, sounding a little distracted.

Kate listened for a second and could hear music on in the background. She practically accused, "Are you guys watching Pacific Rim?!"

"No," said Rachael.

"No," said Denise.

"Yes," said Emily.

Kate sighed in irritation. "I'm coming back." She lifted straight into the air and, flying along the path she and her friends walked time and time again, headed back to the complex. "I've got to work tomorrow."

"That sucks, hon," Rachael commiserated.

"At least I'm not working an opening shift," she rationalized as she flew.

Half an hour later, Kate arrived back at the complex and descended right into the walkway of Denise's apartment. Denise, Emily, and Racheal all came clambering out as Kate took off the helmet. With a sigh, she griped, "Well, that sucked."

"Yeah, well," Denise said as Racheal and Emily helped get the cape off her shoulders. "You're new to superheroing. It'll take some time to get it down."

"There was no superheroing," Kate said as she undid the suit, stripping out of it as she headed towards the bathroom where her clothes waited. "There was no crime. I thought it was going to be like Spiderman or something, and there were going to be muggings and stuff everywhere." She shut the door to the bathroom but continued through it. "There wasn't anything."

"Yeah, well, Spiderman's set in New York, and this is decidedly not New York," Rachael called through the door.

"Yeah, plus he's fictional," added Emily. Rachael and Denise both looked sourly at her, like that was a trivial matter.

The bathroom door opened and Kate stepped out, dressed again in her civilian attire, still tugging her shirt down. "Maybe we should all move to New York then," she said with a tired smirk.

"Yeah, we'll get right on that," Denise told her in cynical deadpan.

"Maybe we can go overseas," suggested Emily, standing in the hallway with the others. "I mean, we don't have to fight street crime, you know? We could go over to Africa and fight Boko Haram or something. You know, the guys that kidnapped all those little girls and forced them into marriages?"

Rachael scoffed. "You mean conservatives?" Denise snickered with her. "Yeah, that'd be sweet," she acknowledged the point before asking Kate, "but it would take you, what? A month just to fly across the ocean?"

"I have no idea," said Kate as her stomach gurgled. She covered it with a disappointed expression. "I'm hungry," she said rhetorically.

"Besides, they've got guns," Denise continued to Emily, leaning against the opposite wall.

"And muggers don't?" asked Rachael, jumping sides.

"A mugger's got A gun; terrorists have got gunS," Denise emphasized the plurality.

"Yeah," Kate said sadly. She yawned and started out. "I'm going to get the bus. I want to get some sleep."

"You sure you don't want to stay over tonight?" Denise asked, a little concerned as Kate gathered her stuff. "I'll kick these two out and you can have the couch."

"No, I'm not…I want to go home," she said. She reached for the door, opened it, and paused. "It kind of sucks, you know," she said, succumbing to negativity. "I've got superpowers…and I've got no use for them." She looked at the others. "Everybody thinks they look fake. Crime doesn't work the way it's supposed to." She shrugged, then departed with a cynical exhale.

Y'marda set the small seed, barely larger than her thumbnail, into the ground. She backed away from the construction site's raw earth and studied the seed's placement. She turned around and faced into the distance, looking into the night. The city beyond was awash with bright lights but nearer to her was just darkness lit by a few street lamps that ran along the construction site. Y'marda glanced back from the horizon to the seed a few times, then held up her hands as if holding an invisible box away from her.

A network of lights extended slowly between her forearms, turning into a display. The three-dimensional screen began to extend and widen, showing a map that included terrestrial terrain as well as details and readings far beyond the tangible world. Y'marda studied the readings, her artificially beautiful face scowling.

"Bah!" she exclaimed suddenly. She dropped her hands and the display disappeared entirely. She stomped back to the tiny seed, the textured soles of her bodysuit kicking up dirt. "This is impossible." She began to wiggle the seed in the dirt. Doing so caused the soil to give way and the seed came tumbling out. It bounced between her feet and rolled into the construction site while she cursed along its whole path. Y'marda turned and tried to spot the seed but didn't immediately find it. "This is--"

"Impossible, yes, I heard you," said Y'dosh. She glared up at him as he sat atop the roof of an excavator, studying the display in his forearm.

"You do it," she ordered petulantly. Realizing that he wasn't, she suddenly grew curious. "What ARE you doing?"

"Monitoring the anomaly," he reported. "Also, mine are already done." He gestured blindly back to the far crest of the construction site.

Y'marda looked around the construction site, aware of but not seeing the seeds. She shook her head, amazed. "How do you navigate this limited..." She gave up with a disgruntled huff. "What of the anomaly?"

"See for yourself," said Y'dosh. He gestured his display towards her. By the time she looked to her own forearm, her suit was showing the readout. "This was a much longer reading," he explained.

"The longest phenomena yet," Y'marda said, studying the multi-colored display. She affected it, turning the readings to glean new insight from the display. She looked to her partner. "We need to find the source of this. We need to get to the bottom of it."

Y'dosh nodded. "I'm working on it," he assured her a little desperately.

Y'marda glared, displeased at Y'dosh. "If it's someone else, their very presence jeopardizes the whole mission."

"I am aware," he said carefully. "A third would warp the results of our plan." He ventured cautiously, "It might not even be worthwhile going through with the event if there's a chance of that happening."

"Precisely," Y'marda insisted, taking his statement as a challenge to resolve, not a caution to observe. She turned back around to the soil and jammed the seed into the flesh of the earth. "Aborting the plan is not an option, is not even possible. We must see our task through to completion. Discover the nature of this anomaly so that we may destroy it." She hastily confirmed the seed was aimed in the right direction and waved her hand over it. A collector sprouted, showing crystals aimed towards downtown. Convinced it would suffice, she closed the seed with another wave of her hand. She resumed placing the subterranean collectors with renewed focus.

CHAPTER TEN

Kate tried to lose herself in exercise. In the middle of her small room, under the watchful gaze of superhero and anime posters, she hiked the heavy kettlebell back between her legs. Her back straight as she bent at the hips, she popped her pelvis forward to swing the bell in front of her. It came to a floating stop at collar-height before gravity tugged it back down. She added a pull with her arms to throw it back between her legs as hard as she could, and repeating the process again and again.

Kate kept popping her hips forward, trying to lose her anger through exertion, but she couldn't find an end to it. She felt like she was turning over a gas can full of her emotions, letting the negativity and anger pour out…only it wouldn't stop coming. No matter how much she emptied her anger and sadness and negativity, there was more to come.

A knock at the door startled her and the kettlebell nearly went flying. Kate snatched it out of the air before she completely lost her grip and pulled it back down. "Y-yes?" she stammered as she carefully lowered the heavy hunk of cast iron.

"Katie, honey," Deloris called through the door. "Don't you need to go soon? You're going to be late for work."

"No, I've got…" Kate said even as she checked the time. It was after 8am. Kate had been swinging the kettlebell for twenty minutes. Twenty minutes straight. Kate looked down at the heavy bell like it was a viper.

"Baby?" her grandmother innocently asked, assuming she hadn't heard the rest of Kate's answer.

"Thanks, Nana, I'm...I'm getting...ready," Kate said as she slumped down onto the bed. The bell only sat there, cold and indifferent. Its weight hadn't changed but what had been a struggle to complete ten times in a row was now a thing Kate didn't need to even consider. She'd swung it like a champ for far longer than she'd intended without even a thought. Her hips and legs weren't even sore.

There was no sense of accomplishment, though. Kate hadn't achieved anything. She felt robbed. She looked forward to that sense of struggle, that sense of daily, incremental progress. Now it was gone. Now, the game she was looking to beat had gotten too easy. The kettlebell wasn't a trial now.

The loss was too much and Kate began to cry. She crawled away from the bell and pulled her legs to her chest. She stared at the metal, growing angrier by the second. The only thing that gave her a daily sense of accomplishment and now it was taken from her.

It took her some time to finish crying.

Tears caking her vision, she looked around her room. Posters covered her walls; each and every one of them of either drawings or people dressed as drawings. Superheroes. Anime. Video games. Comic books. The stories and characters within, and the people who cosplayed them. That was her world. That was her life.

She took out her phone and summoned a picture of her costume she'd flown in the night before. Laying on the couch in Denise's place, it had looked so cool. So magical. Cosplay brought to life, made real. Now, looking at that picture, she realized it looked so dumb. Other people were working. They were saving lives or protecting others or simply making money, not living hand-to-mouth, unable to afford their clothes hobby. Kate grew mad, at herself and at her pastime. Her profession. Her addiction.

A knock at the door broke her out of her heated self-pity. Lauren leaned inside and said, "Hey, hon. Do you need the shower before work? Otherwise I'm going to jump in."

"No, it's..." Kate sniffed her armpit. "No, I'm fine, mom. Go ahead," Kate said, feeling like a fraud out of failure, not intention.

"I'm tapped out until the end of the week," her mom called through the door. "Can you get dinner tonight? Anything's fine."

Kate smiled and said, "Sure thing." It was a sick, financially-exhausted smile. Phone in hand, Kate checked the balance of her account as she wiped away the tears she was grateful her mother hadn't noticed. The usually small number was noticeably smaller. A pang of terror tore through Kate and she had to take a second to keep from shrieking. She scrolled through the transactions from the day, spotting new auto-pay bills. Kate's jaw began to quake as she realized the money from her car was already gone. She stared in terror and fury at the number, ready to either break into tears or throw the phone and scream.

Kate quickly wiped her cheeks, grateful there weren't any new tears. She stood and headed into the living room and found her grandmother watching a morning gameshow. Kate wanted to speak but lost her voice. She looked at the door to the bathroom and weighed the fear of her mother's wrath if she admitted her lack of money or the shame of asking her grandmother for still more money. "Nana," she asked in a half-whisper. "Do you want to do something for dinner?" Before her grandmother could answer, the bathroom door opened. Kate clamped her eyes shutting, ruing her decision.

"Kate," her mother demanded angrily. "Do you not have money to get dinner?"

Kate turned around, her back to her grandmother's chair. "I'm sorry, mom, no."

"You just said—" Lauren snapped.

"I don't mind, baby," Deloris told them both, turning around in the chair.

"I thought I did," Kate defended. "I checked my balance this morning and I had more than enough, but..." She gestured uselessly at nothing. "My phone bill hit and the insurance..."

"You don't have a car anymore!" exclaimed Lauren.

"The apartment's insurance," Kate specified, her voice raising. "I pay that, remember?"

Her mom half-retreated, taken aback by her answer. "Yeah, and..." Her words and her confidence wavered. "And I pay everything else!" she finally shouted.

"I do too!" Kate yelled back at her. "Every dollar I make at my job I put into this place!"

"Girls, don't!" Deloris protested from her seat.

"Then where do all those costumes come from?" her mother shouted. "And all those vacations?"

"From the prints and..." Kate stammered, slowly realizing not as much went to the household bills as she liked to pretend. Realizing she wasn't pulling as much of her weight as she could, she fell silent. "I..." Tears welled in the corners of her eyes. "I..." She had no defense. Money that could have paid for food had gone to buy clothes, gone to buy fabric, gone to pay for websites, gone to pay for photos and prints and gas and travel and lodging and...

The only thing worse than her mother screaming was her mother falling silent. A furious disappointment filled Lauren's eyes and she simply turned away. She stormed into her bedroom, slamming the door. Kate felt in pain and numb at the same time. In a strange, shamed daze, she sat down in her recliner and just stared. She didn't even have the energy to cry.

"It's okay, baby," Deloris said, reaching across the gulf between their chairs to pat Kate's hand. Kate thought how sad it was that her grandmother was comforting a thirty-year-old like she was still twelve. "I'll get dinner," she said. She pulled up her pocketbook from beside her recliner and fished through it. "What do you want? We can get pizza or chicken, or, or whatever you want." She was speaking quickly. Anything to smooth over the heated emotions. Kate just shook her head, trying desperately to keep from crying. "Why don't you get some groceries too, baby?" the sweet old woman told her, pushing the money into her hand.

Kate wanted more than anything to refuse but couldn't. She held the bills in her cupped hand, afraid to ask what this money was meant for instead of food. On instinct along, she asked, "Do you want anything, Nana?"

"Oh, no," her grandmother said rotely. She then paused and said, "Actually, if you see any oatmeal raisin cookies on sale..."

Kate's sad gaze cracked a hint, one side of her mouth curling a bit towards a smile. "Oatmeal raisin cookies?"

"Yes," Deloris said with a little girl's smile on a heavily lined face. "Don't spend too much now."

Kate scoffed at the very suggestion. "Oh, I won't," she promised. But she made a mental pledge to herself not to pass up getting the cookies.

Kate felt an emptiness as she drifted through her partial shift.

In khaki pants and the royal blue shirt of the store uniform, she coasted through the workday without a thought, like some morose ghost haunting the underwear section of the store. She felt like a part of her was missing, like she'd removed an organ or severed a limb.

Without a break or a lunch shift to look forward to, Kate had little to hang her mind on. The store was crowded for once, the result of a mid-week sale bonanza dictated by the corporate office out of state. All Kate could do was glance over to the toy section, wondering what, if any, new action figures were over there. She saw kids going in and out and felt a pang of jealousy that children enjoyed more freedom than she did as an adult.

She could hear a soft, dull buzz of the TVs. She saw Rich and Derek watching one TV, tuned to something other than the in-store promotional videos. She couldn't tell what they were watching, only enough to see a news graphic and the word 'school'.

Certain they were watching talking heads argue about the asteroid, Kate turned back to her section and wandered among the people that she was sure would rather she left them alone. She lost herself thinking about a planetary catastrophe. She imagined a burnt hellscape where society once lay and found herself smiling at the thought. "No more bills," she delighted. Her smile soured. "No more comics," she also realized.

After three hours and fifty minutes, Kate was clocked out. She exited the store and simply stood. Shoppers were walking by her, entering and leaving the store. Some had giant bags full of merchandise. Kate watched one family leave, the husband carrying bags in each hand, his wife with a bag of her own. They were smiling. With them, a young boy was following behind with his own bag of toys. Not toy, not singular; toys. More than one. And through the semi-transparent bag, Kate saw looking back at her the very Supergirl action figure she'd been looking at a week ago.

Jealousy welled up inside of her and Kate felt tears begin to sting the sides of her eyes. With a strange sense of panic, she walked around the store and headed towards the back. She couldn't face people, couldn't face society, couldn't face the world. She turned the corner and began to hurry, to run, towards the loading dock. She burst out into the rear section of the shopping center, only to see two guys getting a smoke break as well as a truck opening up for unloading. More products to go out tonight, while the world slept. More things Kate needed to sell and couldn't afford. She wanted to scream at the truck and the men, for their arrogance to be where she needed to be. Instead she rushed across the parking lot. She shoved through some prickly bushes into the wooded area separating the store from the apartments behind it.

Amidst the junk, trash, and litter that had been discarded among the trees, Kate stood perfectly still. She took long, deep breaths. She tried to stay calm, to push away the toxic fumes of the day at work. She tried to exhale the negativity of her overriding sense of failure like it was black smoke she needed to purge from her lungs.

Once she'd achieved a modicum of calm, she began to think about lifting up. Not flying, not soaring high into the clouds or shooting across the continent within a matter of moments. Just lifting up. She thought about it the way she might think about lifting a foot.

Nothing happened.

Kate looked down at her sneakers on the tangled roots of some knotted tree barely clinging to life in the pollution of the suburban world. She chewed on a thumbnail for a second, and then didn't bother thinking. She just lifted. It wasn't conscious or deliberate, merely instinctive, every bit as natural as taking a step without a thought. She looked down at the ground now about a foot beneath her soles. Curious, she looked up at the trees and kept floating up. She rose into the air slowly, passing branch by branch with gradual patience.

Kate rose into the branches and touched one of the leaves. "I bet you've never been touched by a human before," she told the leaf with a smile torn between childlike optimism and adult nihilism. She left it behind and rose further, finding herself worming between the branches as easily as she might move down a crowded aisle at work.

She reached the top of the tree and looked out. From the treetops, the forest behind the apartments didn't look decrypt and broken down. It didn't look like the trash heap it appeared to be from the ground. It looked picturesque. Idyllic. Like something from a storybook. Kate breathed deeply and found herself smiling sadly. "Why can't you really be like this?" she asked the view, slowly remembering this was no CG-trick or doctored photography. It was real.

Kate happened to glance down and saw a fawn. A small deer wondered through the forest and sniffed at a tire. It butted the tire with its nose and then pranced playfully. As it tried to play with the tire, its mother came up behind the fawn. She sniffed the air intelligently and glanced in a few different directions before looking up right at Kate. Through the trees, the doe found her just as easily as if she'd been on the ground. The fawn looked too and saw her. The doe twisted her ears at Kate, then turned suddenly. Right as Kate started to smile in delight, a gunshot tore through the air.

The two deer dashed off frantically and Kate's heart froze. The echo of the gunshot carried into the air, reverberating on and on into the distance, fading far too slowly. Kate listened a moment longer, but heard nothing else.

Deciding to risk it, she rose still further and crested the summit of the trees. She listened for a moment and spotted flashing lights. She drifted between the treetops, glancing down occasionally to make sure nobody was beneath her.

She arrived at the edge of the apartment complex behind the shopping center. Beyond it, she saw the small but prestigious private school around which the whole community seemed centered. Kate's blood chilled at the prospect, then she heard another shot and a small cloister of screams. Kate descended quickly and dropped to the sidewalk that wound through the manicured property. She rushed through the strange neighborhood to join a crowd of people at the edge of the complex. Two news vans were parked on the street that separated the onlookers from the school property.

At the edge of the small suburban street, Kate saw a large throng of middle and high-school kids along with police, EMTs, and firefighters. The police had surrounded the diamond-shaped school, while a battery of SWAT officers in high-tech tactical gear were motionless but poised to move at a moment's notice.

"What's going on?" Kate asked aloud.

"Some kids brought guns to school," said a woman to Kate's right, startling her. "They've got some kids still in there, with a teacher. Maybe more than one." The older woman had her cell phone out and was filming the entire scene, streaming it onto social media. She wasn't the only one.

"Oh my god," Kate gasped. She looked at the kids on the near side of the street and saw tears of fear and sorrow. Kate feared casualties weren't expected but confirmed.

"I heard somebody's already been killed," said someone else, watching out of morbid curiosity along with the rest of the onlookers. Kate didn't see who had spoken, though. She was focused on the collection of phones recording and sharing the events like it was a moment off reality TV.

"I think the SWAT's going to take the school from the back," said the first woman like she was discussing the scuttlebutt on the neighbors. "About half the police disappeared a few minutes ago."

"If they do, the hostages are going to get killed," gossiped the second woman. "My son used to go there. There's no way they can get into the cafeteria without being seen." The exchange poised to grow juicer, both women turned to address Kate, as if to argue at her by proxy, only to discover her missing.

Two buildings away, crouched behind an air conditioning unit, Kate stripped off her blue over-shirt. She quickly pulled her gray undershirt overhead, turned it inside-out, and wrapped it over her face. She tied her shirt into an impromptu ninja mask that covered everything but her eyes, then she slipped back into her blue work shirt. She wasn't even finished buttoning it when she took off from the ground.

Kate arched into the sky, rising up until she was just a speck overhead. Once she was satisfied she was high enough to not be noticed, she simply dropped. The whistle of the wind in her ears was intense and it made her heart race, but it also reassured her that she was falling fast enough that no one would see her. She waited until her nerves couldn't take anymore and brought herself to an abrupt stop. She looked quickly around, terrified she'd been seen. To her relief, she was in the central garden at the heart of the diamond-shaped school.

Just an inch above the ground, Kate looked around the garden and decided nobody had seen her, or if they had, they were being quiet about it. She rushed to the closest door when from above came a quiet, almost imperceptible noise. Kate reached the wall just in time and she flattened herself next to the door. Above her, she could just barely see a police sharpshooter on the roof. He faced into the garden, his shadow at her feet showing his helmet and hinting at his gaze. He looked for long a second, then his shadow disappeared off of Kate. Encouraged that she hadn't been noticed, Kate slipped through the metal door into the school itself.

Short hallways full of bulletins and banners created an instant confusion. For a school that looked so straight-forward from the outside, it seemed maze-like once Kate was inside. Half-flights of steps created a constant change of height as hallways detoured in directions that seemed at odds with Kate's concept of the school. Disregarding the confusion, she crept forward, at a loss for any specific direction to go. She listened for some clue as to where the events might be found but heard little more than her own heart racing inside her ears.

Halfway down the hall, she neared a science bulletin board. Details about asteroids and meteorites filled the bulletin board, including information about the nearing arrival. More importantly than any of that, Kate saw in her reflection in the case that her nametag was still on her shirt. She began to remove it when a teenager turned the corner.

There was a sudden and abrupt moment of absolute stillness. In the hallway, the only sound the muffled echoes of distant police, a teen boy in a black skater get-up, complete with skull face mask and department store shotgun, faced a busty woman with her hands on her breast and wearing a gray ninja mask made from an inside-out t-shirt. Equal parts awkward and tense, neither one of them moved for a second, both equally frozen. In unison, they both said uneasily, "Uh..."

The teen boy's gun rose as if on its own and pointed at Kate. "Don't move," he told her. His voice shook as much as the barrel. It was down the black end of the barrel that Kate faced and she was utterly stunned at how terrified she was. She'd never faced a gun before and the prospect was more unsettling than she had ever thought possible. "How'd you get in here?" the kid demanded.

"Uh..." Kate stammered like before. The barrel of the gun totally owned her attention.

"I said--" he demanded, stepping forward in baggy pants with wallet chains dangling at his thighs. He put the gun in Kate's face. "How'd you get in here?" he shouted, at the edge of losing control.

Kate didn't mean to move. Her hand just sort of jerked up on its own. Without any intention, she grabbed the body of the shotgun. She twisted it so abruptly, she shoved the boy off the grips and pushed him back half-a-step. He fell to the ground, unprepared for a force that could move him like that. The only one of the two still standing, Kate looked at the gun in her hand, as if its very existence confused her.

Another awkward, confused stillness followed. Kate looked from the gun to the boy. Behind the mask, she licked her lips in fear. She swallowed, her throat like sandpaper, and whispered in her best Christian Bale-Batman voice, "Run."

It came out as a stammer, her voice shaking. All the same, it registered with the borderline child and had the effect she wanted. The boy scampered away with frantic, gangly movements born of teen terror. A second later, Kate heard a door burst open, followed by police shouting 'get down'. She looked at the gun, still unable to get the image of that barrel facing her out of her mind. The crack of a spine played in her head, reminding her of the danger of her new-born strength. She very softly laid the gun down on the floor, leaving it peaceably.

The weapon left behind, Kate headed the other direction. Her sneakers, chosen for silence on the sales floor of the store, provided her the same silence as she reached the end of the hall. She glanced to her right, across the intersection and saw police at the door. Their view was obscured by a fundraiser poster. Their backs were turned as well, all of their heads seeming tilted towards the radios on their shoulders. Convincing herself she had precious little time, Kate turned down the hall to her left and ducked into the first door she came to.

Waiting for her was a classroom with a dozen scared students and another gun-drunk skater kid. The hostage-taker, maybe a hiccup younger than the first shooter, turned a boxy, matte-black pistol at Kate. The barrel was steady but his eyes behind a skull half-mask weren't. He confirmed his grip on the pistol and demanded with deadly seriousness, "Who are you?"

The question hit Kate like a truck. For the first time since she'd abandoned the conversation in the apartment complex, she was confronted head-on that she had absolutely no idea what she was doing. In the absence of any other response, her hands were up like she was surrendering. She fixed on the pistol, its barrel smaller than the shotgun's barrel but no less terrifying. In her petrified mind, Kate conjured every Superman comic she'd ever read, trying to think of how the Man of Steel would handle the situation.

"You can still walk away," she said, surprising herself. She did a double-take simply at the realization that she'd been the one to speak.

"Wh-what?!" the boy screamed.

"You can still walk away," Kate told the boy. Her voice was deeper as she channeled her best Christopher Reeve. She wasn't the one talking to the boy. Some sort of weird internal, Superman-cosplay was speaking to him, speaking through her to him. "Put the gun down and walk out," someone inside of her told him. "Take the mask off," she urged the boy. "And just walk out." She saw a cigarette burn on his bare wrist, as well as slash marks by his thumb. She saw a bruise peeking out under his shirt sleeve. She drew closer to him, not his weapon. "Nobody saw your face," she told the boy. "Nobody knows it was you."

"They know!" he said, his timbre cracking when he shouted. "They know," he repeated as a wet smack.

Kate shook her head. "No they don't." She consoled her fear of the gun pointed right at her with fixating on her Christopher Reeve impression and how poor it was. Being grateful that she didn't sound like Margot Kidder made her smile beneath her t-shirt ninja mask, the levity more than necessary to handle the gaze of the gun barrel. "You can still get out," she promised the boy, pretending confidence, feigning certainty.

As the shooter faced her, someone from the crowd of child hostages said "We won't tell. Promise." The boy glanced fearfully back at the crowd, then back at Kate, then the crowd again. He was clearly able to tell who had spoken, even if Kate couldn't. She looked at the gun and wondered if she was close enough to grab it. Before she got the chance, however, the boy lowered the gun.

His hands fell loosely to his side, but the gun remained in his grasp. "I don't..." he said. Kate saw his eyes tighten and knew all too well the uneasy, jagged breathing that came just before tears would begin to flow. The hostages started to shift, some of the braver boys starting to move, but

Kate held them in place with only a subtle gesture, urging them to stay where they were, that the danger wasn't abated. The boy wiped his face, his chin tightening. "I don't want to get into trouble," he sobbed. Like the child he was, he whimpered, "My dad's gonna kill me."

As if a toddler giving up on playing cops and robbers, the boy just casually dropped the gun on the nearest desk and walked out like a shell of a person, wiping his eyes furiously. Halfway to the door, he broke into a sprint, juvenility taking over. Kate focused more on the gun than him, even when the other kids ran by her in a frantic, hurried escape.

Once the kids were out of the room, there was a lot of noise outside the door. Kate looked from the gun that had so transfixed her. She heard police entering the school, the squeak of boots and buzz of radios preceding them. She turned and saw a window just an inch open and knew what she had to do.

A moment later, the door burst open and in came four officers, all armed and all finding nothing but a single pistol on a desktop in the middle of the classroom. Nothing else was out of place in the room.

CHAPTER ELEVEN

Kate whipped out the kettlebell swings without trouble, effort, or thought. Her eyes burned in thoughts far away as crisp breaths were forced out at the top of every swing. With one snap at the end, like a punch, she remembered the looks on each of the boys' faces from the school the day before. With one snap at the end, she remembered the sound of cracking bones and the way a full-sized man went sailing into the air from Denise's upstairs neighbor's door.

As the kettlebell floated briefly at the top of each swing, Kate wondered if being a superhero meant saving good people, or if it meant saving bad people. As the kettlebell went up and down, up and down, like a cannonball-shaped metronome, Kate brushed her mind over the realization that being a superhero meant submerging herself in an ugly world. It meant surrounding herself with people who were so sick or so desperate or both that they were resorting to crime. Being a superhero wasn't about stopping crime, but about helping those for whom crime had become the last resort.

That troubled her to no end.

Kate finished her routine with twelve get-ups, rising from the floor to standing and back again. There was no struggle to it whatsoever. It almost seemed more of a challenge than before, as if it was harder to maintain good form while using a weight that was unnoticeable. The thought that a 62lb kettlebell was unnoticeable only troubled her further.

Kate set the kettlebell down and felt fine. Not even out of breath. It irritated her to not have the sense of pleasant exhaustion, to not have the sense of strain that rewarded her with thoughts that she was making progress.

The struggle validated her sense of effort and conquering it. Without that struggle, without the sense of incremental progress, she felt lost.

She gave up on the bell and just left it in the middle of her floor. Her alarm still hadn't gone off and she wondered if sleep, too, would become a thing she didn't need, or if she was dealing with simple run-of-the-mill insomnia. She grabbed up her phone and sat cross-legged on her bed. She pulled up the morning social media numbers which, sadly, didn't look good.

From there, she studied her bank account, looking over the list of recent transactions, every purchase she'd made and every bill she'd paid, trying to maintain a running tally of every dollar and cent. She reached the end and, doing some quick math, realized the bank's total was as correct as it was tragically small.

Kate instinctively pulled her legs up to her chest and studied the number critically. Her eyes traveled across the room to the mirrored closet doors and she saw her form in the dim light of her bedroom. Kate looked at her side, and put a leg down. The muscles of her stomach were obvious, even curled forward, but a fold of skin sat on the edge of her pajama bottoms. She pinched the skin and pulled it out, feeling gross at the sight. She looked at herself and could only see a fat blob pretending to be a professional cosplayer.

She glanced to the wall of posters and her eyes fell again to Superman. "Did you ever get self-conscious about love handles?" She looked at his sides, so well-toned and perfect. The muscles of his abs, his obliques, the finger-like serratus under his armpits, all stood out in perfect relief. She looked again at the flaw in her proportions and felt like a complete and total failure.

In Star Wars pajamas and a gray sports bra, she exited her room in a bit of a huff. Bad enough that she was poor, but she was fat too. She went through the morning motions, moving mechanically, not consciously. She showered quickly, grumpy the whole time. Brushing her teeth wasn't an act of self-care but anger at all the meals that had marred her smile. She returned to her room in an increasingly foul mood. Everything and everyone else was beautiful. Not her life and not her.

Not long after, Kate came out of her bedroom, dressed for work, her purse slung over her shoulder. She peeked into the living room and found the TV uncharacteristically silent. Immediately on edge, Kate looked around before spotting her mother out on the patio.

The little submerged space just off the kitchen was a cement-floored cube half-buried with a torn mosquito net screen. Fragments of grass clippings and other lawn debris, along with some minor litter, had blown in and collected in the corners. Two plastic folding chairs faced out, with dusty cobwebs connecting them to the lime-green wall. Lauren sat in the farthest seat, looking between a bunch of letters, the sharp creases lining up perfectly.

"Mom?" Kate asked, stepping halfway out into the patio. "Where's Nana?"

"She's not up yet. I'm going to take her to the senior center for dominoes and to get her haircut," said Lauren. She looked up from what were clearly bills and did not look happy. "I know, last night...I know we..." Her mom gave up dancing around the matter. "Kate, I need your help." Her words were thick with the understatement of an adult addressing an adolescent. "We're really coming up short this month."

Kate exhaled slowly, getting scared. "I thought we'd paid everything for the month. We just needed, you know, food and stuff." Her mom snorted cynically and didn't bother with the minutiae to correct her. "How short are we?" Lauren handed her the answer. Kate accepted the bills and only needed to glance through them. "Oh god."

"Yeah," Lauren agreed. She accepted the pages back. "Is there any chance you can get some more shifts? Do you get paid again before the end of the month?" Kate shook her head. Her mother swallowed, clearly working to not give into the fear of desperation. "Stuff's about to start getting turned off. And I don't just mean the cable," she said for absolute clarity.

Kate racked her brain quickly, but it was hard to push through the fog of fear. "If we can pay some of it and put the rest off until after the 1st, I can try to get some more shifts by then." She deflated. "No, those wouldn't register until the next check."

"Doing that's what got us into this mess," her mother said. "We've got to get caught up on everything. We can't keep paying the minimum and hanging on, or trying to eat late charges. The fees get too much, the interest gets too much." Her voice was shaking, the long-held weight beginning to overwhelm her. They both fell quiet, staring into space, at the nothingness of their options. The street light outside their apartment buzzed in the cold morning air, its stinging light creating hard shadows.

"Kate," Lauren said heavily, "I hate to ask this but I don't see another option." She looked to her daughter. "I need you to sell some of your stuff." Kate hid her utter shock, limiting her internal implosion to just her eyes. "Sell some fabric or some…some whatever you have. If needs be, sell some costumes. You've got a closet full of that stuff, some of which you haven't worn." A tear escaped her mom's eye. "I hate to ask it, honey, I really do. But…but we…" She gave up trying to justify her request.

Mother and daughter said nothing further.

The thought hung over Kate like a specter for the rest of the day. The bus ride to work was little more than a period of motionlessness during which she had no distractions except to stare the problem in the face. Her walk into work, clocking in, heading out onto the floor, it all went in a deluded flash as she tried to work her mind through matters.

Her mom was right, of course. She had costumes she hadn't worn in ages: costumes she couldn't fit into. Costumes that needed repair or upgrades. Costumes that were inferior to what she could and should make now. Costumes that were outdated or for characters that had gone through redesigns. Costumes for characters that she simply wasn't that into anymore.

It made perfect sense for her to ask Kate to contribute more money. In the entire time they'd been living together, Kate had rarely if ever contributed her equal share. A fourth or so of the total monthly expenses was the best she could ever manage. Never mind that doing so usually wiped her out completely, but fair and equal were a different matter.

Her thoughts carried through staff meetings and into the tasks of the day. She strolled through the unmentionables section of the store, adjusting displays and righting misplaced merchandise. She looked at the various colors of bras and wondered who had designed them. Had some artist spent their whole life with that bra's cup style in mind, or was it some committee decision? Or had some highly advanced bra-design computer algorithm come up with it? In either case, how much money had they been paid?

Kate looked at the people in her section, none of whom made eye contact. She wondered why they were buying their underwear here, at her store? Was this the best place they could afford and they were getting date-night, sexy bras? Or was this the cheap store for them, where they bought their granny panties for days when sexiness was the farthest thing from their mind? Were they buying new bras because they finally had the money, or were they like her and only buying them whenever other bras in their collection was ruined by too-long of a life?

Did any of them know they were in the presence of a superhero?

The word felt weird to Kate when she thought it. Hero, definitely not. Super? Maybe. She could fly. She could lift heavy things. She smiled sadly when she remembered she had a costume she'd worn once. Kate looked down at her work uniform and wondered if she could wear the dark blue suit under it. Otherwise, how was she supposed to change in phone booths? She lost half an hour just trying to think of the last time she'd seen a phone booth.

After the store's morning rush had died down and before the lunch rush could gather steam, Kate slipped out of the underwear section and into the toys. She was distracted momentarily by finding an Arcee action figure. Based off the 1986 animated Transformers movie, this version of Arcee – the first female Transformer in the regular cast – was pink and white and overly feminine. Yet she had something of an action hero build to her, something mirrored in the best female heroes elsewhere on the wall of toys.

Kate held the toy she'd quietly hoped would come in. Now that it was here, she not only didn't have the money to buy it, she had the mental block that it would be more irresponsible than usual to buy it. Kate looked at the toy aisle and felt a pang of guilt, confronted with the reality that it would be irresponsible to buy any of the toys. She was an adult. She was thirty. She shouldn't be buying toys. She barely even played with them. That she had to say 'barely' really hurt. She wasn't sure what was worse, that she didn't play with them enough to justify ownership or that she still played with toys even occasionally.

As Kate considered the aisle and the mountain of emotional issues it represented, two young girls came down from the far end. Seeing girls in the typically boys' aisle made Kate smile quietly. The girls picked up some Star Wars toys and looked at them. Kate was about to speak up when the nearer of the two girls said, "God, these are so stupid." Kate's smile shattered like dropped glass.

"Yeah," said the other girl, laughing. Not even teenagers, they practically tossed the toys back onto the shelf, knocking over other figures. "A laser sword's the dumbest thing in the world." It took every ounce of strength for Kate not to correct her. "Only immature little boys like this stuff," said the girl, bypassing Kate like she wasn't there.

Kate turned and watched them head off towards the music section of the store, where once CDs had dominated, now rendered novelties adjacent to the headphones and MP3 players. She leaned out of the aisle and watched the girls almost a third her age grab up some CDs with excitement. "Immature," she repeated, like the word was alien to her, yet somehow also some deeply personal hell.

The word rattled around in her head. Immature. Was she? She confronted the ugly reality that her whole life was playing dress up of make-believe characters so people could look at her. She realized her biggest hope was that people would want to look at her more than anyone else. How vain. She wanted to dress-up as someone else's creation and be loved for it. Be respected for it. For putting on clothes and strutting around in awkward poses in hotel lobbies and conventions centers.

Immature.

Was that just another word for amateur?

As Kate slowly collapsed internally under the weight of her self-loathing, Emily appeared at the end of the aisle. "Hey," she said, too obtuse to notice Kate's mood. "Hey, you weren't answering your cell and class got canceled. And I was in the neighborhood." Kate looked read to burst into tears, but Emily kept on, too excited to notice. "We got an invitation to GiganantiCon!" She followed that with an excited squeal and practically vibrated up and down, beaming. "They want us to help run the cosplay track and do some judging for their cosplay walk."

In her mind, Kate simply wished, 'I want to go home'. Outloud, she said, "When is it?"

There, Emily balked. "So, because of some issue with the convention center, they had to move it. It's normally in mid-June but because of like some fund raiser or something, they got a deal with--"

"Emily," Kate asked her firmly. "When is it?"

The youngest of their group let out a half-sigh. "End of May?" she asked Kate, as if looking for her permission already.

Kate closed her eyes and cursed internally. Her idealism and professional hopes were dashed against the rocks of reality. "I can't go," she said with cynical certainty. "I can't." She started to tear up, which made Emily freak out a little. "Money's too tight right now. I gotta sell some costumes as it is, just to keep from getting evicted." Kate dabbed at her face with her palms, trying to brush away her tears. "I gotta get back to my section." She dashed passed Emily and started back towards the heart of the store.

"Kate, hold on," Emily said, speed-walking to keep up with Kate as they moved briskly through the mostly-empty store. "Maybe we can set up a Patreon or the Kickstarter will finally—"

"No!" Kate burst at Emily, stopping and whirling around at her. "I'm tired of trusting to social media to come save me. I'm tired of panhandling for scraps to try to make it by. I'm tired of...of..." Kate's heart just sank. She turned and said, "I'll call you guys when I get off." She rushed away.

Home offered no respite.

With a metal-on-wood scrape, Kate pushed apart metal hangars she'd kept from dry cleaners and motels a few blocks from conventions. Her stash of costumes hung before her in a just-barely-walk-in closet beneath the single bare bulb. The massive wardrobe was the result of sleepless nights, frugal spending, and a lot of ingenuity. She took down one of her first Supergirl costumes, one she'd worked on with Rachael back in high school. She remembered so vividly the surreal sense of staying up past midnight, the giggles of sleep deprivation, and the energy of conquering the night.

Femme fatale Stormtrooper armor from Star Wars. It was her first foray into more sexy cosplay, a leap from which she never fully returned. The hard plastic had been her first attempt at making armor. It had taken almost an entire spring in college to get it right. She was still making the plates a week before the convention, only to discover she'd made it too small. Denise ended up wearing it instead.

Cammy. Ritsuko Akagi. A borg from Star Trek. Popular figures like Batwoman. Obscure figures like Synergy from Jem and the Holograms. So many different costumes, from so many corners of the fandoms she considered her people, she considered home. Each one wasn't just a performance, a demonstration of her love of the art, a display of her skill. Each one was also a product of who she was in that moment. Each costume she looked upon was a moment in time that she could so vividly remember. And she had to decide which memories to give up.

"I want to go home," she whispered sadly in her bedroom closet.

'Flash sale'

'Making room'

Kate checked the posts all over social media. Facebook. Twitter. Instagram. Pintrest. Everywhere she had a voice, Kate posted her offerings. The numbers after the dollar signs looked so small to her. How could she put a price on her beloved costumes? How could she sell a piece of herself?

Whatever price her memories were worth, she knew what she was asking for them. And she knew what people were willing to pay. The two were depressingly far apart.

Part of her was relieved to see the sales confirmed.

Part of her was relieved to see her bank account grow.

Part of her was disheartened by how little her account grew.

Part of her already feared the empty space those costumes would leave behind.

Rachael's studio apartment was like a museum to all things burlesque and bohemian. Posters covered every inch of the one room's four walls, everything from modern porn stars to pre-WWI blue showings. Autographed pictures dotted the multitude of tiny tables, upon which lay every manner of crafting magazine and implement. There were no lights on, only a multitude of carefully arranged candles and mirrors to give off the maximum of illumination.

Rachael popped the cork on a wine bottle with a bulbous base. She sniffed the alcoholic fumes and gave it some thought, sticking her lips out as she worked. "Eh," she decided and she poured a few fingers worth in Kate's waiting glass. "Should still be good."

Kate took the plastic cup and smelled the wine and crinkled her nose at it. Rachael poured an equal amount into her own glass, then set the bottle aside. She went for a toast and missed but got it on the second try. "To paychecks and paydays." She tapped Kate's glass, hiccupping a bit. "Like men, there aren't enough quality ones in our lives."

Kate sipped and crunched her whole face. She stuck out her tongue and looked at the glass for a second. "What about women?" she asked as she decided that on a day like today, bad alcohol was better than no alcohol.

Rachael emptied her cup. "What?" she asked.

"Quality women? What about quality women?" Kate asked. "Seems like, if one is bi..." She gestured at Rachael. "If one is bi, then you leave the door open for, for other...options."

"Oh," Rachael said. "Well, see, I like girls. And I can date girls. But I couldn't date-date girls, you know? I like cock too much."

Kate nearly spewed out the foul wine, laughing so suddenly. "You foul-mouthed wretch!" she squealed at Rachael.

"Wretch?" Rachael mocked. "Who says wretch? I mean, honestly?"

Kate's laughter faded back into melancholy and she slumped back against the armrest of Rachael's antiquated couch. She looked at nothing but her own sadness in the candlelight-strewn apartment. "Sorry about GigantiCon. I just...I..."

"Pssh, it was too good to be true anyway," Rachael said as she helped herself to a Ritz cracker right out of the tube. Kate saw the crackers and her stomach curled at the thought of the carbohydrate goodness. "Emily jumped the gun. Denise tried to warn her, to remind her we've done that dance before. It's not like they'd be the first con to be all 'we'll give you special guest of honor status with all the trimmings if you'll moderate a few of the cosplay panels'. Two months out, we're signing all their cosplay guests, scheduling the panels and events, organizing and coordinating with the other departments while at the same time, we've been downgraded to us having one room to share, no food or travel budget, a table in the back of the dealers' room, we're a two-paragraph listing in the guide book, and we

MIGHT get to walk out on stage at opening ceremonies. They want us to prep and organize possibly the most visible component of their con, all in return for an 'also attending'? Yeah, no." Another cracker and more wine. "I was born at night, honey, but it weren't last night."

Kate felt almost comforted. "I just...I'm just...sick of working so hard. You know?" Rachael was emptying the bottle of wine into her cup. "I just..." Kate paused and moved some giant knitting needles large enough to be mistaken for wooden stakes for hunting vampires. "I don't want to stop, but I...god, I hate working at that stupid store and trying to..." Her chin quaked. Her face contoured in self-disapproval. "I'm so sick of mom looking at me like that, like she's disappointed in me." She looked at the bottom of Rachael's cup as it was emptied. "You know, I had to spend my birthday money on rent? My nana gave me sixty dollars and I had to use it to makeup rent. And the fact that my nana gives me sixty dollars when I'm thirty goddamn years old is pathetic. And the fact that I was so excited to get that little money?"

Rachael lowered her now-empty glass, licking her lips. She looked around on the cluttered floor and found her tablet. "Let's see what's happening with the pictures."

"I'm talking here," Kate griped. "I'm in real pain."

"No, honey, you're in real life," Rachael said pleasantly as she activated her tablet.

Kate looked around the candlelit apartment and remembered, "I thought your power was turned off."

"I'm using the neighbor's wifi," Rachael said as she got distracted with the news on her social media feed. "Their password is their kid's name." Kate shrugged, realizing it made sense. "Little punk says the Bayformers movies are his favorite," Rachael complained. "I damn-near told him the truth about Santa Claus right there. Godless brat." She tilted her head back and enjoyed the last few drops of the nasty wine. Kate picked up a candle and turned it a bit, letting the flame dance around the wick. She touched it with her fingertip and inhaled sharply at the pain, not sure what else she was expecting.

"Jesus," Rachael grumbled under her breath. "Everybody's going nuts over the asteroid." She turned the tablet's glowing screen at Kate, nearly blinding her. "Did you see this?"

Kate had to let her eyes adjust before she could handle the glare and read the news feed. Alcohol impeded her ability to read quickly, or silently. "Militia takes federal building..." she sounded out. She sat up. "What, why?"

"Because they're protesting the government spending money on NASA or something," Rachael said, turning the screen back to her. Her eyes glowed from the reflection, as did the lenses of her glasses. "I watched something about them while I was trying to hash out a deal or something with the printers. Anyway, some interview they beamed in this morning or something. Like, they think the government is overreaching with tracking this asteroid or something. I don't remember. It didn't make any damn sense. Like anti-vaxxer-level of not making sense."

"Huh," was all Kate had to say. She stared sadly at the bottom of her lime-yellow vacation cup. She wondered about asking for more and wasn't sure she wanted to risk it. At the same time, she didn't want to risk the buzz ending either. "Why haven't they been arrested yet?"

"Because they're white?" ventured Rachael, cynically. "I don't know. They've got this building and it's not like they've got any hostages or anything. There's like a standoff or something. I think they're threatening to release confidential information or something, but it's a Department of the Interior office or something, so I don't know what information they've gotten that they can threaten to release that anybody would care about." Kate slid across the couch and read alongside Rachael. "They're heavily armed, because of course they are," she continued to explain. "The ATF is...I think it's the ATF...they're there but they're not going in because they're afraid of casualties. Not sure what casualties as they're out by the lake, but like I said, they're white so of course they'll be taken peaceably."

"Huh," Kate said. She and Rachael continued to read the story in silence for a moment, then slowly, inch by inch, turned their eyes to one another. They settled identical looks and Kate repeated, "Huh," with a tipsy smirk.

"I think this is stupid," said Emily as she drove. Her hands firmly in the ten-and two position, she checked every mirror obsessively as the car traveled at exactly three miles below the speed limit.

"We know," Rachael said in the seat next to her, rubbing her eyes. "You said. You also didn't have to come."

In the back, Kate's foot appeared between the seats as Denise tugged on the multi-buckled boot. "Harder!" Kate yelled. There was a scamper of repositioning and the foot disappeared.

"Yeah, well, I wanted to come," Emily said, her dark skin shining from nervous sweat. "I think this is gonna be cool. Maybe. Or tragic. Like, cool or tragic. Those are the only possible outcomes here. Or maybe stupid."

"Where's the helmet?!" Kate panicked in the back.

"On the floor!" Denise yelled at her. "Take a deep breath."

"Why?" Kate asked, just before gasping in pain.

"Honey, cool things are always stupid; that's what makes them cool," Rachael asserted to Emily. She pointed suddenly, sitting forward. "Here. Here! Turn here!"

"I'm turning, I'm turning!" Emily exclaimed frantically. Throwing on her blinker while in mid-turn, she narrowly missed hitting the divider post of the park entrance. Emily's car made it only a few dozen feet down the access road before she brought it to a rather abrupt stop right before a locked metal bar across the road. Emily began to panic. "Oh god, the cops are—"

"Would you chill?!" Rachael exclaimed as she got out. She stood in the cool night air and shivered as a brisk breeze stirred the trees. The door behind her opened and Denise got out with her, looking up into the sky.

"Reminds me of Halloween Is Grinch Night," she said with a grin. "You ever see it? It's like the Halloween version of How The Grinch Stole Christmas."

"Original or Jim Carrey version?" asked Denise.

"What Jim Carrey version?" Rachael retorted.

"The live-action one where Jim Carrey—"

"She knows; she's just choosing to forget it exists," said Emily across the roof of her car. "Like all of us." Denise accepted that.

Out from the driver's side rear door stepped Kate. Fully dressed, her helmet under her arm, she looked up at the sky as well, the buzz of the evening's alcohol beginning to wear off. She looked out from the gate they'd stopped before, across a long municipal lake. In the far distance, they could see car headlights. "That must be the standoff."

"Yep. The building is…straight that way," Denise confirmed with the aid of her phone's GPS. "Just up, over, and down," she advised with hand gestures. "Just like you did with the school thing."

"Do you know how you're doing this?" Rachael asked with surprising sobriety.

"Same as the school," Denise repeated. Rachael waved her off with a buzzing noise and focused on Kate.

Prompted to give an answer, Kate theorized, "I'm going to try and find a way in from the roof." She focused on the building hidden by the night, trying to replace heroic fantasies with sane determination. "I'll get inside and cause a distraction, which will allow the ATF people to start their raid. Maybe I can steal some of their guns so they can't shoot anybody."

"Ooh, get some of their guns and bring them back," Denise said. "We can use them for a GI Joe shoot. I want to be Baroness and—"

"Oh my god, that's a felony!" Emily exclaimed.

"Technically, so is this," Denise told her about parking in the state park's driveway. Emily whimpered fearfully and looked worriedly at her car.

Kate took a calming breath, which did very little, and pulled on the helmet. "Wish me luck," she said over the blu-tooth before she lifted straight into the air. Her cape fluttering at her ankles, she rose into the sky. Her eyes adjusting to the dark, she searched the patternless park until she could see the dark building encircled by police cars and other enforcement vehicles. This high up, the situation seemed to swirl before her.

For a moment, Kate floated towards the building, drifting in the sky like a cloud, lost in the darkness of the heavens. She wondered how much of this moment, of being over this building, about to do this thing, was the result of the wine. How much of it was the result of the crushing drone of a life she had made for herself and yet somehow only barely recognized?

Kate decided it would not be questions that drove her tonight, but answers. Not just answers, but action. She began her descent.

Her cape flapped above her as she dropped like a stone through the whistling air. "I'm heading down," she told the others, her voice quivering as she dropped. Just as the very texture of the roof came into view, Kate slowed herself suddenly, coming to a complete stop only inches from the top of the building. She all but stepped down, the roof groaning a bit when she touched it.

She listened for a long moment. Only the wind made any real noise, muffled for Kate by her helmet. Beneath the wind, Kate was aware of without actually hearing the buzz of distant radios and far-off voices, the individual words lost in the distance. She heard no frantic rush, no change or panic. She guessed nobody had noticed her arrival.

Thankful for her nighttime-colored costume, Kate turned to the rooftop access, a square door on a tiny square atop a square building. Kate decided that was the way to go. She took a single step and the roof gave out underneath her.

It didn't feel like some catastrophic tumble so much as simply a missed step when descending a staircase. Kate thought the floor would be there and then suddenly it wasn't. There was a bigger gap between expecting landing and actual landing but otherwise, it was the same. No true sense of panic and no processing of terror. Just a moment of 'wait, this isn't right' and then an abrupt stop. Sadly, that stop was right in the middle of a room full of armed men.

As debris continued to sprinkle down around her, Kate turned to her left and saw three men who had been drowsing in the corner. She looked to the right and saw two men come running in. Everybody was wearing camouflage pants and jackets, along with a few 'Don't Tread On Me' and 'Make America Great Again' t-shirts. Most of them had scruffy facial hair, much of which was turning white. All of them looked confused more than scared.

Kate looked back and forth between her left and her right before finally saying, "Uh…sorry?"

As if the barrier of silence had been all that protected her, one of the men arriving through the door whipped out a pistol and shot her. The shot caught her square in the chest and knocked her off her feet. Kate was blown into the wall, right next to the three men who had been falling asleep. The drywall crumbled mightily at impact and Kate collapsed to the floor.

Half-fallen to the cheap government-surplus tile, Kate groaned loudly, then screamed, "FUCK!" She reached to her chest and felt her collar, then down her chest until she felt the tear right through her costume. "What the fuck!" she shouted. She shoved her hand into her jacket and fished around until she pulled out a flatten disc that had once been a bullet. She held the disc to her helmet's visor and studied it for a second. She panted a couple of times, then looked down at the rip in her costume, able to see a huge bruise spreading over her skin. She looked at the guy, his pistol still held out, the barrel shaking like his eyes. She roared, "You shot me in the tit, you bastard!"

Kate leapt in a fury before any of the militia men could respond. Her forearms locked together, she slammed into the gunman and drove him into the doorframe, the wood snapping, the drywall caving entirely. The man that had arrived with him took out his pistol and shot Kate in the side. She howled in agony and dropped to one knee. She grabbed her side as the bullet fell out, flattened against her bruised skin as well. She turned to the guy and punched him in the chest. On her knees, she struck with no real power, only enough force to knock him into the far wall.

The three men who she'd woken began to frantically grab at their heavily customized assault rifles. They leveled shaking barrels at the masked figure before them. Kate rose on unsteady feet and turned, just in time to see the barrels. "Wait—" she said, her hands raising as the barrels lit.

A deafening barrage of pops and blinding light filled Kate's world as absolute pain overtook her. She screamed and fell to her hands and knees, her costume getting shredded. As she collapsed, however, the tiny discs that had once been bullets dribbled down onto the floor like lost change.

Through the pain blossomed blind rage. Oblivious to the sounds of shouting that echoed from the floors below, Kate rose against the gunfire and roared in fury. The men's guns lowered as they realized their uselessness. Kate burst at them, screaming madly.

On the first floor, the main entrance was knocked in. A police battering ram came flinging back and armed and armored SWAT officers came flooding through the breached door. Weapons and flashlights aimed everywhere, the black-clad warriors entered in a dervish of light.

There was no sign of anyone, however. The cramped federal office building was cluttered with the debris and refuse of the unwelcome occupants but there was no sign of them. Amidst shouts of "Clear!" around the first floor, the SWAT officers rushed up stairs to the second to find a few men at the stairwells, their eyes cast up. The men in camouflage turned their guns on the SWAT but with so many operatives already aiming at them, they tossed down their weapons quickly and surrendered without incident.

The commanding officer approached one of the men as he was pushed to the ground and cuffed. "Where are the others?" he demanded.

"Upstairs!" he yelled in a panic, afraid of something other than the armed men before him.

The commander led the others up the final flight to the third floor to discover utter chaos. Bullet holes riddled the walls. Furniture was destroyed and shards of drywall and pages of government reports covered the floor in chaotic disarray. A few small fires had started from pinned papers catching from the friction of gunshots passing through. Armed men littered the floor as well, slammed into walls and driven into the floors. An entire squadron, it seemed, of armed militia men had been laid out.

As one SWAT officer passed an office, he happened to glance into the room and spotted a shadowed figure. He kept walking as the glimpse processed, then spun back around, shining his light. "Contact!" he yelled, even though his light caught only the thick textured soles of boots and the edges of a cape. The man ran into the room and looked up, seeing only the gaping hole in the ceiling.

Other SWAT officers, along with agents from other enforcement agencies, came rushing in. They all found the crashed-in hole above them, through which their flashlight beams emptied into the night. They all stared with equal parts confusion and growing concern as to what had come through that hole.

CHAPTER TWELVE

The four women were cloistered together with Kate's grandmother, glued to the television set. They watched, entranced as the news came back around from a commercial break. "And local police are still baffled as to what caused the shootout at the federal building last night." The video feed switched to a camera crew sweeping through the destroyed office, bullet holes and destruction everywhere. "Evidence of fighting between the militia men is everywhere, but with so many of them still hospitalized, two in critical condition, no answers have yet presented themselves."

"Wow," Emily said, her eyes like saucers. She turned to Kate who was standing behind her grandmother's chair. "I can't believe it."

"Me neither," said Deloris, shaking her silver head. "Silly little boys, playing with guns. And after that whole business at the school, too."

"Did they say anything about what happened? Like, what caused the dudes to implode?" asked Emily.

Kate waited for a second, then said, "Nana!"

Her grandmother perked up. "Yes, baby?"

"Did the news say what caused the guys to turn on each other?" Denise asked louder for Emily, sitting in Kate's mother's recliner.

"No," she said with certainty, as if her modesty had been questioned. "But anytime you get a bunch of men acting like little boys together, they'll begin fighting sooner or later."

Rachael giggled and said, "Deloris, honey, I love you." Kate's grandmother smiled, as if aware she'd been addressed but not quite sure what had been said.

With the news report shifting to a local wedding chapel that hosted animal weddings, Kate departed for her bedroom. The others followed quickly, all practically bubbling with excitement. Kate waited by the bed until Denise shut the door, then she yanked back her covers to reveal the costume. "So…it kind of got shredded," she said, looking down at the outfit like it was a deflated medical patient.

Denise stuck her finger in the hole on the chest of the suit and pushed it open. She wiggled her finger at Rachael, causing her to exclaim, "Did somebody shoot you in the tits?" Kate pulled down her tanktop to reveal the massive, ugly purple bruise extending from her collar all the way down into her bra. "JESUS!" Rachael exclaimed. She leaned close. "Christ, do you need to go to the doctor?"

"First of all, no, it doesn't hurt that much, except when you touch it!" she exclaimed, slapping Rachael's hand when she tried to press it. "And secondly, no health insurance, so fuck no."

"Geez," remarked Denise, leaning close as well. She reached to tug down Kate's bra. "How far does it go?"

"Guys!" Kate exclaimed, reaching her quota of voyeurism and returned her tanktop across her collar. "We got to fix the suit. And reinforce it or something."

"Honey, it's a costume, not battle armor," said Rachael. "No fabric is going to handle getting shot."

"I'm just grateful you're okay," said Emily. Kate seemed a little curious that she said that. "You got SHOT," she emphasized dramatically. "I mean, we knew you could fly and we knew you could lift stuff, but that didn't mean we knew you could, you know, take a bullet."

Kate looked down at the costume, slowly realizing the magnitude of the situation. "I hadn't thought about that," she said.

Rachael detoured the conversation, however. "Well, if we're going to repair it or remake it, we need to decide what changes we got to make." She dug out one of Kate's old sketch pads from under a pile of clothes and flipped through some pages. And then a few more pages. And then a few more pages. She stopped and turned the page around to Kate. Dean Winchester from the TV show Supernatural was stripped bare, wounded muscles etched in pain, as was his expression. "Really?" Rachael asked. Kate blushed.

"I was always more of a Sam kind of guy," Emily remarked, tilting her head to one side. Kate blushed more.

Denise did the same head tilt and asked, "You really think he's circumcised?"

"Oh my god!" Kate freaked, covering her face.

Rachael giggled but kept looking through the book. Finding a blank page, she took a pencil out from her hair bun and she sat down on the bed next to the suit. Looking expectantly at Kate, she asked, "Alright, perv, what was it like?" Kate blinked, lost.

"How did it hold up in combat?" Emily clarified, sitting on the edge of the bed with Rachael.

"And what do we need to change?" Rachael further added.

Y'marda leaned forward in the recliner, her elbows on her knees, her chin in her hands. She stared intently at the television screen and watched the video replay. Behind her, down the hall of the small apartment, her subordinate came in. "The bodies are beginning to smell," Y'dosh reported. "I fear the authorities will be alerted and we'll have to deal with more of them." He looked back down the hall at the door to the bedroom. He turned back, to say more, only to realize his superior was still watching the television. "What has you so transfixed?"

Y'marda held out the remote and rewound the cable feed for a moment, going in reverse through analyst evaluations and on-the-scene reporters, before coming back to a video of the previous night. She let the video play again as the screen just showed a nighttime roll of a three-story building. The subordinate watched, at a loss. "I don't get it."

The video was punctuated by sudden gunfire from inside the building, followed by the sounds of internal combat. He stepped towards the TV, intrigued by the video but still not following why it was significant. "So? Some of the locals fought amongst themselves. Why is that—"

Y'marda hit pause. The video feed of the building froze. Y'dosh studied the single image for a second, then squinted. He leaned forward, then stepped towards the television of the apartment and touched the screen, just above the building it showed. His finger fell to a strange discoloration against the night sky. "What is that?" he asked in mild confusion.

"A local paramilitary group took a building hostage," explained Y'marda, her face alight from the TV screen. Y'dosh was only more confused. "I don't understand the political significance of it either, but it will hardly matter soon. What DOES matter is that the holdout was undone by what local intelligence sources claim was in-fighting." She pointed at the screen with the remote. "I suspect, however, the real reason was that which you see."

Y'dosh looked again at the screen, growing more confused by the moment. "What DO I see?" Y'marda's scowl spoke of her disappointment. She pointed at the screen again, at the discoloration. Y'dosh looked closer a the pixlated image, then slowly began to piece matters together. His jaw dropped. "You suspect...?" More confusion now, though of a different sort.

"These creatures are incapable of personal flight," Y'marda explained, before gesturing again at the screen. "The only possible explanation is..." She waited for Y'dosh to connect her point. He clearly didn't. "We have company."

The subordinate looked again at the screen. "Is it an ally?"

Y'marda stared at the small male for a moment, genuinely worried the bipedal body was straining his brain. She said with the utmost, condescending certainty, "No. There's no chance of that, because the mere presence of even a single other would undermine our mission. No, I see two possibilities." She rose from her seat and headed back down the hall from which he had come. Y'dosh followed dutifully. "Either someone is here without knowledge that we are, which seems the likelier scenario given that we've had no contact. Or someone is here, to contest us." She pushed open the door to the bedroom, revealing the four dead bodies of the family that had once called the apartment home. "It is likely that this is the source of our anomaly. Whether it is or not, whether they are here independent of us or in spite of us – perhaps even to spite us – they jeopardize our mission and we cannot allow that."

"I agree, it seems impossible that this isn't the source of the disturbances we've been monitoring," concluded Y'dosh. He stepped around her, crossing over the bloody arm of the slain father. "If it was one of us, it would not register as an anomaly. Our sensors would recognize it." He approached the largest collector yet they had set up, this one the size of a small automobile and taking up most of the room. A green crystal faced into the corner of the room, tilted up only slightly. He placed his hand over the crystal and it began to hum. "If our...counterpart, desires to be involved in the actions of the locals, or worse if it IS a local, it signals a gap in our intelligence."

"Or maybe now, perhaps we can track it," insisted Y'marda. She looked down on the bodies as nuisance and nothing more. "We're days out."

"Between eleven and nine, I believe," said Y'dosh absently as he studied the noise and light given off from the crystal. He removed his hand and looked at the bodies, unable to disregard them as casually as she had.

"We must finish preparing," she said as she departed. "And we must deal with this interloper."

"Slower than a crowded bus," Kate muttered to herself as she stared out the window. "Less powerful than a person with self-control," she went on, staring at the street passing by. "Able to leap to insane and depressing conclusions in a single bound." Kate's eyes shifted and she wasn't looking at the street but her own transparent reflection in the window. "Up in the sky. It's a nerd, it's a skank, it's—"

A shout came from the back of the bus.

Kate's head whirled around, afraid of the violence she knew she'd see. Instead of a fight, instead of abuse, however, she only saw a collection of guys being way too loud. Boisterous as they were, they were laughing harmlessly. If anything, they were spreading smiles because of their loud stupidity. Kate turned back around, wondering what it said about her that the instant she heard a loud shout, she thought of violence. She looked at herself in the window and sighed, disappointed at her reflection.

Several boxes were under Kate's arm as she sat on the bus. Marked and ready for mail, all they needed was postage. To Kate, though, they weren't boxes but dreams. They were weeks and months of hard work. The top box, an old cosplay of Cammy from Street Fighter II, Kate had made the costume for almost a hundred dollars. Now, the leotard, beret, and gloves, was going for less than half that. That was the cost of the materials only. She had no dollar value to apply to the hours spent putting it together.

The boxes in the seat next to her, Kate let the rumble of the bus send her into a dull numbness. She looked out at the afternoon and the cars that passed them by. Autonomous adults, capable of traveling at their own speed, in their own direction, on their own time. Once, not too long ago, Kate had been able to do that. Then she'd torn the door off her own car. So much for responsible. Now she traveled when the bus allowed, and only departed when it permitted.

The entire walk from the bus stop to the post office weighed on her. She saw so many people and they were mysteries to her. A mother with three kids in tow, on a school day. An old man listening to a decade-old iPod. Two middle-aged guys talking with laughs as they walked briskly passed her. She wondered about each of them, as they fixed in her mind like stars by which she was navigating an unknown course. They were backgrounds in the comic book of her life, but they no doubt had their own lives. To them, she was the background character, drawn hastily and without much regard. She tried to fathom how two stories could exist in the same place, at the same time.

Up a sloped parking lot, Kate carried the small stack of boxes to the post office. A long line waited for her and Kate sighed. She set the boxes on the counter of the slow-moving line and pulled out her phone. She began scrolling through email after email. Most were messages from social media, most of those were solicitations or lewd suggestions. A couple of emails were from applications she'd put in at new jobs. Everything from same-but-different retail options to pie-in-the-sky real careers, her resume blitz hadn't been discerning. Nor, it turned out, fruitful.

Each step Kate took towards the line to mail away her hard work, sell the fruit of her labor, was another rejection. Everything from form rejection letters to thinly-veiled hate mail for her audacity to apply for a job she clearly wasn't qualified for, it was all sprinkled in among the sexual harassment and backhanded compliments of how impressive her cosplays were for an amateur.

There was that word again.

Kate waited as the customer argued with the register worker over a difference in cost less than a dollar. An anger welled up in her. It was bad enough this man was mailing $20 worth of stuff and nitpicking over a few quarters, it was worse that he was inconveniencing her. She might have places to be. She didn't, not that it mattered, but she might. And that she didn't have such places to be also made her mad.

The guy behind the register gave up and surrendered the difference. Kate watched as he popped open the register and handed over the coins. The customer seemed dissatisfied at the quick surrender but all Kate could see was the stack of $1s, $5s, and $20s. How easy it would be to just tear the machine right off the counter. She could rip it open with her bare hands. And that tray probably held more money than she'd ever made in a single month.

This led her to turn and look out the windows of the post office. Across the street was a bank, like a dozen others within a mile of her. How hard would it be to get into the vault? Or maybe even just one of the window tellers? Or she could bypass the human element entirely. The ATM was right there. She could probably tear out the money and nobody even see her on camera.

"Miss?"

Kate turned around and the overworked and underpaid register guy waved her over. He didn't have the strength or interest to even smile as he asked, "Can I help you?"

She looked down at the boxes in her hands, containing cosplay from across her career, that she was now selling for less than a hundred dollars each. It took more strength than it would to lift a car for her to lift those packages onto the counter. "I'd like to mail these please," she said sadly, handing over the collection.

At the mid-day meeting, Kate zoned out on Walter's speech that customer satisfaction was their utmost priority. The man paced around the circle blocking the entrance to the stock room while Kate stared into the distance.

One of the stock guys walked by, laborers who never went out onto the floor after the store opened, so they didn't need to wear the uniform. A man in jeans and a heavy hoodie, he wore baseball shin pads that covered his knees and insteps. Kate watched him walk from one side of the group to the other. In that span of time, she imagined a dozen different cosplays around the armored guards.

She imagined a cosplay of Yugo from Battle Angela Alita. It was obscure but still visually dynamic, so that die-hard Yukito Kishiro fans would go crazy but casual geeks would see a cool post-apocalyptic get-up. It was the kind of thing that wouldn't amaze anyone but it would lend some more weight to her (hopefully already considerable) nerd cred and also would help her stretch her--

Everybody started in. Startled, Kate stepped forward instinctively, drawn into the huddle. The gathered workers put their hands into a big mass. "On three," Walter said, like he was a football coach and his team were made up of the most disinterested people in the world. "One, two, three, CUSTOMER SERVICE!" He yelled and absolutely nobody else yelled with him.

Kate followed the others as they filed back into the store. The melancholy from earlier was settling into her bones, becoming comfortable with laying over her thoughts like a poisonous snow. She headed towards the unmentionables section but was joined in step by Derek. "Hey," he said with the goofy awkwardness of a nerdy puppy. "So, some friends of mine are having an asteroid viewing party this weekend," he said. "You want to come? BYOB."

Kate didn't hear about a party or the chance to be around people. All she thought was the price of a six-pack of beer. That cost wouldn't make a difference in the monthly bills, but it would add up with a thousand other expenses. "I can't," she said, trying to smile and failing. She left him at the entrance to the toy section. She headed to work, the gloomy cloud of dying alone in ignominy in welfare hospital spread over her every thought.

That night, riding the bus home, Kate was alone. The usual passengers she saw periodically were absent, leaving her alone near the back of the bus, far removed from the driver. She preferred it that way. She wanted to be a specter, a ghost, some incorporeal thing that couldn't be touched. Couldn't be felt. Couldn't feel.

She stared out the window as the bus stopped at a traffic light, a long ride ahead of her. Kate stared through the window, her forehead leaned against the cold glass. Every breath clouded the window a bit, then the opaqueness receded. Outside, she saw an ATM in between two stores along the downtown street. Kate thought about all the money inside and the plastic frame between her and that money. She looked down at her hands and remembered the tremendous strength within. She looked at the ATM and sighed very slowly.

How wrong would it be?

Thinking that way, though, made her think of the militia men she'd fought. She remembered literally throwing them about like they were little more than heavy dolls. She remembered the way they'd gone flying, the way they'd crumpled and collapsed, and then didn't move again. She remembered the way Denise's upstairs neighbor's boyfriend had just sort of bent when she'd shoved him.

The bus kicked into motion and started to take Kate away from the ATM. She was grateful to have the temptation out of sight. It wasn't out of mind.

There was a morose clarity in the late night.

When the world had gone dark and silent, Kate felt like she could think better. She had her closet doors pushed open and she was staring into the clothes. She picking the next costumes to be parted with. The current contenders to be rehomed were three different Harley Quinn costumes, a Sailor Moon school uniform outfit, and a Wonder Woman costume that simply didn't work for anyone over a C-cup.

Kate walked backwards from her closet, walking into view of her reflection in the sliding mirror doors. She looked at herself in the mirror, the room lit only by a single lamp on the floor. Kate looked at herself, really looked. Without any makeup, the lines on her face were evident. Her hair was messy and her shoulders were slumped forward from the weight of her worries.

Looking at her reflection, unadorned and unmasqueraded, she began to cry. She looked at the costumes she'd selected, vividly remembering the construction of each. She remembered the inspiration, purchasing the materials, staying up late to build them, the messes she'd made, the lessons she'd learned. So clear were they in her mind. They were children to her, the cornerstone of her life, a treasured snapshot of who she had been in that moment.

She backed up to her bed and sat down, her crying turning pronounced. She grabbed a pillow and pulled it close, curling into a ball on the bed. She pushed her face into the pillow and didn't fight it. She sobbed into the night, declaring over and over through tear-warped words, "I want to go home!"

CHAPTER THIRTEEN

Kate pushed the eggs out of the pan, unbothered by the scraps of the metal spatula or that she was adding to the collection of scratches on the pan from previous bad mornings. She'd slept poorly and it showed. She was focusing on her bland, healthy breakfast, not really thinking about the world outside her own grouch.

Banal breakfast on the banal plate for the banal morning, Kate passed around the divider into the living room. She joined her grandmother in the recliners and ate quietly. The food disappeared quickly until she heard Deloris say, "Such a shame."

Kate looked up, a little surprised the world still existed. She was more surprised her grandmother wasn't focused on her iPad for once. "What's a shame, Nana?" she asked.

"These poor people," said Deloris, gesturing with the remote at the TV. On the screen, an on-the-scene reporter was bringing up reports about some person. At the bottom of the screen, the title read 'Burn Victim Ruled Suicide'.

A strange sense of prescience washed over Kate as the screen switched to firemen lowered down a wrapped body, covered in heavy gray blankets like some kind of mummy. The two men in yellow and black were carrying the body down the steep ladder, descending into a crowd of their brethren. "What happened?" Kate asked, an uneasy chill going down her spine.

"Some person was driving, to work I assume, early this morning," her grandmother conveyed to her. "They saw what looked like a torch or you know, up on a building." She waved her hand high, almost as if she meant to signify fanning a flame. "But when the police responded, apparently this poor soul had decided to take her own life." Seeing the on-the-scene reporter returning to the screen, Deloris unmuted the TV.

"This is the second such suicide in as many days," said the reporter, brushing back dyed blonde hair as a morning breeze buffeted her, disrupting the audio in her microphone. "Officials fear for copycats and others attempting to follow suit, but as of right now, no known reason is given why these people thought to take their own life, much less in this dramatic fashion."

Kate's gaze narrowed, fixated on 'ruled suicide' on the bottom of the news screen. "Something's not right," she said.

"Something is never right if a person is so messed up inside that they'd take their own life," said Deloris. "Life is too precious to be so selfish with it." Kate opted not to engage her grandmother on the matter. She went for her phone and began to compose a text to her three friends.

Kate wrote: 'Check the news. 'Burn victim ruled suicide'? Seems suspicious to me. Maybe just me, but I think something's up. Text/email me. Conference call when I'm on break'.

She sent the email and looked at the news. The dead person was already being forgotten as the news went back to the studio to talk about this weekend's sports match-up. Kate grew even more upset at the way they moved on, but the news gave her drive. She set about finishing her morning.

Kate preferred to travel without her phone out. She enjoyed the rare moment of digital silence in a connected world, but today was different. She was scrolling through social media, not for validation but for news. Thankfully, the bus wifi was working reasonably well for once. It was never terribly quick, but it had a tendency to be very buggy and often not even work at all. Today, though, it seemed to be working well enough. Kate sat near her usual seat, bent forward as she read over news reports on her phone.

Glancing occasionally to make sure she knew where they were on the bus route and how many more stops she had until work, she combed over every outlet she could find, trying to collate any and all details.

With some direction, Kate powered through the morning. With her mind miles away and up a building rather than fixated inwardly, she hung new bras, sorted the panties, and fielded questions with barely a thought. The rush of opening customers weren't people she interacted with or nuisances she addressed but merely so much background noise as her mind fixated singularly on the burn victim, being carried down the ladder by the firemen. Yet the rush ended and the day began to drag.

Rich turned in the mirror and put his lips out, turning to the side so he could see how the bra fit over his blue work shirt. He turned further, contorting and putting a finger to his lip. Behind him, Derek shared his appraisal of the look with, "Meh. It's not you."

"You need something with pastels," said Kate, both of them at the register, watching the electronics expert study himself in the mirror.

"I'm just saying, women have nicer underwear than guys," Rich insisted. He flailed to unclasp the bra behind his back but couldn't manage.

"I'm not saying no, but I am saying we definitely pay for it," said Kate, coming to his aid and helping him unhook the training bra.

"What do you mean?" he asked. He turned the lacy straps in his hand to find the price tag. "How much is OH MY GOD!" His eyes nearly bulged out of his head at the numbers.

"Yeah, and this isn't even that nice of a bra," she said, taking it from him and returning it to its hanger.

Walter announced himself with his usual friendly demeanor, by practically barking, "Guys, what are you doing over here?" The assistant manager butted right in. "You're supposed to be in electronics."

"Dude, there's literally no one in the store," said Rich, still shopping for a new bra to try on. "Not exaggerating. Literally no one."

"Yeah, you think anybody wants to go shopping when an asteroid is going to destroy the world in a week?" asked Derek, right between Rich and Kate as to how intimidated he was by Walter.

"It's not..." Walter groaned. He looked at Kate. "And you should not be allowing them to mess with the products."

"By law, if they want to try on a bra, they have every right," Kate asserted, still hanging the bra on its hanger.

Walter turned to Rich and looked indignant. "How I dress under my uniform is my business," Rich told him simply, still casually shopping. He began to turn and pull down his pants. "Although, do you want to see my thong?"

"That's inappropriate," Walter told Rich. "I could write you up for that."

Rich snickered. "Go right ahead, man."

When failing at being commanding finally registered, Walter stepped forward, feigning some effort to be intimidating. "I don't appreciate insubordination."

"I don't appreciate your Draconian, fun-killing vibe," Rich said back without any hesitation. "My sales are up, our section carries the store," he said with a nod to Derek. "But please, tell me where you're going to find an electrical engineer that'll work for $11 an hour."

"We don't need an electrical engineer," Walter told Rich.

Rich went from problematic to pissed in a flash. He took a step towards Walter, causing the assistant manager to backup half a step. "That's how you want to play this?"

"Rich," Walter started, simultaneously warning him and trying to calm him down.

"No, let's go talk to Candice right now," Rich practically yelled, his voice reaching the roof and half the store. He didn't wait for Walter's reaction and stormed passed him, heading towards the general manager's office at the front of the store.

Walter's face was pale and his hands visibly clammy as he turned to follow. He started to do the walk, but told Derek, "Get back to your section." He added a glare at Kate, along with, "Get back to work."

Derek watched them disappear across the store towards the front office with a heavy sigh. He feared aloud, "Rich is gonna get himself fired."

"I think he wants to be," said Kate, organizing a rack of underwear by color. "It feeds his martyr complex." Derek agreed wordlessly and headed off. He was almost out of the section when Kate called, "Do you really think the asteroid is going to hit?"

The big nerd only shrugged. "I honestly dunno. I seen people saying it. It looks more and more likely." A chill of fear was shared by them and they said no more.

"Hey, wakey-wakey," said Rachael.

Kate was startled and whirled around to discover Rachael and Emily behind her. She glanced at the time on the register in her section, not quite able to connect the numbers with the time they meant. "What are you doing here?"

"You weren't answering your phone," said Emily.

"I can't bring it onto the floor with me," she said reflexively, off-kilter from her cosplay friends at her dayjob. "I thought we were..." She checked the time again, as if she couldn't process where in the day she was at that moment.

"Well, can you go on break or something?" Rachael asked. "We're going to call Denise – she's going on break shortly – and we can pow-wow about this suicide stuff."

"Yeah, Rach doesn't think it's suicide," Emily said, getting a 'hush' from Rachael.

Kate nodded and said, "I'll meet you in the snack area in, like, five minutes."

"'Kay," Rachael nodded, she and Emily departing.

Kate broke away from her section and crossed to the home furnishings where she found Walter extolling the virtues of color-coordinating the lids of the plastic containers in the storage aisle. Max, the storeroom clerk, looked so bored, he was offended. "Hey, Walter, I need to go on break."

The assistant manager glanced back at her, surprised to be interrupted. "What? You can't go on break. You just went."

Kate was confused. "No I didn't."

Walter checked his expensive-looking wristwatch. "You've been here more than three hours. You take your break at two hours." Kate still didn't quite follow. "You need to wait until your lunch."

"By federal and state law," said Max, "she can't miss a break and she's required to take it."

"Yes, but she missed it and it's her responsibility to keep up with them," Walter told him authoritatively. "If she works during her break, that's her decision."

"Against the law," Max maintained casually.

"It is not," Walter snapped, growing angry at being contradicted.

Kate didn't have the time or the energy or the interest or the loyalty, so she slipped away and headed for the snack section at the corner nearest the entrance. She took off her work shirt, crossing the store in khakis and a black tanktop. She arrived at the glorified vending machine that was the store's snack stop, offering soda bottles, bagged chips, and for a few hours a day, hot pretzels. Kate joined her friends in the farthest booth just as Rachael said, "Okay, Denise, Kate's here."

"Hey Kate," said Denise by way of Rachael's phone on speaker.

"Hey," Kate said, the three girls crowding around the phone in the middle of the table in the corner of the empty snack station near the front of the store. "So listen, this suicide thing is—"

"It's not suicide," Denise interrupted.

Kate blinked. "What?" she asked into the phone.

"That suicide thing is bull," said Denise.

"Yeah, she's right," Rachael nodded with absolute certainty. "The first one was ruled suicide because the victims were found really high up, on top of a crane. The police decided there was no way they could be forced up there, so they had to do it voluntarily."

"Which is bull," Denise repeated, her voice giving out occasionally over their weak connection. "Once, maybe, I could see. Maybe. But twice? In two nights? Come on." The conversation fell into a nervous hush.

"Is there any other explanation besides the one we're all hesitant to say aloud?" Emily asked, mostly at Rachael. Silence. "Okay then," Emily nodded before looking at Kate. "I think you've got company." Kate swallowed as thoughts of stairwells, blue liquid, and pain flashed through her mind. She clinched her eyes but refused to let her emotions sweep her away. "Whatever gave you...whatever did this to you, it must have done it to others," Emily proposed.

"So what does that mean?" Kate asked distantly, her eyes still closed. She remembered tiny metal nails. She remembered droplets of blue beading out on flesh. The memories with no source chilled her and made her sweat simultaneously

"So...if someone has super powers, and they're killing people, then they're supervillains," Emily reasoned. She looked leadingly at Kate.

"We've got to stop them," Kate resolved. The looks on Emily and Rachael's face told her where that burden would primarily be placed. With a deep exhale, she asked, "How do I find them?"

"Guys?" Denise called.

"Hey, we're here, we were just ignoring you," Rachael said into her phone.

"Bitch."

"We're trying to think of how to stop these supervillains that are doing this," summarized Emily.

"Oh, you guys think they're supervillains too?" Denise asked, her voice crackling over the reception. "Well, if they're setting a person on fire every night, then clearly they're trying to get someone's attention. So they're looking for someone or something. So if they want to be found, all we've got to do is scour the rooftops and they'll find us."

"Me," Kate said with a quake in her voice. She looked at Emily and Rachael and said, "They'll find me." She swallowed and looked down at her hands. Her fingers were trembling. In fact, almost all of her was trembling. "Let's get together tonight. The suit needs repairs and, and…" She nearly crumbled into her own fear.

"Yeah," Rachael agreed.

Emily took Kate's hand and didn't try to stop the shaking so much as share it. Kate clutched her hand in return and smiled. In the back of her mind, all she could think of was 'I want to go home'.

When Kate opened the door, she found her mother and grandmother on their iPads, barely aware of the news on the TV, or anything of the world beyond them. "Hey, guys," Kate said, practically rushing in. She tugged off her over-shirt as she said, "I've got to meet with Denise. We're doing a quick photo shoot for a, uh, a charity event."

Lauren looked over the chair at her and asked, "Any bids on some costumes?" She tried to sound conversational, encouraging.

The reminder brought Kate to a screeching halt. She froze for a second, her back to her mother. She clamped her eyes shut and resolved not to get upset. She was just a step away from her room, too. "Yeah," she said unevenly. She turned around to her mom as she fished her phone out from her purse. She checked her balance and said, "I can go by an ATM or just write you a check."

Lauren seemed genuinely surprised by the response. "How much did you get?"

Kate started to say, then handed her phone to her mom. Lauren had to find her reading glasses, then looked down her nose at the digital screen. "And it's how much I'm getting," Kate clarified with the present-tense. "This is just the first half. I'll get the other half of the money on receipt of delivery."

Lauren took off her glasses and couldn't make eye contact, born of equal parts shame and relief. She gave a smile meant for her daughter and said quietly, "I'm sorry to ask it."

"What is she selling?" asked Deloris, finally looking up from her game.

"The check will work great," Lauren told Kate. "I can deposit it on my way to work tomorrow. If we get the payment in before 8am, we can probably avoid the late charges."

"What's she selling?" Deloris asked again.

Lauren leaned around Kate to tell her, "She's selling some of her costumes." Kate's grandmother looked mortified.

"No, it's fine," Kate lied with a convincing smile. "My closet's a little too full anyway." She dashed into her room as she added, "It'll be cathartic to get rid of some of these." She shut her door, and then collapsed against it, about to burst into tears. She slipped down the door, feeling like a volcano about to erupt. "I want to go home," she sobbed once.

Suddenly, she slapped herself. A vicious red mark on her cheek, she glared aggressively forward. "I don't have time for this," she said tearfully before she forced herself back up to her feet. She quickly set about changing into workout clothes, trying to anticipate the night's events.

Just before she began to undress, she froze. She went back out into the living room, neither her mom or grandmother looking up from their games. Kate opened her backpack and retrieved a tray of store-brand oatmeal raisin cookies.

She handed the cookies to her grandmother. When the octagenarian didn't look up from her game, Kate slid them into view. Deloris was startled by their appearance, but once she recognized the treat, she beamed, her heart melting. "Oh honey," she whispered with pride and gratitude. Kate tried to take what consolation from it she could, the burning pain of selling her costumes as well as the financial need that necessitated it still eating a hole inside her.

"I love you, Nana," Kate told her grandmother with strange finality. She gave her a kiss on the gray hair, then repeated the sentiment and gesture with her mom. Back into her room she went with urgency. Lauren watched her   go,   worry   on   her   brow.

Kate landed on the yellow metal supports of the crane high above the city. Her double-sided cape flapping in the brisk urban wind, she looked down on the lights of the city, of the passing cars and the neon glow of the stores far below. The wind whipped around her, but her helmet protected her from much of the sound.

In her ear, the Blu-tooth headset connected her to her friends who sat in Denise's apartment, all crowded on the couch, their laptops open. "Okay, nothing on the police scanners," Rachael said into her cell phone, once again on speaker and placed equidistance between all three women.

"There's a candlelight vigil at a church in the Palms," Denise said, scanning the news streams. She slurped on a smoothie, making Kate wince at the noise over her headset. "Other than that, I don't see anything."

Rachael glanced to Emily and saw her watching a YouTube video. She reached over to slap her, then saw a kitten and an otter playing. She leaned over to watch it too, smiling. Denise glanced over and saw them, then reached over and swatted Emily's hands. She glared at them both.

"I don't see anything," Kate was saying over the handless phone line. "I'm not sure what I'm supposed to be looking for," she said. "I mean, how are they supposed to find me and how am I supposed to—"

There she was.

Kate didn't know how she missed her or likewise how she saw her, but she suddenly saw the woman across the spanning distance of downtown. Nothing more than a speck, the nigh-human-looking woman was somehow

210

clear as day across the distance. "Got her," Kate said as she pushed off the crane and began to soar through the air across the downtown city.

"Got who?" Rachael asked.

"I see the person," Kate said, her hands forward as the wind coursed passed her.

"How do you know it's them?" asked Emily.

Kate hedged in response, but decided to trust her instincts. "It is." She glanced down and reported, "I'm flying towards the bank building downtown." Rachael looked to Emily and mouthed 'Call the police'. Emily nodded and got up from the couch.

Kate drew close and saw Y'marda in the black suit, her arms crossed over her strong body. Kate flew over the side of the rooftop and landed slowly, her feet crunching on the white gravel. Determined to make a strong first impression, she put her fists on her waist, striking the best Christopher Reeve/Superman pose she could.

Y'marda turned her head a bit, looking over Kate like she was surveying a fallen wheel. The first thing the woman said was, "You can fly." It seemed almost a derision, like she was mocking Kate out of a mixture of jealousy and disbelief.

"Are you..." Kate stopped her question when she realized how muffled her voice was due to her helmet. "Are you the one murdering these people?" she repeated, speaking loudly. She worried about the volume hurting her friends' ears but if it did, they didn't speak up.

Y'marda smirked on the left side of her almost-human face, the right side enigmatically motionless. Just over the cliff into the Uncanny Valley, there was something eerie about her, something unsettling in her near-perfect appearance. "And you're female. How..." Her words failed her. Her eyes took on a look of vicious intensity. "Who sent you? How are you here?"

Kate felt her knees get weak. She was trembling. The woman's gaze was terrifying. Had she not had a mask to hide behind, Kate was sure she would have run. "I'm here to stop these killings," she yelled instead. 'Killings' was warped by her voice cracking. Kate winced, clamping her eyes shut in humiliation. Across her blu-tooth feed, the three friends looked worriedly at one another, likewise scared what that flash of weakness betrayed.

Y'marda seemed unsurprised by the vocal betrayal. "Who sent you?" she asked again, stepping forward. Her feet crunched the pebbles beneath her heavy step. Kate immediately stepped back defensively, her hands coming up in her best Shaw Brothers kung fu pose. The woman grew angry. "I asked you a question, thing. Answer me."

"I'm here on my own," Kate told her defiantly. "And you're not going to hurt anyone else."

"Good line," Denise whispered supportively over the phone. Kate's three friends were clustered close, as if proximity to the phone was the next best thing to being there for their friend.

Y'marda was noticeably less impressed. "Worry not for others, only yourself." She stepped forward and grabbed Kate's jacket by the front of the collar, wrenching it tight. Kate shrieked and grabbed her hands but the woman hoisted Kate into the air with one arm and slammed her onto the rooftop. The entire surface shook violently at impact and partitions beneath their feet gave underway. Whole sections of the roof ruptured and cracked as the ceiling bowed in. A great groan came from beneath Kate in the crater of her impact. Y'marda knelt down atop Kate, pinning her to the ground with her knee, her hand still on her chest. "The spoils of our strike will not be shared." She grabbed Kate's helmet, bracing to rip it off her head. Or rip of Kate's whole head, she couldn't tell and didn't care to find out. "We have too much at—"

Kate rolled up her legs and wrapped them around the woman's arm. Straightening her body suddenly, she threw Y'marda away with a powerful thrust. The black-clad woman went sailing back while Kate scrambled to her feet, throwing her cape behind her. Y'marda hit the service access and the wall cracked slightly. Chips of paint crumbled off as Y'marda peeled herself from the impact. She settled a murderous gaze at Kate, inhuman features displaying all too intense emotions. Kate flexed her gloves hands and began to circle the woman.

"Kate, get out of there," Denise warned, only able to hear the fight over the phone. Rachael and Emily both listened, terrified.

Y'marda lunged forward and swung wide at Kate. Kate blocked with her left hand and tried to punch with her right but Y'marda beat her to it, punching Kate in the chest. She gasped in pain worse than the gunshots she'd received as she was knocked to the ground.

Y'marda stomped towards her and drew back again. Kate, from a kneeling posture, kicked up at her foe, catching Y'marda in the stomach. She bent forward like she'd been struck with a battering ram and Kate came at her with a sloppy punch that still hit in the jaw with enough force to knock Y'marda cleanly off her feet.

Kate panted as she watched the woman get up from the punch, more dazed than meaningfully hurt. "Guys, get online, find me a karate school now."

"Yeah, we'll get right on that. RUN!" Rachael yelled into the phone.

Y'marda charged Kate and barreled into her. The two women fell over the edge of the building and went careening toward the ground below. Kate screamed for only a second before the woman punched her in the chest. Holding onto her jacket, Y'marda punched Kate again and again, battering her the whole way down as they fell story after story.

With a terrible crash, the two collided with a squat municipal building across the street. Falling almost twenty stories, they crashed through the roof, blowing wide papers and debris as the fragments of ceiling were splintered beneath them. Kate rolled onto her stomach, howling in pain, but the woman was already standing like the fall had been only a momentary distraction. Standing over the reeling Kate, Y'marda stamped her foot down on Kate's head.

The first kick slammed the helmet hard into the floor. The second kick to her back drove Kate's chest full-force into the floor. She only managed a cough, in too much pain to scream. The third strike was a kick to the side, right into her stomach. Kate screamed for fear that her spine had snapped. Y'marda drew up her foot for a fourth kick but Kate grabbed her leg with one hand and, like she was tossing a pillow, threw the woman into the nearest wall.

"Kate, run!" Rachael yelled into the phone.

"Fuck no!" Kate growled, stalking towards Y'marda. "Fuck this bitch!" She stormed over as Y'marda was getting up. She turned towards Kate, just in time to get punched back down into the floor. Kate knelt down over the woman and grabbed the back of her hair and slammed her face-first into the floor, cracking the cement underlayer. She pulled Y'marda's head up, blood draining from her nose. "I don't know who you think you—"

The woman backhanded Kate. She was sent sailing over desks and debris before she slammed into the wall. Kate fell hard onto the floor, collapsing into a fetal ball. Inside the helmet, she coughed, blood dribbling out from inside of her mask. Across the office, Y'marda rose, furious. She dabbed at her nose, seeing the blood pouring out of her wounds. She staggered at the sight, like the concept of internal damage was an utter impossibility. Her eyes huge with intelligence and malignancy slid off the blood and onto Kate. She screamed madly, "I'll not tolerate a whelp like you, a spasm of matter, upstaging me in my moment of triumph!"

Kate scoffed as she got to her feet. "Please, like I haven't heard that shit before." She swung for Y'marda but she blocked it like a veteran dissuading a novice and punched Kate in the face. Her entire helmet caved in a little and Kate was thrown back into the wall. The woman punched Kate in the chest, then came around the other side to hit her in the ribs. She followed with a close elbow that knocked Kate loopy. She staggered for half a second and then dropped deliriously to her knees.

Y'marda pinned Kate's shoulders to the wall and she struck with a knee to Kate's chest, a loud crack issuing from her sternum. "I will—"

Kate punched her in the groin. The woman howled suddenly and stumbled back, her hands between her knees. Kate leapt at the woman and slammed into her much like she'd done atop a different building and, picking her up off her feet, went charging at the wall.

Unceremoniously, the exterior wall over the street burst outwards like a pimple rupturing. Brick, drywall, and other debris came spewing out into the air, falling into the street, causing cars to go screeching onto the sidewalk and into each other in a futile attempt to avoid calamity. Kate and the woman both slammed hard into the pavement, cracking it and sending it rupturing to the sidewalk. The handful of people out at that hour all backed away in shock as the two figures rose again to their feet.

Y'marda, bleeding worse now and from more than her face, punched Kate in the head, the helmet doing little to dampen the blow. Kate returned the punch to the jaw but it did little more than turn Y'marda's head. She kicked Kate in the side and, without putting her foot down, kicked again and knocked Kate back. Kate managed to stay standing, skidding across the ground until she came to a stop a few dozen meters back. Once she stopped, she called, "Guys, what do I do?"

Only silence.

"Guys?!" Kate yelled into her blu-tooth headset. There was no response. The disassociation from her friends transformed the fight and reminded Kate of the outside world.

A new form of fear hit Kate and she backed away. Y'marda stormed right at Kate, ready for murder. Kate nearly succumbed to terror but at the last second, lifted into the air. "NO!" screamed Y'marda in madness as Kate soared higher, leaving her foe behind. The almost-woman watched as Kate disappeared into the nighttime sky overhead, retreating into the heavens.

CHAPTER FOURTEEN

Y'dosh was working on a central collector. The device wedged between his knees, he was consulting a floating display projected from his forearm. He turned a circular control on the side of the floating interface, counter-clockwise first, and then twisting it along the Z-axis. At the same time, the display changed from a light green to a deep orange. The wave pattern on the screen remained mostly the same, with a few variances. He looked puzzled for a second and tapped a few commands on the bottom of the screen. The variance grew and he was further confused. He kicked back in the recliner of the dark apartment and stared at the screen, trying to ponder through the curiosity.

The apartment door burst open, causing Y'dosh to toss the collector into the air. He frantically grabbed at it, missing it a few times before he finally snatched it safely out of the air, just before it fell passed him on the left side. Panting fearfully, he looked as Y'marda slammed the door shut, utterly furious. "What happened?" he asked. "Is she—" The alien punched the wall, caving the drywall and knocking pictures of the now-deceased owners onto the floor. Glass shattered and the frames broke, to which she was indifferent and oblivious. Y'dosh remarked benignly, "I take it the anomaly still lives."

"Not only lives, thrives!" Y'marda roared, panting she was in such a frothing rage. She whirled around to Y'dosh. "She can fly. What we saw was true. She has no means of conveyance." Her fury overrode her ability to speak, causing her words to stammer. "It is not some technological marvel existing here beyond the confines of the regular populace. She can elevate herself into the air without effort! Without thought!"

Y'dosh's confused look slowly drained into worry. "That's…not possible."

Y'marda scoffed at his logical mind. "She would seem evidence to the contrary," she growled. She paced angrily, nearly spinning as she reached the ends of the room. Her hands shook with madness. "And her strength. She is…she is far beyond what we had hoped for ourselves when we arrived."

"Where is she from?" asked Y'dosh. "Who sent her here? Or placed her?"

Y'marda shook her head, mad in every sense. She spun on a heel and started back around, then slowed. She reached halfway through her pacing when she came to a full stop. Anger warped in disgust. "I…I suspect she is from here." Again shock overtook Y'dosh. "Yes," she reasoned almost frantically, unaware of Y'dosh's horror. "Yes, that is all I can think of." Y'marda sneered with disdain and hate. "She had no grasp of who I was or what I asked of her. And she seemed terribly fixated on the locals and their well-being." She laughed with anger, boiling towards rage. "She confronted me to avenge the deaths of those we'd slain!" She didn't speak, she mocked.

Y'dosh only shook his head, unable to grasp what his superior was saying. "She cannot be local. She cannot be indigenous."

"Far-fetched, though it seem, I see no other likely explanation," said the woman.

Y'dosh laughed hysterically. "Then we must report her!"

Now it was Y'marda who laughed, a sickly, cynical chuckle at her subordinate. "We are here as outlaws!" she told the smaller man. "Need I remind you? We shall not go running to the universe and let them know we've found an anomaly. That would set back plans far above our lives. Far beyond our lifetimes. Ten thousand years have been planned for our mission. And our success is but a step in the larger, true plan." She again scoffed, disappointed in Y'dosh's lack of propriety. "Those that matter –

actually matter – count on us to fulfill our duties so that true success can be achieved where it really counts."

Y'dosh persisted, nearly pleading with Y'marda. "Think not of our plan. If the local population shows any signs of real intelligence, or just the first indications of it, then we cannot proceed."

"An anomaly is hardly a sign of intelligence!" Y'marda shouted.

"Yes it is!" he exclaimed back at her. "Think of the implications! Even an aberration can be an indication of the direction evolution is going. If one – even one – upon this planet shows even a spark of intelligence then we must abort our—"

Y'marda grabbed Y'dosh by the throat and slammed him into the wall. The entire apartment building seemed to shake at his impact as she clamped her fist tight on his throat. "We will do," she seethed violently, "No. Such. Thing." She released Y'dosh with a thrust, tossing him to the floor. "And I'll not tolerate a single mention again of such cowardice."

Y'dosh recovered on his hands and knees. "And what if we go through with our plan?" He looked up at Y'marda, submissive but his resolve unchanged. "What if she is affected like us?" This did concern Y'marda and she looked sternly at the man. "She will not only alert all the universe – by her sheer existence alone – but she will mortally undermine the goals we were sent here to further."

Y'marda was quiet. Her gaze drifted away as she thought through a thousand scenarios. She finally asked, "How long have we?"

"Days," Y'dosh reported with an imprecise gesture. "Less than a hundred hours."

Y'marda nodded, deep in thought. "Then we must resolve this matter before the event."

"You would kill the anomaly?" he asked.

Y'marda glared at him. "I will pluck a weed from a garden, so that our crop may flourish."

"I want to go home," Kate whispered quietly as she huddled on her bed.

Still dressed in her costume, the cape draped half over her almost like a blanket, she hugged her knees to her chest. She sobbed against the fabric, streams of tears dribbling down the sides of her legs and pooling on her bed. She peeked up at the Superman poster across the room from her and glowered at it. "I'm a coward," she whimpered. "I ran away, oh GOD!" she sobbed louder, then swallowed it. She began to hyperventilate, trying frantically to control her volume. The ugly crying continued until somebody knocked on her window.

Kate shrieked and dove against the far side of her bed, scrambling over her blankets and pillows in a startled panic. She froze, even holding her breath, only to hear a light rapping on her window again. She crawled over to the window and very carefully parted two of the blinds to see Rachael, Emily, and Denise outside her door. Kate clamped her eyes shut and whimpered, "Leave me alone."

"We saw you, honey," Rachael told Kate through the window. "Don't make me knock on the door and wake your mom."

Panic at the thought of her mother finding out she was moonlighting as a superhero and not working caused Kate's heart to skip a beat. She got up and stormed off her bed, furious that nobody would let her be miserable in peace. She unclasped the cape as she exited her room, rounded the turn into the empty living room late at night and opened the apartment door.

Kate's three friends were looking right at her. Kate looked at them and just got it over with. "I ran away."

"Yeah, we figured," said Denise. She sort of muscled her way between Emily and Rachael to slip inside. Taking Kate by surprise, Denise hugged her tight. "I was afraid you wouldn't."

Kate did a double-take. "Wh-what?"

"I was afraid you were too proud to run," Denise told her, speaking in hushed tones as Emily carefully shut the door behind her. As the others hugged Kate, grateful she was safe, Denise checked down the hall, making sure no lights were coming from beneath the doors into Kate's mother or grandmother's rooms.

"You thought I was…what?" Kate said, turning back to Denise.

"I was afraid you'd be too proud to run," Denise explained quietly, satisfied the rest of the household slept. "If you got in over your head, I was afraid that you'd be too proud to run and stay when you should get the hell out of there."

"I ran away," Kate practically sobbed at her friend, as if contesting her assertion.

"Guys, guys," Rachael interrupted. She suggested, "Why don't we talk in your bedroom? I don't want to wake up Lauren or Deloris."

All in agreement, the four slipped around the corner for Kate's bedroom. Denise saw the cape on the floor and gathered it up, reprimanding Kate with "Come on, this is serious fabric."

The four women retreated into the clothes-strewn room and Kate shut the door, leaving the four alone. "We still gotta keep it down," she said in a whisper to the others. In the dimness of her room lit by a single lamp on the floor, Kate slid down the door and stared vacantly at her cowardice. "She…she was…"

"Okay, first things first," Rachael said. She unzipped her purse and took from it a small box of fruit snacks. She held the Star Wars-shaped box for Kate to see and then ripped it open. "You did something amazing, honey." She took out a pouch and tossed the box to Kate. Kate caught the box, looked at the pouches inside, and began to tear up again. "Honey, you faced an alien menace that's killing people and gave the bitch what for."

"I ran away," Kate wallowed in disgust.

"You retreated," Emily said. "Running away is giving up, but retreating is a real tactic that the military and stuff uses. You didn't run away."

"Yeah, unless you're giving up," Denise posed at her. She eyeballed Kate. "Are you giving up?"

Kate didn't know what to say. She opened her mouth, unsure of what answer she would give. Before she could, however, Denise looked from her to the poster on her wall. Kate saw her eyes move and followed them to where Superman was looking at her, as if right at her specifically. She looked back at Denise and she was staring expectantly at Kate. All three of them, on her bed, were staring at her. They looked at Superman in the poster, then at Kate. "B-but…" Kate stammered. "My, my mom wants me to sell more of my…"

"It's not like I like the Empire; I hate it, but there's nothing I can do about it right now," Emily quoted at Kate.

"Kate," Rachael told her seriously. "Who else can stop her?"

Kate slowly sighed, sorrow and shame collapsing beneath emotional exhaustion. She looked down at the box of fruit snacks and almost unwillingly withdrew a pouch. She tore it open and selected a piece. Lime green made her smirk with a brief, tiny moment of delight. She looked at her friends and asked, "What do we need to do?" The three went into full support mode.

"For starters, we've got to re-do the suit," Rachael said, finally looking past Kate's emotional turmoil and appraising her physically beaten-up state. "Did she…like, do anything to you? Like shoot lasers or a gun? Did she have claws or something?"

Kate shook her head as she ate the snacks, enjoying them almost against her will. "No, this…" she said, gesturing to the rips and tears on her clothes, "this is all from being tossed around."

Rachael picked up the helmet from beside the bed and studied it for a second. "Reinforcing the helmet won't be too hard. It might take some time, but I know a guy who does armor-shaping for weapons-fighting and stuff. We can use his workshop and make a real combat helmet."

"How much will that cost?" Kate sulked.

Rachael scoffed. "Those boys can make chain link mail out of paper clips but ask them to sew a tabard? Hell, they'll let me use their forge if I just make a new flag for them." She turned the helmet in her hand. "And their helmets are meant to shrug off hits from genuine maces and axes. It should be able to stand up to punches okay."

"Yeah, but will it look as good?" Emily asked, like the aesthetics were a primary consideration. Rachael shrugged, uncertain. She was focused on the work before her, doing a gazllion calculations already.

"It's not just the helmet. We've got to reinforce the whole costume," Denise thought aloud as she studied a torn flap of loose fabric on Kate's arm. "We could do a heavy weave. It would be too heavy for anyone else, but since she can lift half a ton, it shouldn't be too bad."

"Yeah, but that wouldn't be flexible," Kate added. She sniffed but her tears were fading as she lost herself in the logistics of the issue. "Anything strong enough isn't going to be flexible, or breathable." Rachael perked up for a split second before a mischievous grin slowly spread. She fished out her phone, her smile only widening. She sent a quick text which the others noticed. "What's up?" Kate asked.

Rachael began to answer when her phone buzzed. She checked the message and then sent a follow-up text as the others watched. "Sorry," she said quickly. "So, you remember Elliot from the cons? That kinda-skeezy dude who always does Guile and at least one super-saiyan from Dragon Ball Z?"

The others all strained for a second to recall, and then all remembered in unison. "Yeah," they said. They all then sneered like they smelled the same sour milk.

"So, he's got this bolt – a full bolt – of this military-grade, like, super fabric he developed when he was getting his masters or something," Rachael explained. "He was telling me about it at the table at the last con. Anyway, he—" Her phone buzzed again and she checked it, then responded. "Okay, so he's willing to sell it. And he'll same-day it to us. Downside; he wants a lot for it."

"What's a lot?" Denise asked. Rachael showed her the text and Denise did a double-take. "Fuck that."

"And on top of that, he wants a custom picture of the three of you, signed," Rachael added.

"He wants a what?" Kate balked.

"He's a collector and likes having stuff nobody else has," she said. "He won't go showing it off online and stuff, but he wants it." She was smiling like the price tag was a good sign.

"For that much? That stuff's got to be made out of Vibranium or something!" Denise exclaimed.

"When we talked at the con, it did sound like some serious stuff," Rachael acknowledged as she showed Kate and Emily the amount.

"Good lord, I didn't even get that much for more car," Kate lamented.

"Honey, you didn't pay that much for your car when you bought it," said Denise.

"I'm not sure your car was worth that when it was new," Emily said, repulsed at the price tag.

Rachael thought for a moment, as did the others, when she again perked up. She smirked deviously and set about texting. "What?" asked Kate. "What was that? I know that smile."

"That's not a smile," Emily agreed. "That's lips mocking us."

"Hey, Emily, do you still have that blue mandarin dress?" Rachael asked out of the blue, her grin only growing more devious. "You know, the Chinese one you had to wear at your old job?"

"Yeah," she nodded, growing worried as to where the question was coming from.

"Would it fit Denise?" she asked.

"No," Emily said with absolute certainty.

The answer seemed immaterial. "Perfect," said Rachael as she texted.

"Are you texting with Elliot?" asked Kate. "We can't afford that for fabric."

"Yes, and don't worry," Rachael waved off as she giggled at her own ingenuity. "I'm making him a counter-offer." She looked at Kate and one eyebrow cocked up from behind the thick rim of her glasses. "You've submitted a few sets to Cosplay Deviants, right?"

Denise and Emily's jaws both dropped as they looked mortified at Kate. Her face was absolutely flushed with embarrassment as she fixed her eyes straight on the ground. "Y-yeah," she admitted awkwardly, avoiding looking at either of them. "But, I mean, they didn't accept them."

"All the better," said Rachael, finishing her text.

"Oh my god, really?" Emily exclaimed at Kate. "They do nudes!" She whispered the final word like an adult might overhear them.

Kate didn't feel up to defending previous choices. "What are you offering Elliot?" she asked Rachael instead. With a proud smile, Rachael handed over her phone. Kate took one glance at the screen and her eyes flared wide. She read aloud, "How about an erotic photo set with Kate as Cammy and Denise as Chun-Li from Street Fighter II?"

"How about what?!" Denise exclaimed. "I'm doing what?"

"Yeah, Chun-Li's Chinese; that's kind of yellow-face, isn't it?" Emily remarked at Denise.

Denise had a minor conniption. "THAT's the part that jumped out at you?"

"That won't work!" Kate exclaimed, just before the phone buzzed back. Now her jaw dropped. "How many pictures?" she read aloud. She looked stunned at Rachael.

Logistics ruled Rachael's thoughts as she weighed the options. "We're talking a lot of money so I'd say a lot of pictures. Like, at least 80 in the photo set," she advised. Kate looked down at the phone like it was some alien device. Stunned, she wasn't sure what she was doing until she completed the offer and hit send. The three looked at Rachael, almost scared of her. "What can I say?" she shrugged. "Boys can be such easy marks."

The phone chimed again. Kate read aloud in total disbelief, "Deal."

All three women's faces turned towards Rachael, jaws agape. "See?" she told them with a haughty flash of her eyebrows. "Easy marks." To Kate, she said confidently, "Let's get you a new super-suit."

CHAPTER FIFTEEN

Kate smiled as she inwardly wept.

The hippie in every sense of the word said with garlic breath, "Bras are meant as shackles to hold us in bondage." The way she weaved when she said 'bondage' made Kate wonder if that was a good thing or a bad thing in the strange woman's mind. "Boobs are meant to be free, not repressed and averted away, like motherhood denied to the maiden." Kate glanced around, certain she was on a hidden camera show. "Yet because the body was made by a man," the hippie went on, further breaking Kate's brain, "the body cannot support maternity."

Kate regretted it the instant it came out but she wasn't able to stop herself. "What?"

"These are the hours of ill portents," the woman explained to Kate, clutching her dark blue work shirt. "Demons fight for souls while the heavens seek to rain down upon us. The star that was our neighbor has chosen us as a sacrifice!"

"Yeeeeaaaah..." Kate peeled the woman's hands off her collar and said, "Ma'am, if you want help with a fitting, I can do that but otherwise, I'm going to have to ask you to—"

"Ill portents!" the woman exclaimed before she dashed off like a silent film actress.

Kate watched her go before mumbling, "What the holy hell?" She glanced around her section of the store and confirmed it was as empty as always. On the far end of the section were two shoppers, both of whom were avoiding eye contact as they shopped for unmentionables.

Her phone buzzed and Kate slipped it from the cargo pocket of her khaki pants. Rachael had written, asking, "Your head is 22 inches, right?"

Kate grew very worried. She glanced around again to make sure nobody was noticing her and she quickly measured her brow size using her measuring tape. "23 and a half," she wrote back.

"Close enough."

"Why?" Kate wrote. She got no response.

At break, Kate stirred her eggs, seasoned only with salt and a bit of pepper. She ate a cucumber like it was a banana. After taking a crispy bite, she looked at the long green vegetable and wondered how she'd gotten to a point in life where its bland, watery flavor was one of the highlights of her day.

As she chewed, sequestered in the corner of the break room, Kate was joined by two of the cashiers. "What made you say yes?" asked one as she followed her more brazen friend to the refrigerator.

"I figure why not," the woman shrugged with an indifferent look as she fished out a styrofoam lunch plate and a glass bottle. "I figure everybody gonna die soon anyway."

"What?" Kate blurted out. The two register workers looked at her like cheerleaders looking down on a band geek. They departed almost urgently, whispering until they were out of earshot, leaving Kate behind.

Kate passed right through the toys – sparing only a quick glance to make sure nothing new had come in – before she arrived at the electronics section again. "Hey, guys," she said to the two at the counter, doing little and not bothering to hide it. "Some…nut…said something about the meteor."

"Uh, yeah," said Rich, practically laughing at her subtlety. "I don't doubt it."

Kate felt a pang of fear. "What happened?"

They both stared. "Are you for real?" asked Derrick in utter seriousness. Kate's clueless expression said it all. "The meteor's curved," he said like he felt bad for being the one to break it to her. "Its course has shifted. NASA says there's a chance it may hit us."

"No, there's not 'a chance'," Rich argued with Derrick. His acerbic levity was tinged with fear pushed deep. "It WILL strike earth. It's coming RIGHT at us."

"Dude, really?" Derrick argued back. "You think you're rinky-dink setup is better than NASA?"

"I think I'm honest and NASA's worried about a panic, yeah," Rich argued.

"What setup?" Kate asked.

"Captain Nerd here has a super-nice telescope," Derrick said, thumbing at Rich.

"Yeah," he confirmed. "I've had once since I was a kid."

"Oh my god, what kind of a kid owns a telescope!" Kate exploded at him as she spun around. She started back for her section just as her phone beginning to vibrate. She slipped it out, reading the message, "It's happening. Tell work you're sick and get your butt over here."

She stopped in her tracks and said, "Turn on the news." She turned back around to Rich and Derrick, prompting them again. Derrick seemed indifferent but Rich shrugged, curious. He worked his electronic magic on the nearest TV and brought up the local news. The instant he did, his jaw dropped in horror. On the news was a report of a dozen figures suspended around a rooftop, all ablaze. The three stared at the screen, the skyscraper looking crowned in flame. "Oh god," Kate whispered.

Derrick stepped back, bumping into Rich who steadied him. "Aww, Jesus," Derrick gaped.

"It's like some cult thing," Rich gasped. Kate cupped her mouth to keep from screaming. She turned away from the screens, eyes clamped shut.

"Who are those people?" Rich asked, gesturing at figures on the rooftop, walking about.

Derrick stepped close to the screen, squinting. "The feed's clear, why do they look so..." He looked at Rich and at the same time, the two managed to decide on, "weird?"

"That's enough, gentlemen. Shut it off," ordered Walter as he stormed up on them from behind. "That's not appropriate viewing to be watching at work." The snap in his voice conveyed seriousness bordering on vicious.

"Hey, Walter," Kate said suddenly, holding her stomach and milking it a little. "I think I need to go home."

"No," he denied her flatly, barely even acknowledging her existence, much less her fantasy pain. "You're scheduled; you will work your shift."

Kate tried to bury her irritation with him. She glanced at Derrick and Rich, both able to tell something was amiss with her request. "Walter, it's, uh, it's lady-parts related."

"Dude, let her go," Rich butted in.

"You've done enough," Walter told Rich with a threatening tone and a deviant glare. He turned his ire to Kate and said with a finger in her face, "I don't know why you're over here and not at your station. You need to get back over there."

"Walter, I—" she started.

"No!" he yelled, surprising all three of them. "You are not excused from work. You are not allowed to leave. I don't care that you're PMSing or whatever."

Kate looked ready to level him. She informed him, "I need to leave."

Walter told her clearly, "You can choose: your job or your uterus."

Kate didn't hesitate. She snatched her nametag off her shirt, ripping the fabric. Sneering at Walter who was clearly unprepared for her to call his bluff, she crumpled the plastic nametag in her bare hand and dropped it at his feet. She glanced only in passing at Rich and Derrick, as if to thank them for their friendship. She stormed passed Walter, leaving him dumbfounded as she left the store and didn't look back.

Kate's leg vibrated, her knee bouncing up and down as she rode the bus across town. Furious, she glared out the window as the rain dripped down the pane. In her mind, she thought of a dozen torturous ways to destroy Walter. No man in the history of the world died a more painful death than he did, over and over again, inside her imagination.

She arrived at Denise's complex and leapt off the bus. She had to will herself to touchdown to the pavement, lest she just float onward at the apex of her leap. She had so much energy born of anger, she considered flying to the door but thought better of it. Instead, she ran across the parking lot and rushed to Denise's door.

After Kate knocked, Denise opened the door, readied to speak, then asked, "What happened?"

"Men are assholes," Kate denounced summarily as she stormed inside. Waiting for her were Rachael and Emily as well as the brand new suit that lay finished on the couch. Kate's eyes shone and her jaw dropped. "You guys got it done?!"

"Mostly," Emily said uneasily.

"After you left yesterday, we kept working on it all last night and today," Denise said, more with pride than as a complaint.

"We want to add some additional stuff, like, you know, pockets," explained Rachael. "But yeah, the base form is complete." She took out a switchblade and raked it fiercely across the fabric. "It's completely tear-resistant. A samurai sword isn't cutting this thing. Elliot says that even some gunshots won't tear it, so long as it isn't a straight shot."

"It breathes, which is the important thing," Emily further added. "According to Elliot, it'll allow oxygen but nothing larger, so we shouldn't have too much of an issue of particulate debris."

"Me and Emily want to try and actually enclose the suit, but we don't have that kind of time right now," Rachael said. She took from beside the suit a helmet nigh-identical to the previous, handling the weight with some trouble. "Dylan - the armorer dude I know – he came through big-time." She handed Kate the helmet. "It's padded and reinforced inside, just like the stuff he makes for his armored combat boys. The visor is a little bit wider than the cosplay model and it goes down a bit more, so that should help your visibility." Kate dumped the helmet on her head and looked around. "I'm going to be able to actually rig the helmet with Blu-tooth so we don't have to rely on the earpiece, but – again – that's going to take time that we don't have."

Kate knocked on the visor of the helmet. "Transparent aluminum," Emily told her.

"Really?!" Kate delighted.

"Of course it's not," Rachael groaned. "It's the windscreen off a motorcycle helmet."

Kate pulled the helmet off, tendrils of blonde hair falling about. "Who do you know who rides a motorcycle?"

"Pssh, I didn't know his name," Rachael laughed off. Next to her, Emily grew worried.

"The aliens, guys. They're still calling her out," Denise reminded everyone, still by the door.

"I'll get...alienS?" Kate emphasized the plurality.

"Yeah, the news said there are two figures on the rooftop," Rachael said. "Maybe they got it wrong, but...come on. When has your luck ever been that good?"

Kate looked down at the helmet, seeing both it and her reflection in the visor. She looked at her friends and nodded with all the determination she had left.

Y'marda stood at the very center of the building, eyeballing the helicopters that circled the skyscraper. She could see their cameras within, locked onto her but they didn't dare draw near the black smoke rising from the charred bodies tied to the exterior of the building.

Y'dosh approached her timidly from behind. "The bodies are mostly burned. The fires will go out soon." He noted a helicopter flying by. "We may not see her. She may not arrive."

"She will come," Y'marda said adamantly, her arms crossed defiantly as she watched the helicopters like they were flies irritating her.

"There are other factors to consider," he urged, having to speak over the rushing air. "They have warriors here. Enforcers. I do not wish to lose any more lives in this useless display."

Y'marda snapped at a glare at the man, silencing him instantly. "It is not useless when we remove her from the equation and can secure—"

Kate landed on the far side of the rooftop. In her shining new dark gray suit, she stood defiantly before the pair and called, "This has gone far enough."

"Whoo!" Emily squealed inside her earpiece. "That was classy!"

"I got chills, Kate! I got chills!" Denise giggled along.

Y'marda smiled cruelly at Kate's arrival, like a fisher finding a tug on the line. She shoved Y'dosh out of her way and started towards Kate like a runaway train building speed. "Your interference is at an end." She drew back and punched at Kate. Kate stepped back and let the punch swing by, then punched wide for the woman's head. She didn't connect as Y'marda slipped around the punch, then entangled Kate and swept her off her feet.

Kate slammed hard into the ceiling and Y'marda dropped her knee onto Kate's stomach to pin her. A second later, Y'dosh appeared and grabbed Kate's hands, holding her down. "You'll not interfere," Y'marda warned, pulling back her fist. She punched Kate in the chest, a loud crack issuing forth. Kate screamed at the pain as she flailed, bucking the woman off of her.

As Y'marda scrambled to recover, Kate kneed Y'dosh in the head and then flew straight up. She almost made it free of them, but Y'dosh's frantic scamper enabled him to grab her cape, stopping her ascent. "Ha!" he called. "You can't—" The snaps on Kate's shoulders gave and the cape ripped free. "Get away?" the man muttered, looking at the fabric held loosely in his hand. He looked up from it just in time to see Kate coming in at him, flying at full speed.

She collided with him at the speed of a car and the force of a battery ram. He was sent sailing, slamming into the rooftop access of the towering skyscraper, crashing through the brick wall. Kate landed and turned as Y'marda ran at her and threw a powerful punch. Kate did her best Shaw Brothers move to parry the punch and strike the woman in the chin. The technique worked but the blow hit her throat instead. Y'marda suddenly hacked and coughed, grabbing at her neck as she convulsed in surprise.

For an instant, Kate forgot about the bodies and the death. Afraid she'd killed someone, she apologized, "Oh shit, are you—" Y'dosh grabbed her from behind. He lifted her off her feet and threw her to the ground. Halfway down, Kate remembered she could fly and simply stopped in mid-air. Hovering at knee-level, she grabbed Y'dosh's legs and flew backwards, yanking him off his feet, mostly from surprise.

Kate hovered in a defensive ball, waiting as the two aliens recovered. They both neared her, unable to address with any confidence the hovering, defensive posture. Kate watched them close, then she slowly rose up a bit higher to just over head height. The two reacted cautiously, on opposite sides of her, neither sure how to approach. Kate floated closer towards the woman, then abruptly kicked right at her head. Y'marda backed away from the kick and Kate zoomed at her, striking her in the chest.

She turned in the air and kicked at Y'dosh, keeping him backing up with flailing kicks thrown with more imitation than sincerity. He backed up all the way to the edge of the building and stopped, suddenly terrified. Kate also stopped, not sure how to proceed without doing the unthinkable.

From beneath, Y'marda grabbed Kate around the neck. She yanked her down onto the ground and with enough force to stop a charging elephant, drove her into the rooftop. The flimsy surface gave way and Kate was sent careening through the ceiling into the office below. Debris and insulation went spilling everywhere as an entire SWAT team panicked at the sudden damage.

Y'marda dropped down beside Kate but saw the police instead. She barely had a second to speak before someone yelled, "Open fire!" An absolute symphony of gunshots ripped through the air as the black-clad armored men unloaded on the woman, bombarding her with gunfire. Kate scrambled away as Y'marda threw up her hands defensively, howling in agony as the bullets struck on all sides.

A litany of clicks followed soon after as the SWAT lowered their guns. Y'marda, her outfit ripped and torn across her nigh-human body, lowered her hands as absolute fury seethed within her. She screamed at the officers, her rage distorted her face, and ran at them.

Kate crawled on all fours, trying to get up, unaware of the bloody carnage happening beyond her. She began to catch her breath when Y'dosh kicked her in the side. She was thrown up and slammed into a pillar, then stopped there without falling. She hovered in a fetal ball for only a second before flying suddenly at Y'dosh. Ready for her abrupt attack, he punched her out of the air. Kate hit the floor again, the simulated wood cracking and bowing in but not quite giving.

"Kate, what's happening?" Rachael had been yelling over her headset.

Kate coughed and her vision waffled. She saw Y'dosh grab her hand and, keeping it pinned, began to punch at her chest again and again. The punch from earlier made the blows all the worse and Kate howled in agony. Desperate, she shoved Y'dosh off and took to flight. She plowed right through a window and burst into the sky, flying passed helicopters monitoring the entire fight. Clutching her chest as it pained her, Kate disappeared as best she could into the rooftops and buildings of the city.

Back in the skyscraper, the blood-covered Y'marda approached her male subordinate, furious. "The coward ran again," she growled. Unable to control hersef, she screamed ferally, shaking with rage. The outburst made Y'dosh close his eyes, keeping fear on a tight leash. Her scream letting up, Y'marda punched a wall, caving in a portion of the building's supports. "Will she not stand and fight?!"

"We've done her serious damage," said Y'dosh, out of breath. "Her strength is not equal to our own, but her flight is a problem."

The woman only seethed, her anger stoking. She saw a helicopter fly close, getting a clear shot of the two of them through the window shattered by Kate's sudden departure. "Our only hope now is that she will show up before the event and we can ruin her before the cataclysm." Y'marda grabbed up the top half of a SWAT officer and threw the bloody torso at the helicopter, taking some tiny satisfaction in the wet squish of his tattered remains against the windshield. The chopper veered off, undamaged but no less frantic.

"We cannot be distracted any longer," Y'dosh urged. "Twice now she has set us back. If we are to have the network prepared and the device set up, we must—"

"It will be for naught if she is still among the living," Y'marda reminded him as she stepped back through the blood-drenched room full of corpses, departing from the site of the carnage.

CHAPTER SIXTEEN

Kate quickly wiped her eyes, trying to pretend she hadn't been crying, when her bedroom door pushed in. Lauren came inside, closing the door behind her. She had to push some clothes to the wall to have a clear space to stand, before asking, "I need to talk to you about..." She took one look at Kate, with bruises all along her arms and a massive bruise extending up passed her tanktop collar to her neck. "What happened?"

Kate wasn't sure why she knew she had to lie. "A pallet fell on me at work."

"Good lord, are you okay?" said Lauren suddenly, rushing to her daughter. She sat down on the bed and brushed away Kate's blonde locks. "What happened?"

"It's nothing," said Kate, looking away, desperate to not talk about it. Or anything.

"Do you need to go to the hospital?" Lauren asked without hesitation.

Kate laughed sadly. "Yeah, no. The last thing we need is more debt."

"Baby, not if you're hurt," insisted her mother. She turned Kate towards her and made her hold up her hands. She studied her torso through the tanktop, but Kate didn't know what she expected to see. "Are you sure you're okay?"

Kate nodded. "Yeah. They, uh, they let me come home early," she lied. Remembering the destruction of her nametag, she almost started crying again. "I'm afraid they'll..."

"What about workman's comp?" asked Lauren, the crossing of her arms signaling the shift from maternal concern to paralegal pragmatist.

"No, it's..." Kate tried to keep from bursting into tears. "No, mom, it's...it was my fault. I was...I shouldn't have been getting the stuff and the pallet fell, but it was my fault. They may, uh, they may...they said they wouldn't press charges against me."

"Press charges?!" Lauren exclaimed. Kate hated herself as she realized the scrutiny she was about to receive under the glaring eyes of her legal-aid mother. "They're going to press charges after YOU got hurt at WORK?" she exclaimed.

"Mom, it was technically my fault," Kate told her. "I...I violated OSHA or whatever. They might even..." She closed her eyes and lowered her head. "Mom, I'm sorry. Please stop yelling."

Lauren stood up suddenly, mortified. Terrified. Her eyes were huge with realization. "Oh god, they fired you." Kate just nodded, furious at herself with how out of control the lie was spiraling. "Oh god, Kate. Oh god!" Her mother went pale in shock. She backed up to the bedroom door, her hands atop her head. "Kate, god!"

Kate looked at her mother and whimpered, "What does it matter? That meteor's going to..."

"What if it doesn't?" Lauren told her. "Kate, if you've lost your job, then we're homeless." Her mother's voice shook with hysterics. "All three of us are homeless. We can't afford rent. We can't afford your Nana's medicine. We can't afford food. Kate, if you lost your job!" Her mom looked on the verge of panic. "Baby, you NEED to go back and get your job back. You need to get your job back. We can't—" Her mom only shivered. The ageless walls that her mother needed to keep existential terror at bay were crumbling before Kate's eyes.

"Okay, okay," Kate said, standing and almost reaching for her mom. She tried to smile soothingly. "Okay, n-no problem. I can go back and I can talk to one of the other managers. I've been at the store for long enough, I'm sure Candice would..." In the back of her mind, she knew everything she was saying was totally untrue. They probably replaced her already. "Everything will be fine," she convinced her mom.

"Baby," her mother repeated weakly. Nearly in tears, she hugged her daughter, clinging tightly to her. Kate hugged her back, her mind a tangle of thoughts of humiliation, failure, and death. She was going to humiliate herself before Walter just before she died in a painful, agonizing death beneath the crushing heel of a meteor.

Somehow that seemed appropriate.

'I want to go home,' Kate thought to herself as she tried to console her mother.

Dressed in her uniform for work, Kate was crumpled over herself on the bus stop bench. Her superhero costume was bundled in a bag beneath her feet. Cars zipped by, the next bus to arrive at the stop not due for another ten minutes. Kate could smell the fries from the burger joint half a block away and her mouth watered, but certain her tears were ruining her makeup, she didn't want to move.

Her elbows on her knees, her face in her hands, she tried not to cry but wasn't really succeeding. "I want to go home," she repeated, feeling worthless. "I want to go—"

Her misery was interrupted by her phone ringing. Kate snatched it out of the bag, having to sift through the cape to find it. "Hello?" she nearly sobbed into the phone, wondering if Yaya Han ever had days like this.

"Kate? Honey, are you okay? Thank god you're alright. Where are you?" Rachael asked. She immediately reported, "The aliens have set up a machine."

Kate sighed, feeling more irritated than anything else. She looked down into the bag, her outfit looking like nothing but a wad of cheap urban camouflage. Kate started to say something, then her self-loathing got the better of her. "My mom says I can't come out."

There was silence on the phone. "Uh…what?"

"I have to go get my job back," Kate admitted with a shaking lip.

On the other end of the phone, Rachael lowered the phone and looked up at the heavens, as if wondering what she had ever done to deserve this. She inhaled calmingly and then went back to the phone. "Okay, honey, I know things are bad right now, but the aliens have got, like, this giant machine-thing." She looked at her laptop as it streamed the news, showing a live shot from the traffic chopper. "We kind of need you to do something."

"Like what?" asked Kate morosely, checking to see if the bus was by any chance early. It wasn't.

Rachael nearly snapped at Kate, but realized she had no plan. She looked at the giant machine of green metal and a lighter green crystal, the size of a small truck atop the tallest building in the city. She started to answer, then hedged. "Uh…punch them?"

"I ran away twice," Kate practically sobbed. "I'm a coward."

Rachael hedged, not sure what to say. From her bathroom came Denise, asking, "Did you get her?"

"Yeah," Rachael confirmed, holding the cellphone to her chest. "She's being kind of emo, though. Her mom is making her ask for her job back."

Denise nodded understandingly and gestured for the phone. "Hey, Kate?" she said sweetly with a doting nod of her head. "Hey, honey, are you feeling okay?"

"Honestly, I'm feeling—"

"IT DOESN'T MATTER HOW YOU'RE FEELING!" Denise screamed into the phone. "Get off your ass, get over yourself, and go kick these aliens' asses into next goddamn week!"

"But I can't beat them!" Kate griped.

"No, you haven't beaten them yet," Denise insisted. "Just get on your suit and…" Her absolute certainty wavered.

"Ask her what would Superman do?" Rachael prompted.

"What would Superman do?" Denise asked quickly, in total agreement.

Kate lowered the phone and glowered, knowing she was being played like a fiddle and angry that she was going to dance to the tune.

"Okay, so the aliens seem to have constructed seven devices," explained Emily as she sat in the computer lab of her community college. Alone except for the computer science lab-tech who was too busy torrenting hentai to pay attention, Emily was consulting multiple screens of satellite feeds of the downtown area. "It looks like the big device is the primary one, though, because the other six are all surrounding it at, like, intervals of a quarter-mile or something. They're all on top of adjacent buildings."

"Did you get that, Kate?" Rachael asked as she and Denise sat on the floor together in Rachael's living room.

"Yeah," Kate confirmed, trying to be quiet as she rode the bus, heading towards downtown. It was empty except her and the driver. "Nobody's around," she observed.

"The meteor's supposed to make planetfall sometime tonight," said Rachael.

"I bet that's what the aliens want," Emily speculated. The lab tech looked up from his flimsy white particle board and shhhed her. "Maybe they're going to catch it," she whispered, blushing for making too much noise in the empty computer lab.

"If they were that benevolent, they wouldn't have killed a bunch of people just to get Kate's attention," countered Denise.

"Maybe the meteor's actually like an alien invasion ship," Rachael proposed.

"Meteor, I can't do anything about," Kate said, trying to channel her best Christopher Reeve. "Aliens. Let's focus on the aliens. What are the police doing?"

Rachael and Denise both checked the laptop. "Nada. Nothing," said Denise. "They can't approach the machines. The six smaller ones, according to some pictures from a news chopper, it looks like the rooftops are kind of crushed a little? Like, the access to the machines is physically blocked or something."

"They can't fly; how'd they do that?" Kate asked.

The others didn't offer any explanation. Denise just continued. "The police have cordoned off downtown and stuff. They're going evacuation-o-riffic, but they can't seem to even get close to the machines, or the aliens. They've called the military but who knows when they'll show up."

"What are the military going to do?" asked Emily, searching through her screens.

Rachael and Denise looked at each other. "Uh…military stuff?" Rachael proposed. Denise shrugged, unable to offer a better theory.

"Okay," Kate said. "So, if the police can't get close, how am I getting in there?" she asked.

Silence.

"Right," Kate sighed. "We're winging it."

"Pretty much, honey," Rachael told her.

Kate sighed and lowered her head. "Can we please just go back to being cosplay losers?"

"After you use your superpowers to beat up the killer aliens, sure," Denise promised her.

Kate wiped her eyes, too irritated and depressed and scared to be sad. "Okay, so there are seven machines, six around the big one, right? What if I take out one of the machines? Maybe even the big one?"

Silence.

"Will that do anything?"

Silence.

Kate sighed and her shoulders slumped. "We really are winging this, aren't we?"

"Big time," Rachael acknowledged sympathetically.

Y'dosh paced around the machine, studying the display projected from the forearm of his suit. He glanced up at the late afternoon sky and studied the clouds that dotted the heavens. He sniffed at the air, burned by the electrical discharges from the giant crystal behind him. He turned and took a step, then jerked when a pulse of lightning shocked him. He yelped and shook his hand, glaring at the device.

"Why the discharges?" asked Y'marda as she came around the far side of it.

"People in the city are dying of other causes," said Y'dosh, going back to his device. "Don't worry. They're in small enough numbers to not burn out the crystals, or really even register against it." He gestured at the arcs of lightning. "That's what the electricity is. Discharges of necrotic energy."

As he gestured, Kate landed out of the sky. Y'dosh only sighed and groaned, "Here we go."

Y'marda was more enthused. "Have you come to finally stand your ground and face me?" she demanded, storming towards Kate. "Have you come to finally accept your inevitable fa—" Kate punched her in the mouth. Not hesitating like before, Kate followed by punching the alien woman in the stomach and shoved her into Y'dosh. They both hit the ground and skidded across the rooftop to the edge.

Kate turned and faced the giant machine. Its metal frame looked structurally dubious, with spindly supports at odd angles. It looked more like an elaborate spider's web than a sturdy structure. Meanwhile the giant green crystal seemed almost comically oversized. She looked it over, unsure what to do, then just approached it and knelt down beneath it. She squatted down, catching it on her shoulders. She began to stand, the machine groaning as she pushed up beneath it.

The roof gave out beneath her feet and Kate fell halfway before she caught herself. Flying now, she rose back to the machine and caught it with her hands. Pushing hard against the base, she began to fly harder, pressing into the machine. The metal body groaned and then warped inward with a loud crunch. "Damn it!" Kate cursed, giving up on that approach.

Y'marda slid under the machine like she was sliding into first base and kicked Kate into the broken roof. Kate caught herself on the roof and whirled around, backfisting the woman and then dropped willfully through the hole. Kate was about to fly out a nearby window, only to be surprised to see a SWAT team yet again. She froze when she realized she was in a room with a dozen heavily armed officers in black.

"Keep them distracted," said one man in a black ski mask under an armored helmet. "We'll blow the machine."

Kate didn't know what to say but relieved somebody else had a clue what to do, she nodded and looked at the roof. She burst up threw it like she was charging through drywall. She erupted back into the rooftop, surprising Y'dosh. "Where's—" asked Kate, just before Y'marda grabbed her from behind.

Y'marda grabbed entirely onto Kate, wrapping her arms across her chest and her legs around her waist. She clinched tightly, trying to crush Kate by sheer strength and hatred. Instead of fight her, Kate kept flying. Despite being entangled, she flew at Y'dosh who backpedaled in surprised terror. Kate wrestled free her left arm and grabbed Y'dosh's collar as she barreled into him. She flew and fell simultaneously over the edge of the building, taking her two foes into the open air with her.

The two aliens barely had a chance to realize what was happening before Kate when spiraling for the ground. Rather than fly, she let herself fall, surrendering to gravity. Above them, a loud crack of sound tore open the sky. The two aliens saw above them a fiery display as shrapnel from the device was sent coursing in flaming streams across the top of the city. Y'marda's screams turned into howls of fury when she saw the rooftop covered in the explosion. She shoved off of Kate just in time to collide with the pavement.

Asphalt gave way as the three slammed into the ground like speeding cars through a brick wall. Kate broke through a deep sewer pipe beneath the city and into another beneath it. She finally stopped against dead earth, only to battered with firehose intensity. She held her hand up to block the hard blasts, but was quickly submerged in murky, brackish water. She opened her mouth to scream but instantly began to drown.

Panicking, she rocketed straight up into the air, water splashing from her as she rose out of the ground. Kate gasped and hacked. She dropped onto the broken street and coughed, unable to clear her windpipe. She tore off her helmet and hacked again, water gurgling from her mouth. She hit her own stomach, forcing herself to vomit up still more water.

Kate gasped frantically and collapsed to her side, on the cusp of losing consciousness. She flopped onto her wet cape and stared straight up. She felt like death was circling her. All she could do was fixate on the smoldering remains of the machine at top the building. She laughed with relief as she saw the flaming streaks coursing from the right side of her vision to the left. However, one streak of flaming light was moving against the explosive remains of the device.

Against the first shreds of twilight, Kate rose onto her hand and stared up into the sky. High above, far beyond the ceiling of the city, she could see a fiery star descending from the heavens. Kate tried to fathom what she was seeing, and her eyes went wide in horror. The meteor had arrived. As if to punctuate the horror, it let out a loud crack, like a single gunshot ripping through the air. The clouds overhead were pushed away, leaving only the clear sky above. The tail of the meteor was not long and the great flaming ball was growing larger by the second. It wasn't falling in a wide streak; it was plummeting as if straight for her city.

Kate rose slowly, looking up at the heavens to see the falling visage of death. She looked at the city, seeing no one but still somehow aware of all the occupants, like they were the combined people of earth. All eyes were faced above, she could feel it. Everyone stared at the tiny speck of fiery light that was growing brighter. Another explosive pop echoed from above, like an announcement of the inevitable.

From behind, Y'marda tackled Kate, slamming her into the very building they'd been fighting atop not moments before. She spun Kate around and punched her across the face, knocking Kate to her knees.

Y'marda hit Kate in the face once again with her knee, then elbowed straight down atop her crown.

Kate didn't fight back but leapt high, knocking the alien away. Y'marda rolled back and screamed furiously at Kate, mad beyond all reason as Kate lifted into the air beyond her reach. Behind her, Y'dosh approached but he looked to the sky as well, following Kate's view to spot the meteor. He smiled and said, "Finally." Kate turned horrified to him. "It will strike momentarily," he told Y'marda. He looked at Kate and said, "A third each of the world's deaths, instead of the half we planned, is a tragedy but it will still shift the scales of the war."

"The world's deaths?" tried to reason Kate. She looked again at the meteor as it fell, a growing ball of fire in the sky. Her eyes glazed over in terror. Somewhere from deep within, she discovered a resolute adamancy. Her eyes fixed, she simply whispered, "No."

In the span of feet, Kate broke the sound barrier.

Rocketing into the heavens like a missile, Kate soared straight at the meteor. Air tearing around her, she fired into the sky with focus that burned away all other concerns. Into the heavens she flew, to meet the meteor as the great falling death shot as if right for her. Flying faster and faster, Kate screamed as she achieved speeds she never could have imagined.

Coursing through the heavens, she flew higher than she'd ever gone, passing clouds and the world itself. She entered the very upper atmosphere itself, left in a cold silence with nothing between her and the massive chunk of rock that had invaded her world. Before her, looking down on her and her world itself, the meteor loomed. Despite speed and distance, what had first seemed only a tiny speck, and then a smaller boulder, quickly blossomed into a world-killer. Fire born of friction succumbed to velocity and the flames gave way. Before Kate was the massive, pocket-marked body of the meteor as it fell. Looming larger before her, the dark stone death was ringed in flame as it blacked out the nighttime sky.

Kate neared as speeds unknown to her as the meteor's size continued to spread until it enveloped her entire vision. The size of a building and giving off enough heat to burn the air in her lungs, the meteor seemed fixed straight at her, and she at it. Arms locked together and determination set, Kate accelerated.

The heat growing intense until she couldn't stand it anymore, Kate screamed and slammed full-force into the meteor. Another crack tore through the sky, this time like every roll of thunder within a hurricane, striking all at once. A burst of air ruptured from around the meteor, but its intensity was not abated. As soon as she'd hit its iron surface, Kate was flattened against it, her own speed dwarfed by its might.

Pressed against the hot globe of death, Kate mustered the strength to flop over onto her back. "NO!" She screamed, pressing against the meteor. As if digging her heels into a ground that wasn't there, Kate tried to resist its force. The intense heat was lost to her as she focused only on the coursing, unending, unturning velocity of the massive invader. Screaming madly, she pressed back with all her might as beneath her, the ground zoomed to meet her. All her might, all her power, all of her was focused on stopping the death of the world. Clouds rushed past. The air grew thick against her. The continent, the land, the city, were zooming in faster than seemed possible. "No!" Kate screamed in the acrid heat coming off the meteor. "No! No! NO!!!!"

The instant Kate saw the buildings of her city, she knew she was too late. Without the focus to stay balanced against the meteor, she was thrown from its path, the force of its descent too great to resist. Kicked wide, she was left behind in its wake. The tailwind of the meteor batted her about, all while her hysterical screams against the death of the world were lost in the falling fury.

Passing Kate by, the giant flaming ball of stone slammed into a skyscraper and toppled it. The meteor ripped through metal and material with ease, bursting through the far side with a sky-shaking crash. It plowed through the urban air and slammed into the side of the city's baseball stadium. Clipping a piece from the coliseum-like wall, the meteor slammed head-on into the solid dirt of the outfield. A tidal wave of artificial turf shot over the stadium like a tsunami of over-priced sod and slammed into the highway beyond. The grass caught fire and the stands erupted in an intense blaze. But the meteor stayed put.

Fires exploded from the stadium like tendrils of devastation, flaming loops cascading into the nearby streets. The toppled skyscraper collapsed into its neighbors, shattering glass windows and collapsing in a black cloud of devastation that blanketed out between its city neighbors like the shadow of the Grim Reaper. Debris and industrial materials showered onto empty streets, destroying cars and shattering pavement. The whole of downtown shook as if struck by an earthquake. Dust fell from buildings and panes of glass cracked. The pillars of the world shook but remained standing. But the meteor stayed put.

A surreal calm fell over Kate and the city beneath her feet. Post-calamitous silence saturated her as she finally processed the destroyed baseball stadium, at the heart of which was the giant porous meteor. Smoke and steam rose from the ground around it as fires burned but was contained behind the wall of the sports arena.

Kate slowly lowered, staring in awe at the devastation not wrought by the meteor. She couldn't process the world still standing. Downtown was damaged, but still there. The city was harmed but still standing. The world would keep on turning. It was only with that realization that Kate thought to finally breath. The gentle exhale of relief was followed by a sudden, abrupt gasp and she realized she was practically choking. Kate panted as she lowered from the sky, descending among the buildings shaken but not toppled by the meteor's impact. Exhaustion began to reach her and she winced, her entire body aching like she had never known.

A flash of light caught her attention.

Akin to being woken early and abruptly, Kate jumped with an unsteady start, looking deliriously about. Vertigo hit as she thought for a moment she was upside down and ascending and not lowering towards the ground. Beneath her, on the streets removed from the fighting, was a sea of blinking lights. Confused, Kate looked above and was able to see the half-moon amidst the dark city sky, confirming she was returning to earth. She looked out again at the streets and slowly the realization dawned on her: the flashes were from people.

Filling the city streets, hundreds of people – maybe thousands – were beneath her. Clapping. Cheering.

Taking photos.

Each flash was from a camera, their symphony of light only scant hints at the multitude of devices capturing her image as she floated above the city. Kate realized a thousand images of her were about to flood the Internet. Any hope of keeping her suit and her identity separate was gone. They could all see her. All the world could see her.

All the relief she might have felt for stopping the meteor was gone, washed away by a numb, sick feeling of being exposed. The only thought that went through her head was, "I want to go home."

More of Robert V Aldrich's work can be found at his website,

TeachTheSky.com

Made in the USA
Middletown, DE
15 January 2018